BARCELONA
SHADOWS

MARC PASTOR

BARCELONA SHADOWS

Translated from the Catalan by
Mara Faye Lethem

PUSHKIN PRESS
LONDON

Pushkin Press

71–75 Shelton Street, London WC2H 9JQ

Original text © Marc Pastor 2008

Published by arrangement with the Ella Sher Literary Agency

English translation © Mara Faye Lethem, 2014

Barcelona Shadows first published in Catalan as
La mala dona in 2008

This translation first published by Pushkin Press in 2014
This edition first published in 2014

0 0 1

LLLL **institut
ramon llull**
Catalan Language and Culture

The translation of this work was supported by a
grant from the Institut Ramon Llull

ISBN 978 1 782270 63 8

Set in Monotype Baskerville by Tetragon, London
Printed and bound by CPI Group (UK) Ltd, Croydon, CRO 4YY

www.pushkinpress.com

For Eva, Miriam and my parents,
who are always there.

Let my death be a greater birth!

JOAN MARAGALL
Cant espiritual

The boundaries which divide Life from Death are at best shadowy and vague.

EDGAR ALLAN POE
The Premature Burial

Sanguinem universae carnis non comedetis, quia anima omnis carnis sanguis eius est: et, quicumque comederit illum, interibit.

LEVITICUS 17:14

"Didn't hear what the bet was."
"Your life."

CLINT EASTWOOD
For a Few Dollars More

1

NOW I'M A VOICE INSIDE YOUR SKULL. Or the recitation of someone you love beside the bed, or a classmate who can't seem to read in his head, or a memory dredged up by a scent. I'm man, I'm woman, I'm wind and paper; I'm a traveller, a hunter and a gentle nursemaid (oh, the irony); who serves you dinner and pleasures you, who beats you up and who listens to you; I'm the drink that burns your throat, the rain that soaks through to your bones, the reflection of the night in a window and the cry of a baby before suckling.

I am everything and I can be everywhere. I behave more like a man (if *behave* is the appropriate word) than like a woman. And I am referred to across cultures by many different names: The Dark Angel, The Inexorable One (I particularly like that one, it's from *One Thousand and One Nights* and I find it quite poetic). But all the Romance languages describe me in the feminine. That has a pretty logical explanation though. Women are the essence of the species, the beginning of it all. Women give life. You are the opposite of everything I represent. We are two ends of the rope. I don't hate you (I have no feelings, merely curiosity), but I am not like you. I'm more of a man: destructive. Men only know how to annihilate, negate, in all possible senses: to dominate and to kill. But without men, there would be no babies, you could argue.

Nonsense. Men don't give birth. They only possess the female and leave their seed in her, their destructive trace. In a way, he kills her and she sacrifices herself to create a new life. It's women who give birth and raise the children and make sure everything keeps going. That's why I wanted to explain Enriqueta Martí's story to you. Because, despite being a woman, she's different from the rest.

So, forget about the skulls, the dark robes and the scythes; forget the medieval imagery of gnawed flesh and empty eye sockets, the thick fog and the groans of pain, the chains, the evil laughter and the ghostly apparitions. I'm not the bloke with the cart piled high with corpses, the Supreme Judge or the hooded executioner... even though I can be that. All that is what you are, all of you with your fantasies, fears and nightmares.

I'm not the end of the path: I am the path.

But enough talk about me, which isn't worth the trouble and doesn't get us anywhere, and let's get started, with the story that I've come to tell.

And those who know nothing about it say that the first shovelful of dirt is always the worst.

Blackmouth tenses up his body, his ears pricked up like a greyhound's. He's surrounded by the scent of damp earth, of One Eye's sweat, of the salt the breeze pulls off the sea. His hands are frozen on the handle, his eyes bulging, round like the moon whose light splatters the cemetery debris.

The cry of an insomniac seagull frightens them. What was that? Nothin', nothin', some bird.

One Eye, tall and lanky, bereft of his right eye from a bullet during the Tragic Week, with a gap-toothed smile and ulcerous skin, digs beside Blackmouth. They hadn't been to Montjuïc together looking for bodies since the summer. They'd come in

One Eye's carriage, which in the daytime he uses to drive meat from the slaughterhouses to sell in the city, and they've tossed the shovels over the fence before jumping over themselves. A single oil-lamp sun is visible from any point on the peak, so they don't light it until they're shielded by the forest of funereal sculptures. Don't want to get caught by the nightwatchman or the coppers, or I'll end up with the nickname No Eye.

"What does the doctor want with these bodies anyway?"

"What does it matter?"

"He pays us pretty good for something he could just take from the hospital."

"What do you know about medicine? So let everybody do their own job. The doctor can do his doctoring, and we'll stick to carting off crates."

The hole grows deep. The pair of two-bit thieves dig harder and harder; they've almost reached the box.

"But he'll never go to the clink. He's a doctor and we're a couple of lousy crooks."

"Shut up, Blackmouth, and don't jinx us. You don't need to worry about him going to prison. You worry about the cops catching you and sending *you* to the clink. Come on, pull out that grape juice, I'm dripping with sweat."

Blackmouth pulls the wineskin from the sack and passes it to him. When he gets it back he takes a sip. Experience rules, and his partner had certainly had more whippings over the years. In the end, Blackmouth is just a lad, a chick fresh from its shell, abandoned by his father, mother and God. With no money, eking it out in a pigeon loft on Lluna Street, eating when he can or when he robs, which usually amounts to the same thing. The only company he has is an old blind chap in his building, who gives guitar lessons to children and makes ointments and pomades for adults, which he assures cure all type of ailments, even though he's been blind and crazy for years. León Domènech is his name, and he never complains when one of the pigeons goes missing. Why do they call you Blackmouth, lad? he'd asked him once, unable to see his teeth stained with dried blood and the dirty feather in his hair.

Hurry up, hurry up, we're almost done and the sun's coming up.

Like galley slaves, they focus on their shovels, silent for quite a long while. A thump tells them they've hit wood. They wipe the dirt off the surface and search for the nails. Blackmouth pulls two out with his fingernails, bloodying his hands. One Eye works the slit between the lid and the coffin with the shovel blade. Crack, splinters, the door is halfway open. Blackmouth gets excited and lifts it up. He can't hold back a horrified scream.

"Shit!" mutters One Eye.

"Is this the one we came for?"

"Yeah." He unfolds a small piece of paper he'd been carrying in his pocket. "Have a look for yourself."

"I can't read."

"It's a map…"

Standing with the headless corpse between his legs, Blackmouth declares, "Whoever this is, he didn't die of fevers."

One Eye comes out of the hole and rests his chin on the shovel handle. He closes his eyes. He's thinking.

"The doctor's not going to want that."

Blackmouth grabs the corpse by the underarms and sits it up.

"Now that's what I call dead weight."

One Eye isn't in the mood for jokes.

"It's not even fresh. Look at all those worms!" He brings the oil lamp closer to Blackmouth, who discovers that the worms

12

are crawling up his hands and falling onto his trousers. Some of them are making their way into his shoes. He looks inside the corpse's neck and finds more life there than he was expecting. He searches through the entire coffin for the head.

"Is it a man or a woman?"

"You're not thinking about keeping it?"

"If I clean her off good…"

"It's a man."

"Oh, forget it then, I'm no poof."

Silence. The seagull approaches them and looks them up and down. It seems to be saying: if you blokes aren't interested, I won't turn my nose up at it.

"Maybe the lady will want it."

Blackmouth turns around, frightened. From inside the tomb, on his knees, the image of One Eye with the shovel and the oil lamp up there, talking about her, makes his blood run cold.

"The lady?"

"Screw up all your courage and let's get it out of here."

With the decapitated cadaver inside the sack, they walk to the fence. The hole remains open, with the seagull inside, nibbling on the remains.

"I don't like the lady," Blackmouth finally dares to say.

"Don't start getting daft on me, lad."

"I don't like her. You know what they say about her."

One Eye turns his head to look at him, poor lad. Once they're in the carriage, he gives him the brass crucifix they took from the corpse's pocket.

"If you had garlic for supper, then you've got nothing to be afraid of." And he bursts out laughing.

*

"Giselle, you're the best French whore of all the French whores born in Sant Boi."

Moisès Corvo sits to one side of the bed, on the wrinkled sheets marked with other clients' stains dried onto them weeks ago and giving off a stench of sex that floats around the room. Her body lies naked on the bed, curled into an S, with scratches on her back and two bruises on her inner thighs. Her hair is on the pillow and her attentive gaze on Moisès, without any trace of emotion, but also devoid of the fear she usually has after going to bed with whoever can pay for her supper. Moisès Corvo treats her well, as well as that big hunk of man knows how, almost six and a half feet tall and with a thundering voice, strong as an oak tree and arms long like a circus monkey. Giselle caresses his back while he dresses. He's already put on his trousers, the braces hang on either side, his shirt like a handkerchief in his gnarled hands. He turns his torso, and his mouth smiles in defiance of his deep blue eyes. His face is like an El Greco painting, with messy hair and eyebrows pointy as a notary's signature, and an aquiline nose as pronounced as his lower lip. You're like the king, his wife tells him when he's home. And he's never sure if she's referring to his appearance or to his fondness for the ladies, the more naked and dissolute the better.

"Are you coming tomorrow?"

"Who knows. I may be dead tomorrow."

"Don't say those things."

"Then don't ask silly questions."

"I'm scared, Moisès. I wish you were here more."

"Scared of what? Not that scoundrel again, the one who…" Moisès can't remember his name. Just the sound of ribs cracking beneath the vaulted arch of l'Arc del Teatre.

"No. I'm scared of the monster."

"The monster?" His hand at his fly, without thinking.

"The streets are full of them. Children disappear. I'm worried about my Tonet."

"No child has disappeared, Giselle. That's just gossip from the old crones that hang around in doorways, sick of the gangs of youngsters shouting and jumping around."

"Dorita's daughter."

"Who?" Moisès, standing up, already dressed, cleans his spats with a cigarette between his lips.

"Dorita. She has, she had, a little girl, just four years old. She hasn't seen or heard from her in two weeks."

"I've never seen that girl."

"That's because she doesn't show her off. You think us whores hang around on the corners looking pitiful with our little ones?"

Giselle, nervous, has also got up and wrapped herself in an old, moth-eaten robe.

"Don't shout at me." Moisès heads for the door. He's got enough headaches from his wife, he doesn't need more from a hooker.

"Don't leave!"

"And what am I supposed to do? Stay here all night, waiting for a ghost to show up?"

"I won't ask you for anything else. Take care of my Tonet."

"Goodbye." With a shrug he puts on his jacket and leaves the room.

He's on the top floor of the La Mina bar, on Caçadors Street. Everyone knows full well what those stairs lead to, but he walks down them with feigned dignity and makes his way to the bar. There's so much smoke you'd think you were in a railway station. Lolo, short, bald, with the eyes of a sick fish and grease on his shirt, rushes to take his order.

"An anisette."

"Wasn't she enough for you?"

"It's to wash the taste of you out of my mouth, you fuck Giselle too much."

"It's a business relationship," laughs Lolo, and turns tail when another customer calls for him.

Moisès Corvo drinks his glass down in one gulp. Eight o'clock in the evening, too early to start working and too late to head home. Balmes Street is far away. If he waits a while he'll surely find a friendly face, because everyone there is familiar, but it's best not to make eye contact, not start any unwelcome conversations. Five minutes later Giselle comes down the stairs, withdrawn, as if she had gulped down all the brazenness she flaunts up there. After an exchange of coins and glances, Lolo blows her kisses and Giselle runs off. She passes Martínez, who looks her over before ordering a nice warm beer and starting to chat with Ortega, who's so soused that he doesn't even care that his wife is at home with "Three-Ball" Juli. He's celebrating having just robbed a couple of British boats stuck in the port, with the help of Miquel, who is now eating a salami sandwich at the corner table (dry bread, incredibly dry meat). Basically just another day at La Mina.

"Lolo!" shouts Moisès over the murmur of voices. The barman comes over to him.

"Another one?" Lolo is about to spit into the glass, to clean it before refilling it.

"No, no. It's a question." Lolo leans his head forward attentively. "Have you heard anything about a monster that's spiriting away children?"

Lolo sucks his teeth.

"Giselle already told you about that… didn't she?"

"Have you heard anything or not?"

Lolo hesitates, looks from one side to the other, and confirms that everyone can hear them. What can ya do?

"Yes. The girls are pretty nervous. They say that it's eight little ones now that have vanished. But since they're… well, you know, since they are what they are, they haven't reported anything."

"They're whores, and the police only want whores for one thing."

"You said it."

"Do you know any of the…"

"Yeah, Dorita."

"Any other one?"

"Àngels."

"Àngels the Hussy?"

"Do you know any other Àngels? Josefina disappeared two weeks ago. Poor thing, only two years old. Àngels hasn't left the house since."

"And how did it happen?"

"Who knows. She must have left her with someone when she was drunk, or she lost her at the market, or God knows where."

A man with a first-rate moustache leans with both arms on the bar, next to Moisès.

"Lolo, bring me one of whatever this bastard's drinking."

"Malsano, I knew it wouldn't be long before you showed up." Moisès doesn't even look at him when he speaks.

"Anise or piss and vinegar?" asks Lolo.

"Isn't that the same thing in this bar?"

Lolo heads towards the other end of the bar, wondering whether the joke didn't have some truth to it.

"We've got work, Sherlock."

17

"Call me Sherlock one more time, Malsano, and I'll rearrange your face."

"Hey, hey, hey…" Juan Malsano lifts one hand, peacefully, and with the other he pulls back his jacket to reveal his revolver. "Don't get all worked up, 'cause we're six against one here."

I move closer to One Eye without him realizing, poised to collect his soul. He doesn't know I'm about to ensnare him. I watch as he hides on Mendizábal Street, waiting for the performance to end. She likes the opera and money. People pretending to be somebody else, the opulent costumes, great passions, tragedies and miseries. A fake world of appearances, convention and protocol, far from reality. A world of masks. At least he isn't ashamed of who he is, doesn't need to pretend to be something he's not. Because he's no worse than the riff-raff that now paw at their imitation jewels at the end of the show, he says to himself. The pretentious music, which can be heard three blocks away, is over. In a little while, when all the lies have been said, when the mistresses have set dates with the respectable businessmen in some little apartment in the Eixample for a couple of hours from now, the procession will begin. That's why One Eye hid a few blocks up, because there are too many beggars on the Rambla. The municipal police will be busy beating them back to allow Mr Sostres's car through, no one will pay any attention to One Eye in this foul-smelling alley behind the Liceu Opera House. Sostres is the city's next mayor (even though the Lerrouxists and the regionalists tied in the 12th November elections, and he won't be chosen until 29th December). No one notices One Eye except me, but he can't see me or hear me now because I'm just a shadow waiting for his soul. One Eye doesn't get what it is the filthy rich see in that German chap, some guy named Bagner. How many times have the same clowns looked on as some singer bellows out fucking opera, in German, which not even Christ himself understands. Good music is hearing whores scream in a warm bed, he thinks. And he laughs, revealing his missing teeth. Today he won't rob anyone, even though it'd be like taking sweets from a baby. Today he has come to see her, which is why I've come to find him. He has something she might be interested in, because opera and money are not her only passions.

He hears the clip-clop of the horses and knows they are on their way. He can almost see them, dripping with jewels, with their fur coats and their husbands by the arm. How he'd love to have his way with some of them, to show them what a bravura performance is. One Eye shields himself from unwanted glances, in the darkness of the lampless street, until he sees her pass by. She is different from the rest. She walks alone, her head held high, with short, quick steps. Her lips pressed tightly together, her face impassive, like a wax figure. She has her hands crossed over her breasts, which are wrapped in a spectacular deep-red dress, a fancy number that goes all the way down to her ankles. Her hair, pulled back in a bun, reveals a long neck that resembles a column of smoke. One Eye licks his lips in desire. Approaching her is like leaning out of the highest window in a building: the sensation of being about to fall is as powerful as it is irresistible.

One Eye goes out onto Unió Street and follows her for a bit, while there are still people around. It is dark, but not yet dark enough to be the witching hour. The people of ill repute are getting ready to start the night. The worst of them all has just left the Liceu. When she turns onto Oleguer, he quickens his step. He pants, he's too old for this, goddamnittohell, and shouts, "Ma'am!"

She turns and glances at him, but doesn't speak. One Eye runs towards her, unaware that it is the last thing he will do before he dies.

When Moisès Corvo and Juan Malsano show up there, two hours later, the narrow street is jammed with people.

"Sherlock Holmes is a pedant. A piece of shit who never leaves his office, thinking he can solve every case like it was some maths problem, just because he's educated."

"But he does solve them, right?" Malsano plays along, fanning the flames. He knows how to provoke him.

"He botches it from the very beginning: for him everything is logic, logic and more logic. Even the most irrational."

"And that's not how it is…"

"No! You already know that! The world doesn't work that way: there are errors, misunderstandings, improvisation. Holmes underestimates the surprise factor."

"But he solves the cases," declares Malsano.

"Literature. It's impossible to arrive at the solution to any case by following a chain of deductions, there will always be someone to break it. Criminals play by their own rules."

"And Holmes doesn't." Beneath Malsano's moustache lies a mocking little smile.

"Not Holmes, and even less Dupin."

"Who?"

Moisès Corvo pushes aside a man on tiptoe who is trying to catch a glimpse of the dead body. One of the few men, in fact, since most of those present are women. They wear revolted expressions but don't want to give up their front-row view of One

Eye. The outraged man attempts to challenge him, but when he realizes that stocky Moisès would probably just lay him out as company for the deceased, he decides to pipe down and hope that none of the coarse women start laughing at him.

"Dupin, Edgar Allan Poe's detective, is even worse than Holmes. Holmes, at least, is seen through Watson and Watson's got a constant crafty streak, even though Holmes is a bully and treats him like shit. Ma'am, out of the way, goddamnit, do you know how late it is?" he scolds. "Dupin is a some sort of crime-solving machine who's never set foot on the street. I'd like to see him out in the real world, off the page, where all the murderers aren't stupid monkeys."

"There must be one that you like…"

"Lestrade. I like Lestrade. A Scotland Yard detective who does his job even though Holmes insists on humiliating him."

"Moisès, you read too much."

"And you talk too much, Juan… for God's sake!"

They reach the cordon made up of two policemen. They can make out the body, or at least its shape, beneath a blood-soaked sheet. The female spectators just cry and grumble disjointed sentences, as if they really cared about the poor wretch laid out there. A cutpurse slips into the unguarded pockets of the few men present who are consoling the women, hugging them close, feeling their breasts heaving against them. Moisès smacks his hand and the pickpocket scurries off like a mouse. One of the municipal policemen, when he sees them arriving, asks the crowd to move aside, but they don't pay him much mind. He gets tough, furrowing his brow, and finally manages to clear a small path with a couple of threats.

"Asensi, fuck, what happened?" asks Moisès.

"You're asking me? What do you think? One Eye, who must've been waiting for folk to come out of the opera and didn't know that today he'd be the star of his own show."

"How'd it happen?" Moisès moves closer, and Juan lifts up the sheet, which sticks to the victim's body for a few seconds.

"We don't know. No one saw anything until they found him like this, all sloppy."

"So no one's been arrested."

"You don't miss a beat."

Moisès shoots him a look and Officer Asensi understands that he's used up today's quota of familiarity. The body is in a puddle of blood, twisted, its hands stiff as claws, with one eye staring at the sky and the other, the empty socket, stuck in hell. He looks like a white cockroach.

Moisès approaches and squats beside Juan, but he's distracted. All he can hear are the comments of the ring of people, who seem even more excited by his arrival. You fear me, but I'm your favourite spectacle: when I show up, you can't look away.

They always come when the evil's been done, he hears a slender woman say.

"Isn't it too early for this stiffness?" asks Juan.

Moisès touches One Eye's cold fingers, which now have as much life in them as a banister. His face is out of joint and pale as a candle, his mouth a grotesque grimace. He bled to death, thinks Moisès, but he doesn't see any wound. His neck is stained with blood, and in the darkness it looks like tar.

"It's the panic. His death was so sudden that the panic paralysed him." He rolls up his sleeves, revealing his forearms. "He has no defensive injuries, but from the position of the body it seems the killer was standing right in front of him."

"He wasn't expecting it. But how did he bleed to death?"

A monster, hears Moisès. The rumour grows around him.

"Asensi, get all this riff-raff out of here, fuck, they don't belong at the scene."

Asensi does as he's told, but the people basically ignore him. Fascinated, they retreat a few feet and come right back when Asensi's gaze returns to the dead body. Moisès grabs a hand-kerchief and cleans the blood off its neck until he finds what he was looking for. A ripped-off piece of flesh, with the skin flapping over it. Moisès sticks his right-hand index finger into the wound, confirming for Malsano, once again, that sometimes Corvo is crazy.

"Right at the jugular. However it was done, this attack was direct and brutal."

The buzz on the street grows. He's white! They drained all his blood!

"But this isn't a knife wound, and it wasn't made by a firearm either, Moisès," Juan says, stating his fears out loud. He senses what made that wound, but he doesn't want to believe it.

"The cut is semicircular, but not precise. As if it had been made with a small saw. But a saw would have been more destructive, and there would be signs of struggle. The body has no other visible blows. In any case, we'll have to wait for the autopsy…"

"Do you think it's possible?"

Moisès turns the cadaver upside down, as if he were hauling a sack. And, in fact, that was what it was for him. Just a sack, nothing more than work. He takes off the corpse's jacket and, with a small knife, strips the shirt off its back. A screech from the crowd gets Asensi worked up again and he is about to pull out his truncheon. But he's curious too. Moisès carefully looks over the arms. He asks for a lantern, which the other municipal brings him. On his upper right arm there are four small bruises in the shape of a crescent moon. On the left arm, there are three.

"They got him from the front. The aggressor grabbed him from the front… and bit him."

A woman faints. Moisès turns when he hears the uproar.

"It's a mouthful," continues Juan looking at One Eye. "They pulled out that piece of flesh with a bite."

A reporter arrives, equipped with a notebook and pencil.

"Inspector Corvo!" he shouts.

"Not now, Quim."

"Come on, man, it's still warm!"

Juan stands up and addresses the journalist.

"Do you want to feel how warm my fists can get?"

He shakes his head.

"Then shut up."

From the Ronda de Sant Pau to Ciutadella Park, the rumour spreads that the monster is hungry.

While Judge Fernando de Prat is arriving, a couple of babies cry for their mothers' attention. As if it were a factory whistle, the spectators begin to file out. Some of them want to make sure their children are at home, sleeping beneath the blankets, even if they're full of lice. Others would rather not meet up with the magistrate face to face, in case he reminds them that they're due in court one of these days, that they owe a fine or have a sentence to serve. There are those who suspect that it's now questioning time, that the police will start interrogating anyone who has a mouth and eyes and, in this neighbourhood, it's best to be mute and blind. Surely better than being one-eyed like the poor stiff, which is starting to stink, if it didn't stink to begin with.

When he sees Don Fernando de Prat step out of his Hispano Suiza car into the commotion on Sant Pau Street, with an inhospitable expression, smoking jacket over his pyjamas and a pipe at his lips, Blackmouth turns tail and heads down Om Street towards Drassanes, where One Eye's carriage sits, still carrying the body they dug up in Montjuïc. He takes it to the port, where the topmasts sway to the slow, deliberate rhythm of the sea breeze and, making sure there are no prying eyes around, gets rid of the body by dumping it into the water, with a crashing noise like a rock falling from a mountain. Blackmouth runs off, leaving One Eye's carriage. He won't need it now, he says to himself, and he heads home, to the pigeon loft on Lluna Street, wary of the dark, which is where vampires hide.

Don Fernando de Prat looks obliquely at the body, without much interest, and starts up the usual shop talk with Moisès and Malsano. He acts as if he wants to know what happened, but he's only thinking about going back to bed once this damn on-call shift is over.

"If we at least had cameras," laments Corvo when de Prat asks him to prepare a report on what happened for the next day.

"Draw, like you've done your whole life."

"Sometimes life ends, Your Honour, and we move on to a better one. I would recommend you ask our guest for tonight, but I think his reply would be too cold."

The magistrate ignores Corvo's sarcasm because the doctor has just arrived.

"Tell me he's dead, I want to go home and sleep."

Doctor Ortiz, moustache held high and satchel in his hand, is a man of few words. He crouches over the body and puts a little mirror in front of its mouth.

"Maybe you'll have more luck with the neck wound, doctor," says Corvo, who gets no response.

He checks the pulse, looks into the eyes and stands up.

"Take him to the Clínic for me."

And having said that, he shakes the judge's hand and heads off from whence he came. He can dispense with formalities. Don Fernando de Prat, Moisès and Malsano know him well enough. Just as they know each other. They've all met up many a night around a corpse. And so the judge decides that that's enough for today and that tomorrow's another day, God willing. The two detectives wait alone on the street for them to cart off the body, with no more company than a limping dog that groans and stops to lick the puddle of blood off the paving stones.

At number twenty-nine Ponent Street, not far from where One Eye was found, Salvador Vaquer has only been in bed for a short while. He was in the study waiting for Enriqueta to come home. His eyelids were heavy. Then he got up and went to the room of little Angelina, who was sleeping. He locked it with a key and opened the door to a large closet, where Dorita's daughter sat on a straw mattress. She was crying.

"What's wrong, pretty girl?" Salvador approached her and caressed her short, clumsily cut hair.

"I'm scared," she whimpered.

"Why? You don't have to be scared of anything." Salvador slid his fingers down the little girl's neck and then her chest. She's four years old, at most.

"I want my mummy…"

"I'm here, sweetheart, I'm here."

Salvador now smells his fingers, which hold the girl's scent. From the bed he hears keys at the door and the woman entering.

A twinge makes him feel guilty, and despite the cold he starts to sweat. He pricks up his ear, like a hunting hound, and he imagines her going first through the dining room, then the kitchen and finally the large closet, where she stops. Silence.

Enriqueta opens the door to the bedroom and Salvador pretends to be sleeping. She undresses in the dark and gets into bed. She embraces him from behind. Salvador bites his lips when she lays her cold fingers on his ribs. She breathes deeply and lets out a whistle from between her teeth that makes him think of a snake. The woman bites his ear and then runs her tongue along the nape of his neck, while her hand slithers down his pubic bone until it catches its prey. He turns and kisses her: her mouth is hot and salty.

Like blood.

2

G REASE SLIDES ALONG THE TILES. The sink is stopped
up. The brazier's embers trace shadows that sway to and
fro in a spectral shivering. These are the few signs of life, as mis-
leading as they may be, of the morgue at the Hospital Clínic.
On one of the tables lies the sewn-up body of One Eye, white
and rigid, with contusions on its back, arms and legs. Less dead
than the decapitated body that rests on the table beside it, judg-
ing by its smell. They found the corpse very early, floating in the
port, beneath a mountain of seagulls. In fact, they wouldn't have
even noticed it if it weren't for the din of the big birds screeching
and fighting for a piece of rotten meat in front of the statue of
Columbus with its outstretched finger. Doctor Ortiz believes that
the discoverer of the Americas was pointing out the dead chunk,
as if asking them to get it out of there. Now the doctor taps the
floor with his feet, first the right, then the left, to drive out the
cockroaches that smell a banquet.

"Have you started the party without us?" bellows Moisès after
coming down the spiral staircase that leads to the autopsy room.
"I hope I won't have to dance with the ugliest girl…"

And he looks at the headless body. Doctor Ortiz furrows his
brows and shakes his hand. He does the same with Juan, who
comes down behind him.

"Good evening."

Everyone knows it's a figure of speech. Doctor Ortiz doesn't think this is a good evening. He doesn't even think it's a good anything. He called them in because he wants to show them something on the corpse with the bite mark.

"Let's get down to it, doctor," pressures Juan. "We've hardly slept today and I'd like to take a nap before the shift is over."

"I think there are still some free beds, if you want, and even some company, the kind that doesn't complain much," replies Moisès.

"Is the comedy show over, gentlemen, or am I going to have to start charging admission?"

"And what about this one? Do we know what it's doing here?"

"He just came in a little while ago." The doctor pats the chest of the body, since it has no head, and a stream of insects splashes onto Juan's feet.

"Goddamnittohell!"

Moisès leans over the corpse, covering his nostrils and mouth with a handkerchief that has his initials embroidered on it. It is the only thing of his wife's that he carries with him.

"Here we have the best proof that, indeed, there is life after death. A lot of life."

The stench is almost unbearable, and with the brazier it is asphyxiating. Doctor Ortiz knows how to make sure visitors don't overstay their welcome.

"As I said, he had already been a *client* of mine. A poor wretch who threw himself onto the railway track and ended up like this… well, not quite like this."

"And what was this Marie Antoinette doing in the port? Now even the deceased are in on this stupid swimming craze?"

"Mr Corvo, I'll pretend I don't hear your insightful comments and I'll refer you to your colleague, Inspector Sánchez, who is handling the case."

Buenaventura Sánchez. The perfect policeman. If Juli Vallmitjana wrote about the coppers instead of about the plebs, Buenaventura would be the main character. Tall, handsome, with spiky hair and light eyes, a hypocritical smile and pat on the back, a guy who knows everything about crime and how to fight it. A policeman so perfect that he's the apple of his boss's eye. The district chief of Barcelona, José Millán Astray, can't stop listing his virtues while Buenaventura brings him warm milk and tucks him into bed. With everyone else he acts like a know-all, like someone who knows he'll go far, or at least thinks he will. Juan Malsano can't stand looking at him, and Moisès Corvo has already broken his face once.

"Has Inspector Sánchez been here? I think I can smell his perfume…"

"He came this afternoon, Inspector, with Doctor Saforcada, who did the autopsy on the subject I called you here about."

"And what did Doctor Saforcada find?" asks Juan.

"Your monster. It's human. Or at least, a human with necrophagous tendencies."

"So we can rule out the Wolfman or Count Dracula?"

"Inspector Corvo, come here." He stands beside the table and grabs One Eye by the arms. "Four ecchymoses on one arm and three on the other. What does that tell you?"

"That they held him down before he died, from in front. Someone with some strength…"

"Don't tell me something we all know already. Think. Why are there three on one arm and four on the other?"

"Because the killer has missing fingers?"

"Ectrodactylism. That's a possibility. And it would definitely limit the search field."

"Our fingerprint archives are still small," says Juan, running his fingers over his moustache. He has been breathing in that same air for so many years now that he barely smells the odour of putrefaction except when he takes off his clothes in the morning, before getting into bed.

"Yes," continues Moisès, "Professor Oloriz is just now supervising the archives' creation. And to top it all, there's all sorts of people coming back from the war against the Moors missing a hand, with their trousers knotted up at the knee, or in a pine box."

"I said it's a possibility. What's the other?" Silence. "That one of his hands was busy with something else."

He moves One Eye's body like a dried-out baguette and pushes it closer to the lamp, revealing a fourth bruise, smaller and longer than the rest.

"He was carrying a knife?"

"A knife would have left a cut. It must have been a pointed tool, like a bodkin."

"But there's no bodkin wound either."

"Not at first glance, but we didn't bring him here to sing us a zarzuela, did we?"

"If you want your part of the ticket money for the show, doctor, all you have to do is say so," grumbles Moisès.

The doctor positions himself to touch One Eye's head, shaved and sewn up clumsily, and opens the neck wound. You spend half your life seeking me out and the other half running from me. You rough up the corpses, jab at the flesh, looking for explanations inside the bodies that bear my mark. Who? How? Why?

The answers are within these men's reach, these men that shuffle around dead bodies like someone looking for the answer to an arithmetic problem.

"This is a human bite. We can tell from the diameter, from the way the skin is broken and the teeth marks, which fit with a human odontogram. But the killer's first attack wasn't the bite. He would have to have been a real big brute to just grab somebody, even a very weak victim, and bite off a piece of their neck."

Moisès looks inside the opening, but doesn't make out anything.

"Here," continues the doctor. "This cut on the inner part isn't consistent with the bite, but with a lacerated-contused wound stemming from a weapon, such as a bodkin."

"Such as a bodkin."

"Or a hairpin."

"What murderer wears a hairpin?"

"What murderer drinks their victim's blood?"

Moisès Corvo closes his eyes and the memory of Rif comes flooding into his head, as vivid as the warmth of the room he is in. Soldiers who eat human flesh in order to survive. Were they monsters then? He himself had cut off the enemy's fingers and ears as some kind of stupid souvenir of his tour of Africa; was he a monster?

"Who could do something like this?" asks Juan.

"You two are the policemen, gentlemen. I'm just a doctor. There you have the clothes, which haven't been inspected."

Moisès picks them up off the table and separates them. He starts with the wrinkled jacket, then moves on to the shirt. It feels like parchment where the blood has already dried, and slippery where it's still damp. There doesn't seem to be anything useful, until Juan pulls a crumpled piece of paper out of the trousers.

It's a map, written in pencil. On the back, they couldn't have had a better stroke of luck: it's a doctor's business card.

"Doctor Isaac von Baumgarten," reads Juan. "Do you know him?"

"No."

"But you're both doctors…" he replies, annoyed.

Doctor Ortiz bites his tongue. They'll be leaving soon and he'll be left with the only company he gets along with, the dead, who are considerate enough not to spend the night saying stupid things and expecting a nice response.

Barcelona is an old lady with a battered soul, who has been left by a thousand lovers but refuses to admit it. Every time she grows, she looks in the mirror, sees herself changed and renews all her blood until it's almost at boiling point. Like a butterfly's cocoon, she finally bursts. Distrust becomes the first phase of gestation: no one is sure that he whom they've lived with for years, whom they've considered a neighbour, isn't now an enemy. All of a sudden they put up walls, making obvious the differences among Barcelonians, and each one takes refuge in his own universe, prepared to defend or attack. And this is how violence, the second phase in the metamorphosis from bug to butterfly, becomes an irreversible phenomenon. Over some petty thing, some groundless motive, some made-up excuse, the old lady is once again covered with scars and burns; she screams madly and pays homage to me. These are days when I stroll openly through the streets of a city devoted to me, and I enter a thousand bodies anxious to please me. I collect souls in abundance, without paying attention to names or faces. Slain Jews and monasteries in flames. Blood and fire create the soot that will be the make-up Barcelona smears on to become old again. Renewal as the final step, the pretence that nothing happened although now everything is different, will make the city both a wiser woman and, at the same time, a more aggrieved one.

And thus, along these scarifications that are the narrow streets of the old quarter, Moisès Corvo and Juan Malsano search for the origin of the evil that is now more than just a rumour, that is breeding fear. And only three years have passed since the last wave of violence. They head down Raurich Street—a dark, damp ravine that's misty around its amber street lamps and cloaked in sepulchral silence—and stop at number twenty, the address of Doctor Isaac von Baumgarten.

Just as the half-asleep doctor opens the door slightly, a whore crosses Tres Llits with a customer. Malsano thinks he recognizes him as a famous politician, and so he turns his gaze, trying to summon up his name, just in case some day it comes in handy. Later he'll jot it down in a notebook, beside all the notes on strange Doctor von Baumgarten.

Isaac von Baumgarten is short and thickset, not really fat. His blond hair is always well combed, but not now, not at this hour. Gentlemen, what is it that you want, his eyes are puffy with sleep and he wears a robe over his pyjamas. It's cold; he shivers and shakes when they identify themselves as policeman because, holy shit, they've caught me.

"Doctor?" says Malsano with his foot prepared to keep him from slamming the door shut.

"Yes?" He is afraid.

"Do you know One Eye?" Corvo isn't up for playing games. It's night, it's late and he's a cop; he's not going to beat around the bush.

"No," he lies, but his small ice-blue eyes, puffy with sleep, give him away.

"Then how do you explain this?" He shows him the business card, the full name clear as day, wrinkled but intelligible.

"Where did it come from?"

"Can we come in?" Malsano's legs are cold. Besides, it's awkward talking to half a face. Doctor von Baumgarten still hasn't replied when Moisès Corvo pushes the door and enters.

It isn't quite a doctor's office, but it's not a private residence either. The entrance is austere. Its sagging walls are clean, with greenish wallpaper, and illuminated by an electric lamp besieged by an insomniac moth. There are no personal photographs, not even the slightest trace of any family life, notices Moisès.

"How do you know him?"

"He helps me." He doesn't know where to hide his hands, Moisès also detects.

"Helps you what?"

"He just helps me, that's all."

"He works for you?"

"It's not exactly that, but he does some errands for me. Would you like some coffee?" An unidentified accent makes its way through his "s"s.

"If I said yes, you'd have some too, and then I'd have to nail you to the wall to keep from getting seasick with all your shaking."

"I, uh…"

"Work alone?"

"Me?"

"One Eye."

"Yes… I mean, no… I haven't seen him in two days, since I sent him to pick up a corpse from Montjuïc. The card is his, that's for sure, on the back is the sketch he drew. Sometimes he comes with a lad. A youngster who barely speaks. He's never crossed the threshold. He stays outside, like a little dog, waiting."

"Do you know who he is?"

"I'm foreign. I don't know anyone, and those I do know, I'd rather not."

"Well, now you know us, doctor, and it would behove you to start remembering." Malsano inspects the entrance and stops in front of a closed door. Doctor von Baumgarten carries the key in his pocket and he caresses it with his soft fingers.

"How long have you lived here?" Corvo continues his questioning.

"Can you tell me what happened?" The doctor approaches the exit.

"Did you not understand me?" responds Corvo.

"Two years, not quite. I'm Austrian."

"And what brought you here?" Malsano is getting tired. He opens a drawer. No bodkins, no fangs. It doesn't look like the doctor dresses up as a vampire for his evening walks.

"Friends?" ridicules Corvo.

"I am a doctor. You've already seen that on the card."

"An Austrian doctor. You wouldn't be one of those psycho-analysts who are everywhere these days, would you?"

"No, no. Those are a gang of illusionists who think they're practising science when they chalk everything up to fucking. I am a phrenologist, of the positivist school."

"Aha, Lombroso," says Moisès. "I know some of his theories on anarchy." He doesn't add that he read them at the printing press where his brother works, flipping through *Criminal Man* to kill time and because the title amused him.

"Will you tell me what happened? Is he dead?" Doctor von Baumgarten takes the lead.

"Why do you ask that?"

"Because if he weren't, I don't suppose the police would be waking me up at this hour of the night."

"We came to bring you a glass of warm milk, so you can have sweet dreams," growls Corvo. "But you must not be very thirsty. What's the name of the boy who comes with One Eye?"

"I only know his nickname. He always called him Blackmouth."

"You see, how it's all coming back to you?... Where can I find him?"

"It was always One Eye who came to see me."

"We would have liked to invite him, but he had a small problem of... how would you say it... death."

Now I would be smiling. I liked Moisès Corvo, with his sense of humour that was so dark, so dear to me.

"Gentlemen, it is late and I can't be of any more help to you. Please forgive me, but I am going back to bed."

Moisès Corvo slaps on his hat and buttons his coat. That was enough for the first round, but this bloke knows more than he's saying, we'll meet again.

"Farewell, Inspectors..."

"Corvo and Malsano," answers Juan on their way out of the door.

They walk towards Ferran Street, where there is more foot traffic. It's the weekend, and sailors hungry for nightlife have left their boats docked in the port.

Let's go to the Napoleón, says Moisès Corvo out loud. The cinema on the Rambla Santa Mònica, closed hours ago, is the roof under which Sebastián, the projectionist, sleeps as well as works. When the screenings are over and the audience has gone home or to bed (which aren't always the same place), he opens the doors of the booth to the policeman and lets him in. They chat while he puts on one of those Italian movies that are all the rage now, he brings him up to date on the latest gossip which, in the long run, is often significant, and they smoke like chimneys until the projection moves from the screen to the wall of smoke they've created in the seating area. Sebastián has known the inspector since the war, they were in the same levy, and a few years back he found peace at the Napoleón. It was Corvo who arrested him at the start of the century when he stole, from a train in the North Station, a shipment of paintings that had been forged in Belgium, and it was also Corvo who found him the job at the cinema when he got out of prison. No grudges held, you do your job and when you nabbed me it was nothing personal. Now Sebastián, with his blue eyes, hooked nose and two daughters he hardly ever sees, has mellowed but he still lusts mightily after women. And that makes Moisès, womanizer that he is, feel comfortable.

Today both the inspectors will go and wake him up, put on a film and sit to chat for a while. It is starting to be time for the wall of secrets closing in on them to be hammered down.

They can't even begin to imagine the horror hidden behind it.

3

I T'S A FROZEN WINTER MORNING, Christmas is drawing near and the street is filled with youngsters playing. Near them, in the shadow of doorways, hand over hand on laps and attentive gazes, circles of women watch over them while the men are at work. Corvo sleeps, far from the racket, in his flat on Balmes Street, but his wife is nearby, watching over him as well, in her way, searching through the pockets of his jacket, sniffing his shirt collar and checking the starched feel of his underwear. Luckily for the detective, the smell of rotting corpse is so strong it drowns out the scent of shady intentions and sex for money, and Conxita is left to think that her husband has only been seeing cadavers and criminals. Conxita is a bit thick, but she doesn't know it, so she's happy.

Blackmouth went down to the street with the four coins León Domènech gave him for breakfast. He would rather not have left his den, because he has the feeling they're looking for him. He doesn't know what he's more afraid of: the coppers or her, the Bloodsucker. If the flatfoots link him to One Eye, they could accuse him of having killed him (there's no motive, there's no evidence, but since when do coppers need that?). If One Eye,

may he rest in peace, said anything about him before passing...
he doesn't even want to think about it. He buys some curd
cheese from a vendor who carries the cheeses in a cart covered
by a rag, and he smiles in appreciation. When she sees his teeth
she makes a repulsed face and gives him the change as rudely
as she can. Shorting him, obviously. Blackmouth puts the coins
away in two different pockets: one for León—that curd cheese
gets pricier every day, he'll claim—and the other for him. When
the cheese-seller isn't looking, he filches a bit of cheese from the
cart and licks his finger.

"Good day, ma'am," he says in parting.

"Piss off, wretch."

It will be a bad day for Blackmouth, which isn't terribly
surprising if you take into account the fact that his life is a long
series of frustrations and fears. He can't complain, in the end;
someone with no idea of what it is to live well can't compare it
with his own lot. And everything he has he gets from those who
can afford to lose it. It's nature's law, he says to himself, in a world
where the law is written on the wind.

He can hear León's guitar from the street. Today his student
is Isabel, the sixteen-year-old daughter of the milkmaid of Xuclà
Street, hideously ugly and with as much musical talent as the
cockroaches just crushed under Blackmouth's boots. Maybe a
bit less, even. Isabel is under the mistaken impression that if she
learns to play the guitar she can join an orchestra, perform on
Paral·lel (which is truly a pretty futile ambition to begin with), meet
a good man who will sing her to sleep every night and never have
to work again. In the end, it's León Domènech who does most of
the "playing", and just then Blackmouth spies in silence from the
entryway. León plays at coming very close to the girl, stroking and

sniffing. He's blind, but he's plenty well equipped with the other senses. Blackmouth grows stiff as he watches and says to himself, how clever is this bloke, the whole neighbourhood hears him scratching out chords and he still pretends he's a teacher. If he's lucky, he'll corner Isabel and suggest, who knows, that she suck his willy (that's how Blackmouth refers to his knob: deep down he's still a boy), because today he feels lucky. He is very wrong.

Once the girl has paid León and said goodbye with a kiss on each cheek, the old blind man has him come in. I know you were watching, pig, and I haven't forgotten, about the coins, you can hand over that change. Someone's knocking at the door, it must be Isabel, probably left her book of sheet music.

"Go and open up," orders León, and Blackmouth, accepting his role as a servant, is there in two strides.

It is Salvador Vaquer on the other side of the door. He had come looking for him.

"Enriqueta wants to see you, now."

Blackmouth and Salvador head over to Ponent Street, and the boy lowers his head when they pass a couple of municipal policemen running to some emergency on Peu de la Creu. Salvador Vaquer notices and says they're not looking for you, not yet, and Blackmouth feels a shiver.

The most merciful way to define Salvador Vaquer is to lie. There are certain people whose absence, if they disappeared without a trace from one day to the next, nobody would notice. Salvador Vaquer is so insignificant that it's not worth the trouble even including him on such a deplorable list. Fat, lame and lowly, he hides his baldness beneath a hat that's too big for him and a substantial moustache that leans over the abyss of lips that don't speak so they won't be answered. He lives in the shadow of Enriqueta, with an

41

inferiority complex over the notable influence of her former husband (another piece of work) and her father. I'll tell you more about them all later, and you will see how they talk, how they think and how they lie. Salvador Vaquer gets it from all sides, but he never has the pluck to rebel. It could be said that he's doing fine, that he doesn't need to be a person, that someone has to fill the role of fall guy. He's not ambitious, he's not sly and he never raises his voice. But he's not a good man, either. The flat on Ponent is at number twenty-nine, and it is one of the three that Enriqueta uses to carry out her activities (the other two are on Picalquers and Tallers, but she doesn't usually live in them). Light manages to sneak in through the balcony, until it ignites into sparks the scrolls of fine dust that dance in the air. Yet Enriqueta remains in shadow.

Blackmouth grows pale, as if the blood were fleeing his body out of fear of the woman. She savours it, because she knows she has that effect on people. She knows she is feared.

She says nothing, merely studies him from the darkness. Blackmouth can make out small eyes, fallen, as if sad. He shivers when he realizes that Enriqueta's gaze is no more dynamic than the dust that floats before her. You called for me, ma'am, he states, to hear his voice, since he can no longer hear his heart beating. She doesn't respond, not yet.

A girl cries behind a door and then Enriqueta, placid and inscrutable as a caryatid, has him sit down and she sits beside him. Blackmouth is a bag of nerves, shrinking like a mouse into a corner when the lights are turned on.

The screams and wails have become scratching on the wood. The black metal key is in the lock and it trembles.

"You're handsome," she says, with a cracked voice. "And very young, but I think you're not getting enough to eat."

"No, ma'am."

"You want to eat?" And with a hand gesture Salvador disappears and returns with a tray filled with biscuits. Some are butter biscuits and others have fruit.

Blackmouth grabs three at once and brings them all to his gob. He chews greedily and is about to choke, while Enriqueta watches him and smiles for the first time. He is surprised, because it is a sweet, friendly smile. Another hand movement makes Salvador appear with a glass of beer, warm, but beer. Blackmouth swallows the lump.

"You want to eat more?" she repeats.

"No, ma'am, I'm full."

"You didn't understand me: do you want to eat more often?"

"I don't work for nobody, ma'am." Blackmouth doesn't yet know if he is doing the right thing by refusing Enriqueta's invitation.

"I'm not asking you to work for me. I'm suggesting you help me. One Eye did me a real service, yes, but now, the poor bloke… has died on us."

There couldn't be more cynicism in her words, but she doesn't bother to conceal it. Blackmouth looks her up and down. The fearless face, the nostrils widening as her eyes close, as if trying to smell his fear. Enriqueta bites a lip, Blackmouth feels tired. Talking to her is exhausting because he has to show his strength at all times, that he's tough and won't cave. She is a bloodsucker, he thinks, but then blushes, believing she has read his thoughts.

"What would I have to do, ma'am?"

Enriqueta is about forty years old, but when she draws close to Blackmouth she resembles a sculpture thousands of years old, a marble body without a soul. He sees her small, sharp teeth, which emit a barely perceptible whistle.

"One Eye never told you what he did?"

"Never."

He didn't need to. After every visit to Enriqueta, One Eye seemed more hypnotized, stuck in a spider's web he didn't want to extricate himself from. She is captivating and horrifying all at the same time. Salvador Vaquer, standing in a corner of the dining room, is just a slave, a zombie.

Enriqueta gets up and smoothes her skirt with twisted, malformed hands, like claws. She opens the drawer of an old side table that creaks and pulls out a machete. Here, she offers it to the boy, and he accepts it. He fears what will come next, but he can do nothing to avoid it. Salvador opens the door and Blackmouth sees a dark girl, little more than four years old, with clean but knotted hair, her face covered in snot and clothes that look new. She stops screaming and only whines, and Enriqueta takes her hand.

Blackmouth kneels, but he cannot look the girl in the eye. He caresses the machete handle just as he smells something delicious coming from the kitchen. The bubbling of the pot works its way into his brain. Enriqueta closes the window and the blinds so the screams won't be heard out on the street.

The next day, Moisès Corvo and Juan Malsano find Blackmouth on the roof where he lives, and Corvo fractures his incisor before saying good evening. His fist hurts, the lad is all dried-out skin and rock-hard muscle, but over the years the policeman has learnt that a little pain in the knuckles right at the start saves him saliva in the end.

"One Eye is dead and you are the last one he worked with." Malsano reveals his intentions before Blackmouth gets up off the floor, his chops bleeding.

"Who are you?"

Since he knows full well, but is playing dumb, he earns himself a blow to the nape of the neck. This time with the back of the hand and without damaging any teeth, but with a warm, foul taste of blood on his palate that he doesn't entirely dislike.

"I don't know nothing."

The third blow is like a very full glass of beer, thinks Corvo, it always loosens the tongue of the person you bought it for.

"One Eye worked for a foreign doctor on Raurich Street. He'll know what happened to him."

"He's the one who told us you were with him on the very night he was killed," says Malsano, calling the shots.

"No, no, no. We had an argument. I wasn't working with him any more."

"And the body you stole from the cemetery?"

"What body?"

Corvo grabs him by his nape with one hand, like an eagle hunting a rabbit, but a pathetic, emaciated rabbit, and drags him over to the railing.

"You decide. You learn to fly in less than thirty seconds or you can start talking." Corvo's not joking.

"I don't know what you're talking about! One Eye was mixed up in some very strange business, and it scared me too much."

Corvo leans him over the street. The boy's torso is suspended over the edge, he flails his arms, searching for something to grab onto.

"You guys steal a headless corpse and One Eye shows up dead and bled dry. It's not so much that I find your tomb-sacking reprehensible, it's that I don't like you randomly scattering the city with dead bodies. It's a bother, and it makes a stink almost as bad as your crotch right now."

"Black magic!" It's the first thing that comes into Blackmouth's head. The reply must not convince Corvo, because he lets him fall a bit further, making his balance increasingly difficult.

"You think I'm an idiot. Remember that idiots have bad memories and sometimes they forget they're holding somebody up over a four-storey drop."

"No, no. I'm not lying," he lies. "One Eye wanted the corpse for black magic, for witchcraft."

"One Eye couldn't tell the difference between electric light and a pile of horseshit. You want me to believe he was a necromancer?"

"A what?"

Corvo is about to let him go. But he is the only means he has for resolving a crap murder with a crap victim. Who cares who killed One Eye? They should build whoever it was a monument. Normally he would have made a toast to the son of a bitch who'd taken him out of circulation, one less lowlife on the streets. A wretch and wastrel, a grave defiler and a war amputee. Definitely a lowlife. But it could be that something different is hiding behind that death, one of so many that happen every day in this city of masks and lies. It could be an open door that leads to the monster, or that man that passes as one.

"One Eye dealt with strange people. Healers, charlatans, people like that."

"Have you ever seen an execution by hanging, Blackmouth?"

Corvo pulls him away from the drop and throws him against the terrace tiles. Some pigeons wake up and coo, but the city keeps pretending nothing's going on.

"No." Blackmouth is no longer afraid. It seems the danger has passed.

"Of course not. Because it's been a while since the executioner has been working his trade around here. And you know why? Because when I ask questions, people tend to talk. And if they don't talk, then I make sure they never do again. I'm the jealous type."

"I'm talking, I'm talking. I'll tell you everything I know."

"You should know more." Blackmouth hastens to invent a good story. The two policemen look at him, expectant.

"Some Negroes…" he says, but he knows he has to be more specific. "I don't know their names, but they're two big Negroes, from Africa, who came to Barcelona a few months ago. They knew what One Eye did for a living and they asked him for bodies."

Corvo pulls out his revolver and opens the cylinder. He has six bullets, perfect. He closes it and points it at Blackmouth.

"With this shit you won't even make it to the gallows."

"It's true. They are two huge Negroes, from the area around the Santa Madrona gate. Ask whoever you want, you'll see I'm not lying. They have the Cubans and the Filipinos scared out of their wits. They threaten to keep their souls and things like that. One Eye got mixed up with them, but I didn't want to have anything to do with it, that kind of stuff gives me the jitters."

Blackmouth is lying, but not entirely. The two Negroes he is talking about are two Guineans from the colonies who extort their fellow countrymen and other unfortunates who believe that if they don't pay like a good Christian should, excuse my irony, they will turn them into zombies, into walking dead who owe their masters obedience. Blackmouth got into it with them once when they caught him stealing their money, and his ribs still hurt.

"And they killed him?" asks Malsano.

"I don't know, I haven't seen One Eye for a while."

"But you were seeing him to go to the doctor's house. What kind of neighbours do you have, who are only interested in rotting bodies?"

"I can take you to them. I can help you catch them."

"Now you want to work for us?"

4

M OISÈS CORVO IS A DOG: nobody pisses in his territory. And if that means stinking up the whole neighbourhood with the cloying stench of urine, he has no problem with that. Moisès Corvo quit walking the beat some time ago, quit being cannon fodder, with a blindfold over his eyes and a yes sir on his lips, to become the gun dog he is now.

He's no longer the defender of the good folk, because he no longer believes in good folk. In Corvo's specific world there are only two types of people: the ones that are like him and the ones who aren't. And he devotes all his efforts to taking the second group out of circulation, without questioning whether, in that crusade destined for defeat, he himself has switched sides. His whole life he's swum through the filth, and you know that if you stir shit up, something's going to get stuck under your nails. The difference between him and the others is that he is convinced there is a difference.

Corvo is an old dog, grim-faced and filled with vices, but he isn't ready to give the streets over to anyone. And much less to these newcomers that Blackmouth wants him to believe killed One Eye and who are abducting children for rituals they've imported from their savage country. As if we didn't have enough with the riff-raff that are from here, now they come from abroad, exclaims Corvo every time the conversation goes down those paths. The detective is of the opinion that the city's not big enough for everyone, that these guys come to do wrong, that any day now the city's going to blow up in their faces, but this time the target won't be churches and convents, which is practically a tradition in Barcelona. The mark will be shopkeepers, workers who get up early each day, the midwives and the tramcar drivers. The police… we coppers are already used to the blows, we've got tough hides and lean flesh. Even still, Corvo's thoughts are pure bar ramblings, cheap Lerrouxism that dissolves the second he remembers Ismael, the little son of a bitch who drives the druggists crazy, or Vicente, a real bastard who steals pieces of industrial machinery to resell them by the kilo; when he remembers how those two mark their victims' faces with rusty knives, or beat people up just for fun, then he curses all the criminals born in this country, in a society where the rich get richer and the poor get poorer, blah blah blah taken from the last book he read or some newspaper headline that caught his eye.

Blackmouth gets another blow to the back of the neck from Moisès Corvo, which makes Juan Malsano burst into laughter.

"What was that for?"

"Just in case."

They are on a roof near the Santa Madrona gate, pitch black, sea salt in the icy air that freezes the jangle of the watchman's keys. Corvo can't get the Apaches out of his head.

It was barely over a year ago that Moisès Corvo took part in an operation to round up a group of Frenchmen who crossed the border to rob jewellery stores in Barcelona. They were the Apaches, a clan that had formed as a criminal gang on the outskirts of Paris and just kept growing. The reason for their name was quite simple: they acted as a group and they were very violent and merciless, like the American Indians were rumoured to be. The description they had to work with was as flimsy as "they've got moustaches and speak French", so both Moisès and his colleagues spent weeks waiting outside jewellery shops and in coach houses for the Apaches to show up. After hanging out on a corner for four hours, keeping watch over the entrance to Dalmau Jewellery on Casp Street, Moisès no longer knew where to hide. He had already drunk six anises to combat the cold and, with his head foggy, he came to the conclusion that the operation was as foolish as any of the houses those new two-bit architects were building everywhere. You tell me if a municipal cop couldn't handle this, he said to himself, as Mr Dalmau, who knew nothing of the surveillance, came out again and again to make sure that that tall, moustachioed loner who was a bit tipsy didn't speak French.

He was so fixed on Moisès, and Moisès was so fed up with standing around there without any good spot to stretch out for a nap, that neither of them reacted when a small, stocky individual, dressed entirely in black and with a bowler hat bouncing around on his head, went into the jewellery store and punched Mr Dalmau in the eye, just like that, as motivation. His wife screams, and a second man comes in with a young bloke, both in rigorous black, like someone heading to a funeral. While the little guy beats Mr Dalmau on the floor, the second man asks his wife, in terrible Spanish, to give him everything, I mean everything, that she can grab. And even though what she can grab is none other than the lad, who keeps manhandling her while ignoring her screams and moans and begging, the poor woman leads them to the back of the store. It was in that moment that Moisès Corvo came in, sweaty, panting, and threw himself on the Apache with the big bowler hat, who wasn't hard for him to pin down given their size difference. One, two, three punches, and when he started bleeding from the mouth it was time to rein himself in, there had to be enough to go around. Trusting, he didn't realize that two other Apaches were coming out from inside the store, and when they saw their partner laid out, with a big ole bloke on top of him, pulled out two revolvers and started shooting. Only one of the bullets hit Moisès Corvo's body, in his neck, grazing his carotid, enough to splatter everything with blood, including the Apache with the oversized bowler, and leave him unconscious. I was about to take him, but Moisès Corvo's soul clung to life. I went with him to the Hospital Clínic where he awoke a few hours later, anaemic, weak and hung-over. Sometimes there are people I go to collect who resist and get away from me. It doesn't happen very often, but when I find one, I feel drawn to them. I follow them and savour the taste of their survival. Moisès Corvo woke up awfully close to the autopsy room. Those few metres of distance between a cold bed and a warm one are like kilometres, but they can be covered in the blink of an eye.

And that's why, on the roof now, watching the people come in and out through the Santa Madrona gate, while Blackmouth talks and talks and says that Negroes have a special smell, like sulphur because the devil breakfasts on sulphur and biscuits, now, Moisès Corvo feels a stab in his neck and remembers me vaguely, and the last thing he wants to do is splatter any damn foreign thief with his blood. If any of the Negroes went out that dawn, they'll go in there and pull them out of bed, out of their coffin or wherever the hell they sleep. If they sleep at all.

Corvo and Malsano wouldn't have continued investigating One Eye's death if he hadn't been drained of all his blood. Deaths like that happen every night, and Corvo has enough experience to determine which ones are worth the bother and which ones aren't. During the day it's the gangsters who are the copper's favourite customers, but at night the knives, razors and pillow smotherings multiply, oblivion in kilos of piled-up shit, and bodies floating in the port. I killed him because I love him, I can't take it any more and I'm going to hang myself, give me back my money ya bastard, you won't live to see the dawn. I guess that's why I like Corvo: we know each other so well, when we look into each other's eyes I know he understands me. He respects me, but he doesn't take me too seriously, and that makes me feel at home, because I'm not always welcome everywhere, and I usually keep my distance.

The arrest, in the end, is quicker than anyone expected, and it's all wrapped up in the blink of an eye. Literally, because Blackmouth was already sleeping when Malsano pinched him to confirm whether the guy who'd come out to piss on the street, who?, that Negro, imbecile, was one of One Eye's murderers. Yes, yes, he lies, and then it's all a chase and a pipe in the hand, stop police, the Negro is still, ironically pale, a punch to the temples and we've got him on the ground. Searching through his colourful clothes, Malsano grabs the keys to his flat, Corvo cuffs him and both are up. Key, lock, door, kick and two more men to the ground, with their heads amid hens clucking in fear. The policemen find everything they're looking for and more, because it's perfect for them to shut the case so quickly: knives of all sizes, a stinking, emaciated dog hanging in a kitchen cabinet and a couple of earthenware bowls filled with blood, half thick, half coagulated, under the bed, where there are also all kinds of bottles, some filled with bugs, another with worms, one further on with rats' legs and who knows what else. Corvo finds a bodkin and he knows he can already go before the judge, that these three will sleep in prison and he'll get another notch on his belt. Case closed, we can head to the whorehouse.

"What evil creatures!" shouts Blackmouth, when he goes through the whole house, among lit candles and drawings and scribbles on the floor and walls. "See, I told you they were bad people!"

One of the detained, who hadn't received as many blows as his buddies, earns one to the back of his neck from Corvo when he looks at the lad, recognizes him, insults him and curses him.

"Is something wrong?" asks a neighbour lady from the doorway.

"Police, ma'am, you can go to sleep," replies Malsano.

The woman disappears behind the door across the hall and a few seconds later returns with a little cardigan on, it's getting chilly. Two minutes have yet to pass and there are some thirty people on the landing, and it's not until after ten that the night-watchman shows up.

"Balondro!" Corvo gestures to him with one arm. "Go to Conde del Asalto and tell him to send a police van."

"You're taking them to the station?"

"No, I want to show off my wheels. You should already be on your way back!"

The entire street is awake. Sometimes Corvo wonders if the people of Barcelona really sleep or just wait around for tragedy to strike. But when he shows up with two more policemen, who take the Guineans, he has his answer: people live for bad news. When he hears on the rebound someone linking these arrests with the disappeared children, his cheeks grow red and warm despite the freezing temperatures on the street. Without a good visual inspection of the flat of One Eye's murderers and without confirming whether the blood in the bowls is human or animal,

Corvo saw no indication that makes them think that any child was around… because they aren't around.

The night drags on, and all morning Corvo and Malsano are busy with red tape. Reports, bureaucracy and stamps. Half asleep, they wander through the station, where everyone seems busy. They go down to the lock-up to talk to the detainees, but they can't get a single word out of them. At midday, Barcelona's head police chief, José Millán Astray, appears in the office of the criminal-investigation brigade and finds them struggling to keep their eyes open. Their breath smells of coffee, but Millán Astray's shaving lotion is so strong he doesn't notice. He is a dry, lanky man, with a tough character and a soldier's bearing. It's unusual to see him speaking to officers, or even detectives, but he likes to make an appearance when a murder has been resolved, and in case there is a medal involved his chest is ready and waiting. No one can stand him, but he's the boss, as Malsano says in his Catalan-inflected Spanish, and you have to put up with the boss, listen to him and forget him.

"I would congratulate you, detectives," begins Millán Astray, looking out on the horizon of a wall covered in papers, "but in the end you were doing your job, and I'm not one of those who congratulates people for doing what they're supposed to."

Why the hell did he come, then? wonders Moisès Corvo.

The chief continues: "The prompt resolution of this case is without a doubt a fortunate…"

"I appreciate that you prepared a speech, boss," Corvo sat down after realizing that standing at attention isn't the best position for someone who's been awake that many hours, "but what I want to hear is that we get the rest of the week off."

"If you weren't so arrogant, Inspector Corvo, I could consider the suggestion. Your constant insubordination makes you worthy of only one day's leave. Don't come to work this evening. Inspector Malsano…"

"Yes?"

"Come back on Monday, go with your family, rest."

Juan Malsano is as much a bachelor as the Pope, but since it's the first time Millán Astray speaks a word to him, he's not going to insist he have exhaustive knowledge of his private life.

"I wouldn't know what to do with myself, so many days with the wife," says Corvo, when the chief leaves the office. "He's done me a favour."

"That mouth is going to get you in trouble, Moisès."

"That's not what my lady friends I'm planning on visiting tonight tell me."

But that night Moisès Corvo is at home, unable to sleep, putting up with a chewing-out from his wife, who is certainly less indulgent with him than Millán Astray.

The next day, tired of being reclusive, Corvo passes by Dorita's place after a light lunch of vegetable and anchovy broth, because he can't eat much when he's just woken up. Dorita sometimes offers him something else to eat, but today she's not in the mood. In a flat on Ferlandina Street, shared by the mice and the sub-letting ladies, the prostitute opens the door and looks Corvo over from head to toe. She remembers him. She lets him in. She doesn't offer him any food or drink or her usual services, because she finally knows, taking a deep breath, that someone has come to listen to her. They sit on a mattress that smells of sperm even though a man hasn't lain there in two weeks. It is a room without windows, without hope.

"They told me you have a girl…"

"Ay, Mr Policeman, the sweetest little girl in the neighbour-hood, and they've snatched her from me."

"How old is she?"

"Just four, just a little woman."

No, it's not the idea that Corvo has of a little woman, but maybe it is the one whoever took her has.

"How did she disappear, Dorita? Did you see anyone?"

"No, no. If only I had seen the devil that took her, because I would have followed him to the very gates of hell to get back my Clàudia."

"Where did they… make off with her?"

"Sant Josep Square! I was buying vegetables behind the Boqueria, and the girl, who is very obedient, was right by my side. Ay, poor little thing, they've stolen her from me, they've stolen her away!"

"Calm down, Dorita." Corvo knows it's useless to ask her to calm down, but he does it out of inertia. "When was this?"

"The 27th of November, what a dreadful day!"

"In the morning."

"Near twelve, before lunch."

"No one saw her leaving? The vegetable-sellers?"

"Ay, no, I tell you he's a devil. He moves among the shadows and nobody can see him. He hides and waits and looks for children and, ay, ay, ay, I'm going to faint… when nobody's looking he wraps his wings around them and takes them to his den. Ay, ay, ay…"

Dorita isn't the harlot who lets you kiss her butt cheeks whom Corvo's familiar with. Now she is a mature woman, with watery eyes, begging for the only person she loves in this world. And she truly believes that the girl is in hell. I know that that's not the case, but close.

"I've never seen Clàudia."

Dorita is silent, the reply seems obvious. You didn't have any business with her.

"Do you have a portrait of her?"

Dorita leaps up, as if an inner spring were set off, and she runs towards the dining room. Corvo follows her along the hallway, a cluster of closed but attentive doors, of colleagues who don't want to see the police out of fear, but don't want to miss a single detail of the story. On a trunk there is a framed photograph of three girls dressed in their Sunday best. One of them, with a bow in her hair, stares at Corvo. Help me. The policeman has to look away.

"Can I hold on to it?"

Dorita is about to burst into tears. She grabs the frame and kisses the glass, leaving something more than damp lips there.

"She is still alive; I'm her mother and I know. But the devil wants to drag her into the darkness. At night I hear her scream, she says, Mama, Mama, come find me."

Dorita hands the photograph to Corvo. He can't believe it, but she still has enough energy to muster up a smile.

Outside, on the street the only devil is tuberculosis. Moisès Corvo walks to the Rambla along the labyrinth of streets that seem to be clearing their throats, unable to sleep. Outlines in the doorways betray indigents I will soon come looking for, spitting out spots of blood on the cobblestones. They've been dead for a while now, when they were forgotten by the last person who knew them. The model city doesn't hide its detritus because, after all, it's as if no one could see them. The policeman crosses the cemetery of the living and reaches the Plaça Reial, lit up by the outside tables of cafés where bohemians converse as if they were in Pigalle. Some stop their chatting when they see the detective pass with a pale face and an undertaker's expression, his back slightly curved, and they murmur, shit, isn't that the king? When he is about to leave the square on Lleona Street, he changes his mind and enters the Aigua d'Or, a tavern run by Miquel Samsó. He orders a mug of the particularly bubbly house beer, which clambers up his palate to his nose. He wipes the foam from his moustache with his sleeve and asks Miquel if he knows Isaac von Baumgarten.

"If I know him, it's by a different name, Inspector." The owner is always behind the bar, night and day, wiping a glass with a rag that hangs over his back. It doesn't matter if the place is empty: he is always washing a glass.

"More or less blond, almost a head shorter than me, with glasses and a foreign accent."

"The doctor?"

Moisès Corvo smiles and takes another slug of beer.

"What do you know about him?"

"Not much."

"Not even his name."

"No, he's a... strange bloke. I don't see him much, but when I do, he's usually alone, he has a couple of beers and he leaves."

"He doesn't talk?"

"He says: a beer, please."

"And then he orders another one."

"Yes."

"Did you ever think about becoming a policeman?"

Miquel touches his belly, which is like a football stuck to his body, about to burst through his apron.

"Man, it's a little late for that, isn't it?"

"Maybe the lad will have a chance, if he inherits his father's prowess." Corvo points to his protruding gut.

Miquel furrows his brow.

The policeman is debating between just shutting up and directing his questions to the wine barrel that's his table. Miquel Samsó suffered very bad migraines when his fifth child was born, with fevers and delirium. A quack trepanned his skull and amputated a part of his brain. He hasn't had migraines since, but he hasn't stopped wiping glasses. One after the other. I've taken his four children (Cuba and Morocco) and his wife (syphilis), and he hasn't batted an eyelash, as if he were only around to make sure the glasses were as crystal-clear as his gaze.

"Have you ever seen him with anybody else?"

"No, he's always alone."

Moisès looks at the clientele. A drunk at each corner, like sentries. He won't get anything more out of the Aigua d'Or.

"Where's Margarida?"

The one daughter he has left. Corvo knows that, no matter what he says, it's not going to register with Miquel.

"At home."

"Tell her to wash the towels, this morning I almost scraped my balls off."

"But…"

He stops polishing the glass, and Moisès leaves through the door, in time to hear an "I'll let her know".

He gets to Raurich and the doctor's light is still on. When he opens the door, Corvo doesn't find the nervous individual he spoke with a few days earlier. Doctor von Baumgarten has had time to work up an alibi, gather strength and wait for the policeman's return.

"Good evening," he greets him, as if it were perfectly normal to receive visitors at two in the morning. He has him come in and sit down, again in the vestibule. The doors are closed. "I read in *El Diluvio* that you've arrested the murderers of that poor wretch. That's real diligence! I hope I was helpful in some small…"

"Shut up, please, you're going to give me a headache."

"What can I help you with?" he asks, annoyed.

Moisès Corvo stands up. He doesn't like to threaten sitting down.

"I'll let you lie to me, but no more than necessary."

"Excuse me?"

"I have four questions for you. You can answer two of them with lies, but for the others you have to tell me the truth. If I catch you trying to trick me more than twice, I'll arrest you and you'll spend the next twenty years in the clink, as an accessory to murder. Those Negroes must be wanting some company, surely."

Doctor von Baumgarten is dumbstruck, even though he doesn't suspect that Corvo's terrible at sniffing out lies.

"I have no reason to lie, Inspector."

"Don't start by wasting what advantage you have, please."

The doctor is a card-carrying snake-oil salesman. With a tiny bit of preparation, he knows what to say to make his questioner happy. A full-blooded coward, he doesn't usually look for confrontation, but he will end up sticking a knife in your back. He's always got nice words, always with a yes on his lips, sharpening his blade as he speaks. But he needs time, and Corvo wants answers now.

"I'll be honest."

"What do you want the bodies for?"

"What bodies?"

Moisès Corvo raises his index finger. One.

"What is an Austrian doctor doing in Barcelona?"

"Oh, it's a long story, Inspector,"—the doctor doesn't know how to keep his eyes still.

"Invite me in and we'll have a chat."

"It's very messy in my house." He places himself in front of the small door.

"I'm a very understanding person." Actually, Moisès is quick to lose his temper.

"I have Catalan blood. A little bit. My great-grandparents supported the Austrians in the war, and they went to Vienna with the emperor, where they started a new life. Now I've come back."

"That doesn't answer my question."

"But it's not a lie, either."

"If I had come here to play, Doctor von Baumgarten, I would have brought cards."

"Great, I love blackjack."

Doctor von Baumgarten doesn't see the blow that closes his left eye coming.

"I think that you're not very conscious of who you're talking to."

"No, I'm not very conscious, now."

"Third question: do you have any family here?" He takes off his jacket and leaves it on a wicker chair.

"What do you mean?"

"I was trying to insinuate if anyone would miss you."

"Uh, no…" OK, von Baumgarten doesn't know where the next one is coming from, and that makes him nervous again.

"I'll ask you the fourth question inside."

Corvo gives the door a kick that makes the hinges jump. The wooden plank, weakened by dampness, bounces back and reveals a small, poorly lit parlour, with four bunks with dirty sheets, like the hostel on Cid Street, but without any indigents sleeping there.

Towards the back, a half-open curtain allows him to glimpse a single bed surrounded by books, and what look like plates with the day's dinner. A mouse comes running out towards him and scrabbles into a hole in the wall. Moisès Corvo looks at von Baumgarten, is that a friend of yours?, and the doctor's facial pigmentation reacts. His skin turns reddish, with the little blue veins quite prominent, and the blow to his eye turns a dismal shade of purple.

"You can't do that! This is a private home."

"Answer the fourth question!"

"I'm telling you everything you're asking for!"

Moisès moves among the empty beds. The scent of boiled sweat pricks his nostrils. The smell of putrefaction, of spilt blood.

"What do you do with the bodies?"

"You already asked me that."

The policeman pulls out handcuffs and opens them. He doesn't make a big display of it, but he knows the effect they have on the Austrian.

"OK, OK, OK. I'll tell you everything."

Not far away, Blackmouth wanders. He isn't used to thinking, he's only used to lying, in a less sophisticated way than Doctor von Baumgarten but more convincing. He's looking for a child for the woman. She asked him to bring her one, between ten and thirteen years old, older than usual, but it's too late and there are no longer children on the street. With a lot of freckles, she had added, and big eyes. Blackmouth knows he won't find any but he keeps looking, because the strumpet is watching him and can read his thoughts, and will do the same thing to him that she did to One Eye. She is very convincing, and if she says she needs a child it has to be now, not in a day or two. What she wants it for, he doesn't know, but the taste of blood comes back to his palate after each intake of freezing air, like a reminder, like a bow that ties him to her and which only she can undo. Blackmouth falls asleep on Corders Street, right beside the gallows I've visited so many times.

There are coincidences that are revealed to be the product of a hidden hand, of an evil stagehand, who's always drunk and has a very unique sense of humour, who tugs on the pulleys like a madman until the play mixes together characters who otherwise would never have met. I have nothing to do with it, even though most times these coincidences end up affecting me. Don't blame me, I'm usually just an observer, calm and patient, despite my reputation as an opportunist. There are no more universal secrets than the ones you already know. No one is so important that the universe conspires against them, nor will the gods intervene in their favour. Basically because there are no gods or anything at all, and things happen because they have to happen and that's all. There's no need to worry about it so much. Don't do what Moisès does, thinking that the stagehand has placed strange Doctor von Baumgarten, a two-bit charlatan, before him to resolve the case he's working on. He doesn't even know what's going on, and he already thinks he's tying things together. The last thing he needed was for von Baumgarten to confess that he studies and hunts the most… extreme—that was the word he used—humans.

Isaac von Baumgarten explained that he has been studying the causes behind human behaviour for years. He's not satisfied with the Lombrosian theory of atavism. He wants to know where the true root of evil lies, and so he must do an exhaustive study of all types of bodies. He has to dissect them, he can't do any experimenting while they are alive. He won't fall into the same trap as the Italian master, who only studied Italian inmates without realizing that most of them came from the southern part of the country and therefore had a similar physiognomy. Doctor von Baumgarten wanted to study every race and in Europe there are few cities where they mix together. Barcelona has a port, and everyone here is passing through. And the dead don't point fingers at anyone. I'll go to Africa, he announces, convinced, because it seems that violence runs free there, and there are none of the social constraints of the West, all this religion and all this shit, as Corvo says. Von Baumgarten crosses himself and explains that along the way he has come across some real monsters.

"Monsters?"

"What surprises you about that?"

"You're a doctor, a scientist. You shouldn't believe in monsters."

"I don't believe in them, Inspector. I search for them and I study them. I try to find the difference between a regular human being and a beast."

"The difference is some dig up bodies, open them up and rummage around in them."

"That was a low blow. I need these bodies, and nobody's going to miss them. What's the harm in it?"

"Have you thought about the families they've left behind, who have to see the tomb of their father or their sister profaned?"

"Wouldn't you want to go out on the street and know that the shoemaker you just said good morning to will one day kill five prostitutes? Surely if there was a way to know that and arrest him before he could do anything, the families won't care too much about profaned tombs. These are people who have enough problems eking out an existence every day without worrying about those they've left behind."

"Do you know who Doctor Knox is?"

"Pardon?"

Moisès Corvo mentally jots down that he has to look around his house for the story *The Body Snatcher* by Robert Louis Stevenson.

"Do you like to read?"

"I don't have much time, but I guess you could say I do." The doctor is modest: he has read a lot, to an unhealthy degree. But not the Stevenson story about grave robbers.

The policeman stretches out in the armchair and observes the faded wallpaper, as if the doctor might as well be living in a stable. Or in a crypt, he thinks, and smiles.

"There's no such thing as monsters, doctor."

"You know that's not true. Think about the most evil person you've ever met."

"My wife? She's cruel and ugly, but I wouldn't call her a monster. I can have her come over, if you want to dissect her."

"Inspector…" Von Baumgarten smoothes his moustache and leans back in his chair. It is late, he's sleepy, but he has company. And he no longer seems hostile.

"There are plenty of sons of bitches in this world."

"Haven't you ever spoken with someone who you think couldn't be more of one?"

"No. Each one is a son of a bitch according to his possibilities."

Isaac von Baumgarten sucks his teeth, Corvo is like a wall.

"I don't understand why you're wasting your time with me, usually people don't give a hoot about my comings and goings."

Moisès Corvo rolls over, making the chair leather quiver. The hairs on the back of his neck are mussed and one of his ears is red. He looks as if he's either drunk or he just got out of bed; or like a drunk who's just waking up.

"A hoot? You learnt that pretty well, for an Austrian. Have you dissected a teacher's corpse recently?"

The doctor gets up without answering him. He walks to the bathtub in the corner and then says loudly, without looking at him, you want some ice? Corvo says yes, with a bit of whisky, in honour of Doctor Knox, who's Scottish. He pulls the glass and the bottle out of a cabinet. The bottle is full and its cap is encrusted with crystallized sugar. He doesn't drink, thinks Corvo. He pulls three pieces of chopped ice out of the bathtub and drops them into the glass with a tinkling sound. He rummages around and pulls out a larger piece from between a tattooed arm and two heads with empty eye sockets, torn lips and open skulls. Without blinking an eyelash, he covers the chunk of ice with a rag so that Corvo doesn't see it's covered in blood. He brings the dressing to his face, where his bruise is stinging something fierce, throbbing beneath the skin. Thank you, says Moisès when the doctor hands him the drink.

"I'm not a fool." He sits back down in the chair, tense. "I've heard what people are saying."

"And what are people saying?"

"That there's a monster."

"You're wrong. You are a fool."

"Who makes children disappear."

"Don't be so gullible."

"What?" He lifts his eyebrows, he doesn't understand.

"Don't believe everything you hear. When there is fear, the first guilty party is always the unknown."

"Then you agree: there is fear. And there is a monster."

"Not everything's that easy, doctor."

"It never is, but I'll make you a deal."

"You have nothing to offer me."

"I can help you catch him."

"In exchange for what?"

"Freedom to do my experiments. Fresh bodies from the Clínic."

"And how could you, a quack, help me, a policeman, do *my* job?" He is thinking it over, but he doesn't want von Baumgarten to know that.

"Because, as you said before, I *believe* in monsters, and that's the first step in hunting them."

The screech of metal blinds rising, like eyes filled with sleep, is the first thing Blackmouth hears. His lower back is stiff from the cold and a hard blow to the ribs. A man is standing, waiting for him, backlit, about to kick him again. Blackmouth protects his face with his arms, and then the man speaks.

"You didn't find any."

"Who are you?"

Rigid posture and a sports jacket buttoned all the way up, from which emerges a silk handkerchief. Joan Pujaló puts his hands on his hips and lifts an eyebrow that the boy cannot see, being bathed in shadow. He speaks without moving his lips, hidden beneath a large, gravity-defying moustache, and he compensates by opening his eyes so wide they look like cue balls with a small chalk mark as the retina. Joan Pujaló doesn't live, he overacts.

"Come with me," he twists his head and offers an arm to help him up, "before you freeze to death."

Blackmouth looks around, frightened. Workers in grey jackets and with cigarettes hanging from their lips head to the factories half asleep, paying them no mind. The scent of coffee is almost as intense as the stench of manure from a dairy a few metres away.

"You're no policeman."

Joan Pujaló lets out an utterly false cackle.

"Neither are you."

5

THERE ARE THOSE who live happily in tumultuous times, with blood on the streets, because it allows them to slip amid the violence and drink it in at their pleasure. In anarchist Barcelona—the "Fiery Rose"—everyone does their own thing: some struggle to have food to put in their mouths, others fill their pockets and make a display of it; the beggars sleep in a tavern because they don't have a pot to piss in, the rich travel to Sant Sebastià for a medicinal dip at the beach; there are those who speak to no one out of fear that their secrets will be discovered, there are those who chat about everything in their search for company. Enriqueta has found Barcelona's seams and she travels along them comfortably, alone, knowing she won't bump into anyone else, because there is no one who does what she does. Who cares about one more cadaver, when the corpses of the destitute don't stink during the winter cold? Who cares that there's one less child, if his mother can't feed him? She is up and down, satisfying everyone, giving each what they deserve and, above all, what they are looking for, whether they want it or not. She has everything she wants, but she always wants more. It's never enough. And now she has this lad, Blackmouth, who is young enough not to raise suspicions and whom she managed to enslave in a single night. Blackmouth can't turn tail, and his only way out is to obey her until she tires of him.

The boy walks beside her, but she doesn't ever glance at him. Enriqueta has a dignified bearing, with her head and back held up straight, like an important person, which is strange to see because she dresses in poorly sewn rags, one on top of the other, hiding her figure. Only her face is revealed, pale, moribund, extremely angular, her little eyes with pupils dark as wells. Joan Pujaló, Enriqueta's ex-husband, accompanied Blackmouth to the Plaça Catalunya, where they met up with the woman. You can leave us alone now, Joan, she had indicated, and without saying a word the man had headed down the Rambla, because it's still early and surely he'll find someone gullible enough that he can paint his portrait, separate him from his wallet or sell him a bridge. The other two headed up Balmes.

"Where are we going, ma'am?" Finally, Blackmouth decided to speak.

"To run some errands."

Blackmouth looks at his grimy fingernails and rips off a bit of skin from the side of his finger. He lowers his gaze and kicks a stone towards a horse-drawn carriage that comes down the street, lifting up dust. Whip in hand, the driver glares at him, it was really nothing, and then he looks at the woman, just as their paths cross. That evening the driver will not remember her features, but he won't forget the unpleasant feeling that ran up his spine.

"You have to know people," she says, like a continuation of her thoughts.

"I don't know anyone."

"That's just it. You have to have acquaintances. Never friendships, they always bring problems. You have to know people's names and figure out what they have a weakness for, that way you'll always have them in your pocket."

"But I don't—"

"If you know enough people you can have it all: money, power, respect…"

"Sex?"

She doesn't turn her gaze towards him now either, but it's clear she didn't like the comment. She thinks it over.

"Sex is power."

Blackmouth doesn't understand. Sex is sex. Shagging, fucking, screwing, getting off. He doesn't always have the opportunity, because he doesn't always have money. There have been times when he's waited beside a woman until drink left her groggy, and then he'd had a ball. There is a girl, over on Lluna Street, whom he often sees passing by and one day he's going to corner her and—every time he thinks of it he gets hard. He can almost smell her scent. He imagines her in his claws. He is overcome with such a desire to get some action that he can't walk normally.

"Will I meet girls?"

"I can introduce you to girls, if that's what I have to do to get you to focus."

I like to disguise myself as a man, cloak myself in your skin and pass as one of you. I can talk to whomever and open up their soul like a pomegranate, without them suspecting who I really am. I let them think they have the upper hand, I establish trust, and they start spilling. That doesn't mean they aren't lying, though. You shouldn't believe half of what Joan Pujaló says: he's a blowhard.

My wife was a whore and, in her own way, she still is one. That's something you never give up. No, no, it's not just a bad habit: it's ambition. Joan Pujaló bristles his moustache and looks at the empty glass, dirty with foam. He stares at me, squinting his eyes, as if he didn't believe a word of what I had told him, and he continues chatting. She already was one when I met her. Enriqueta was young, but a big, strong, well-formed woman who was all business. The customers came in through the door and blew their wad before she took off her blouse. Not me, I gave her pleasure, and I could be there for hours. I had as much money as stamina, because I've always been an athlete, I don't know if I mentioned that.

Sometimes she pretended she wasn't there, even though I heard her talking with Dionisia, there on Riereta Street, behind the door, because I left her so burnt out she couldn't work for a week. Did you know Dionisia? No? She was very clean, she was, and she took very good care of the girls. She had six, and at first I went there for Rosaura, a gypsyish girl with enormous eyes who never opened her mouth but let you do everything, you know what I mean. Rosaura had small breasts, soft like egg custards and—well, the thing is that one day, when I got there, Dionisia told me she had a new girl, and she introduced me to her. I saw her come into the vestibule, with a gauzy little dress that hinted at some powerful hips and that gaze that singles you out, and introduced myself.

"Juanitu, at your service."

But, really, she was the one serving me.

I visited the brothel on Riereta Street more and more; it's closed now, a municipal policeman lives there with his wife and children, ain't life strange. That was around '94, you know? Barcelona was very different. Every so often an anarchist would shoot somebody on the street, but normally it was somebody who deserved it and I didn't feel too sorry for them. That was around

the time of the bomb at the Liceu Opera House, that guy sure
had balls, that Santiago Salvador. I knew him, and one day he
came up and asked me: listen, Juanitu, if you wanted to bump
off some middle-class folk, where would you go? To the Liceu, of
course, I told him, but I didn't think he'd follow my advice to the
letter. Poor bastard, he was a good chap. I saw him sometimes
around Riereta. I guess he didn't blow off enough steam that way
and so he ended up exploding there in the audience.

Enriqueta has something magnetic about her. You don't know
why, but you need to go back to her again and again. When she
speaks you're struck dumb, she hypnotizes you like one of those
snakes from the Orient, those ones that come out of a basket.
What are they called? Cobras? Yes, that's it, cobras. Every time
I went to see her I brought her flowers, some chocolate, those
little details women like. But her expression never changed. It
was if nothing excited her, except when she had me between
her legs. The flowers withered in the other girls' rooms, and I
ended up eating the chocolates myself. But I insisted and insisted,
because Enriqueta was more to me than just a whore. It's not
that I didn't want to pay, eh, it's that I was falling for the minx. I
could get anyone I wanted, I could get Empress Sissi into bed if
I tried. Well, maybe not now, but then, that time when she came
to Barcelona, I could have for sure. But Enriqueta was unreach-
able, as if she were always hiding more than I could discover.
She was a challenge.

"Marry me, Miss Enriqueta."

Because I called her Miss, of course, you've always got to
mind your manners.

"And what would I do, married? Don't you see, Juanitu, that
I need to make my bits and bobs?"

"You can retire, I'll set up a little flat and paint your portrait."

"The portrait I can believe, but where would you get the money for a little flat?"

"I have my contacts, Enriqueta, and pressing the right keys—"

"I know those contacts well, and for all their groping and sweating and their I love yous, in the end they never lift a finger for me."

"Ay, don't say that, you'll make me sad."

"You're quite the actor, Juanitu. Don't cry, what I'm selling, you're buying, and so it would be a really bad deal."

"Come with me to the stall, help me with my business and leave behind this world of vice."

"I've got to give it up, but you don't… I know how you are, Juanitu. Like every man. If you married me you'd have a tart to do what I do for you now, and you'd end up leaving me and I wouldn't have the body or the desire to earn a living for myself any more."

"Don't be cruel, Enriqueta, I want you to have my children!"

Big cock-up. I didn't know then that she couldn't—you know, that the Lord our God didn't want her to procreate. It's not my fault, I'm sure, because more than once or twice I've had to run away from a swollen belly and an accusing finger.

"I said no, and I don't want to hear another word about it."

But there were more words about it.

You've got to have women on a short leash, because you know they are very fickle and hot-blooded by nature, and yours truly kept on Enriqueta until she caved. It wasn't easy, or cheap, and we came to an agreement. I would set her up with a stall and she'd leave Dionisia. Enriqueta had always liked herbs and unctions and she had a lot of books around the house with remedies and unguents and potions. I set her up with a herbalist's shop on Sindicte Street. It goes without saying that she never showed enthusiasm, because that's how she is, and the store didn't last long. She wasn't up to the task and didn't have much interest in selling.

"That doesn't make money."

"It's a small but honourable business, and keeps us afloat."

"It's like we're begging for alms, with the few bits of lemon verbena we sell each week."

"Don't look at it that way, woman."

I think Enriqueta lost respect for me the day I stopped calling her Miss.

"And how do you want me to look at it? I used to have enough to live on and I could even allow myself a few indulgences. Look at me now, in these rags."

"But that was no way to live, my love."

"Don't say such stupid things, it's as if you're an actor in a comedy, you're pathetic."

She was cruel. She is cruel. Enriqueta knows how to cut you to the quick. I found it entirely unfair, because I had rescued her from a world where, day after day without fail, they beat her, humiliated her and took advantage of her. I know that she wasn't happy, because Enriqueta doesn't like... well, she likes to fuck but not like a man, you know? You know what I mean: we could spend all day in the honeypot, but women are different, and Enriqueta even more than most. I don't mean she's some nun, and she's certainly not delicate or fragile, not by a long shot. I told you before, she's a real animal in bed. But she doesn't need it. Or she doesn't need it physically, I don't think. I discovered before long that she'd returned to some flat on the sly, and was back on the game. She's not wanton, believe me, but it's as if the money she made with me wasn't enough. And I don't earn a bad living. Have you seen my paintings? Later I'll take you to my studio so you can see them, I'm sure you'll buy one off me. Some say I make Ramon Casas look like an amateur, and that's why he's embarrassed even to brush past me—ha, ha, ha. Brush past me, you get it?

The thing was I had to get her out of that world, and I took her to Majorca.

Blackmouth and Enriqueta enter Àngel's, a pub on Balmes Street that was so full of people so early that morning that anyone would have thought that they'd abolished the working day in Barcelona. Around the large barrels that serve as tables there are circles of men chatting, with a cigarette in one hand and a drink in the other, and the waiter bustling about, serving Ratafias and conversation to whoever stops him first. Everything about Àngel is big: his head, his eyes, his hands, his heart and his dishes of soused anchovies, and when he walks it seems the place moves around him. He greets the woman and the boy who've just come in and he continues busily serving up breakfasts. Enriqueta points to a corner and Blackmouth looks over there.

"Do you see them?"

"See what?"

"The children."

Blackmouth glances and counts three children of about eight years old.

"But this place is packed."

"That means nobody's looking at us."

"Ma'am, I… how can we?—"

77

"Shut up. Talking will only draw attention. Act as if nothing's going on."

Àngel passes in front of her and questions them with his gaze.

"Bread and cheese," she says, "and water."

Àngel pulls a face. Water? In this cold?

They remain still, not chatting, contemplating the customers like someone at the picture show, distant, until after a bit Enriqueta elbows Blackmouth in the ribs. A man leads a boy by the hand (the same curls, the same nose; his son, obviously) to a door in the back, beside boxes filled with eggs. They go inside, and after a few seconds the man comes out alone.

"Go there now."

"To the urinals?"

"Don't waste time."

"But the father is—" Blackmouth sees the woman's decisive look, he gets up and walks towards the urinals.

"If you can't do it, you're of no use to me," she murmurs, almost imperceptibly.

In the urinals there is, besides the boy, another man, and Blackmouth stays still as a wicker man. The boy is distracted, picking his nose with his finger, and his father reappears at the door.

"Aren't you supposed to be peeing?"

The father enters and starts to get angry; from what it seems this isn't the first time. The other man goes out and passes by Blackmouth, who turns his face and is forced to go to the wall to pretend he is urinating. He doesn't know which of them has less of a desire to piss, him or the boy, because he's lost all pressure in his lower belly and he whistles to play it off, while the father undoes the boy's pants and lowers them, smacks him hard on his bum and leaves again.

Blackmouth is left alone with the boy, who has quit digging in his nostrils in order to focus on his crotch.

"If you don't think about it, it'll flow easier," says Blackmouth, as if he were an expert, and the boy looks up.

Blackmouth kneels and extends his arm.

"Do you want me to help you?"

They are both scared and silent for a few seconds. Blackmouth thinks that half the pub will surely come through the door any minute now, but he keeps drawing closer to the boy. He almost has him. Now all he has to do is take him without anyone seeing.

"Do you want a chocolate?"

The boy nods his head.

"If you come with me I have a cart outside filled with sweets."

The boy laughs, gap-toothed. Blackmouth laughs too, but out of nervousness. The boy is frightened by his dark teeth and turns off his smile. He hears a sound at the door and sees his father come in.

"What the hell are you doing?" he bellows.

"Help… helping the boy," he stammers and stands up, but his pants don't follow suit, remaining around his ankles.

"Sick son of a bitch!" he shouts even louder, and a friend of his comes in and, quickly evaluating the situation, takes the boy by the hand.

"No, no, no." Blackmouth pretends that it's all been a misunderstanding, but you can see right through him.

Àngel, the owner, comes in, with a rolling pin, the king of clubs.

"Narcís, a woman told me that you should watch out for this bastard, that he likes to touch…"

No, no, no, moans Blackmouth, his trousers down.

The three of them pounce on the lad and beat him harshly,

that'll teach you a lesson, and end up throwing him out on the street, in front of a horse-drawn carriage that had to move heaven and earth to keep from trampling him. Blackmouth gets up in pain, his nose is bleeding and he thinks one arm is broken, even though he can't tell which, and he decides to march up the street before some municipal shows up or the blokes from the pub rethink things and come back for more; he's already suffered plenty and it's not the time to tempt fate any further.

When he reaches Provença Street he finds Enriqueta sitting in a doorway.

"Now you know the risks," she says, getting up and turning her back to him. "Let's go, we're not finished for today."

Salvador Vaquer was at his workplace, the tramcar from Colom to Pujades, the morning he tried to steal my wallet. Being lame, and with the complexion and dexterity of a barrel of wine, Vaquer went pale when I caught him red-handed. I knew he'd do it, just as I know that he was raised in a poorhouse to the age of twelve, or that he'll never have children, that he likes to eat chicken more than his pocket allows, just like I know the date I'll have to come looking for his rotten, vacant soul. I know the story. But I prefer that he tell it to you. That's why I'm insisting. It's not that I'm not nice; I'm not compassionate; I haven't got any empathy. But direct testimony is much better than some omnipresent narrator such as myself. In the end I'd be boring you, you'd get tired of listening to me going around, bragging about knowing everything, I'm sure, because I'd end up distancing myself, get distracted and start explaining things that aren't relevant.

"Mr Vaquer."

"Eh… do we know each other?"

"We've met here and there."

He bristled his eyebrows, thinking back, but there is a vast void behind his pupils.

"I'm a friend of Enriqueta's."

"Ah!" he smiled, but he still hadn't placed me. The phrase "a friend of Enriqueta's" could mean too many things.

Half an hour later he was confessing, "Pujaló is a son of a flea-ridden bitch. He took her down a bad path. Do you know that poor Angelina spent days and days alone at home?"

"Angelina?"

Enriqueta and Pujaló's daughter, a delightful creature, very affectionate. He'd take my Enriqueta out drinking, and drinking and drinking, and they'd sleep it off on the streets, like two cadgers. He with that big moustache and that unfinished portrait of Lerroux he's always going on about, boasting about his elegance and, in the end, losing his dignity in any and every corner.

The big jerk tried to get her to sell herself again to pay for his gambling! They won't let him into any of the casinos, they all know him too well.

When I met Enriqueta, she had already stopped loving him… well, it's just an expression, because you must know how she is: she never loves anybody much. Even I'm aware that, the day she decides it, we're over. It will be difficult, because like all couples there are secrets that keep us together and shouldn't get out, but with her you never know.

Salvador Vaquer, the poor soul, didn't mention anything about the fact that she was in jail while we were having that conversation. She was there for a few days, not many, because they had caught her stealing costume jewellery from the Nourés family—I'm innocent, I swear, this isn't what it looks like—with whom she'd built up trust and whose drawers she'd been milking until they found her with the great-great-grandmother's necklaces, may she rest in peace, in her hands. Enriqueta froze like a deer, her eyes fixed on Mr Nourés, but he was more scared than she was. For a couple of stones it wasn't worth bloodshed, she decided in seconds, and she burst out crying, the most repentant and false she could muster, with dry tears and begging forgiveness on her knees from the father of the family to see if the situation could be solved in the simplest possible way, even though she knew it would be useless.

And Salvador, when talking to me, lied just like everyone else:

"With me Enriqueta had found stability, for a woman her age that's the best thing. She wants for nothing: food, company and a warm bed."

It was true: at the women's prison on Reina Amàlia Street she had all her needs covered.

"Where is she now? I haven't see her around much lately," I provoke him.

"She's had the flu,"—it's midsummer—"and today she took advantage of the fact that she's feeling better to go clothes shopping."

Oh, so that's what they call it these days, being in the clink. Salvador Vaquer, fat, ugly and unkempt, must have a wardrobe that's the envy of tailors everywhere.

Blackmouth wonders why the hell she did that to him, the strumpet. Walking two paces behind, he looks her up and down and wants to kill her. Pounce on her, strangle her from behind, grabbing her neck hard, pressing until her eyes pop out of their sockets and she is laid out on the ground, crying blood, and people will come over to congratulate him for having killed this murderer, the new hero of the city, the guy who helped in the arrest of the Negro sorcerers and then killed the ogress.

As if she could read his thoughts, she turns and looks at him without stopping.

"You have to get used to it. If you can't be invisible, you have to be strong. If you can't be strong, you're dead."

Blackmouth, like a lapdog, follows her and remembers One Eye's words: you'd best carry garlic on you. As long as he's with her, he'll be in danger; but if he distances himself, he's done for.

As they approach Calàbria Street the sound of the city grows muffled by the distance. The street is empty, the walls lose their posters advertising events (a cabaret, a bullfight, Raquel Meller at the Arnau), and the stores with awnings disappear to make way for closed doors.

They arrive at a small house, barely a few beams thrown together, with a baby's crying coming from inside, mixed with the sound of a bubbling pot.

"Manuela!" calls out Enriqueta, shrinking herself down. She now seems ten or twelve years older and more fragile, her gaze weary.

Out comes a woman about thirty years old who looks much older, dressed in mourning and with her hair pulled back in a bun run through with a rabbit bone, hello Cinta, haven't seen you for days.

"The dizziness kept me from leaving the house."

"Ay, yes." She brings her hands together, half entreaty half applause, one hundred per cent histrionics. "When I was pregnant with Carmeleta I couldn't lift a finger, you don't have to tell me."

Manuela notices Blackmouth and arches her brows in question.

83

"He's my nephew," says Enriqueta. "Maria's son, who helps me on my walks and makes sure I don't fall."

"But the boy is skin and bones! Come in, come in," she invites them. "A bite to eat will do you good."

Manuela Bayona is the level-crossing keeper on Calàbria Street, and every day she goes to the Model Prison to pick up the leftover food. At midday she brings it to her little home, heats it up, sets aside one plate for her and one for Carmeleta, and the rest she distributes among the indigents who visit her and keep her company in the evenings, since poor Serafí can only chat with the angels in heaven who have him in their glory, a train ran him over and all I had left were a couple of pieces of smoked flesh, no good even for the wake.

Enriqueta sits in a wicker chair, ay yi, my bones hurt, I'm too old for this, and Blackmouth remains standing by the door, actually truly in pain but with his feet ready to run away, today he's had quite enough. Manuela is a trusting woman, with the smell of stewing meat stuck in her hair and the steam from the broth scratching at the ceiling, who just wants to have someone to chew the fat with for a while. She keeps one eye on the food and the other on the girl in the crib (literally, because she is well cross-eyed), with a smile that could be a grimace, because it doesn't fade even when she explains how she sold her husband's body to the Clínic for the students to chop open, rummage around in and sew up, since the doctors at the hospital were always so nice to him in life and he would have surely wanted to help them in death.

Enriqueta drinks a bowl of broth, bites her lips and says ay, it's burning hot, while Manuela prepares a little bundle of boiled veggies and a bit of meat.

"Don't you want to eat?"

He doesn't think twice and drinks the soup in one gulp, not caring that it's liquid fire, and devours the plate of innards Manuela has just served him. Carmeleta cries, and Enriqueta goes over to stroke her face.

"Oh, she's so cute…" It's Snow White's stepmother speaking.

"She's got my Serafí's face, God rest his soul." She crosses herself.

"She's a gift from God, Manuela."

"You can say that again, Cinta."

Enriqueta has been visiting the level-crossing keeper for some time now, since the day she found out that she was pregnant. She approached her on the street and offered her some salves for a good pregnancy and an even better birth. They call me Cinta, she added.

"It must be very difficult to raise a girl all on your own."

"She's very good. She doesn't cry much and, when she does, she calms down quickly."

"I've never had any children," confesses Enriqueta mournfully. "The closest I have is this lad, my nephew. And now I'm past the age, and I have a void here inside." She closes her fist over her stomach.

Manuela lifts Carmeleta from her crib and rocks her.

"Do you want to hold her?"

"Ay, I wouldn't want to hurt her."

"No, woman, no. Babies are strong and we women know how to hold them."

"I don't know if…"

"Here." And she places the baby in Enriqueta's arms, who now doesn't look so weak.

Blackmouth stands up and goes close to the door, prepared

to flee, but it doesn't seem she's planning to take her, because she whispers honeyed words and kisses her and strokes her hair.

"Ay, Manuela, how happy I would be with a little one like this."

Manuela extends her arms to take her back and, seeing that Enriqueta won't let her go, she grows impatient.

"The girl has to sleep."

"I can put her to sleep, you'll see. I would be a good mother."

"She can only sleep in her crib."

"Let me try."

Blackmouth locates a bread knife on the table. If things get ugly, in one step he can grab it and in a matter of seconds slit Manuela's neck with the blade. Enriqueta guesses his intentions and shakes her head no.

"I think it's time for you to be going, Cinta. I have a lot of work to do, still, and the train—"

"I'll buy Carmeleta from you."

"What did you say?" She is alarmed.

"I've got some money saved up, I can pay you."

"But... but..." Anxious, she sees how Enriqueta has moved away from her and is protecting the baby against her chest. "You don't even have money for food."

"How much do you want?"

"She's not for sale!" She is about to cry.

"I could make her happy," mutters Enriqueta. "You are a widow: this little angel would grow up without a father, with a mother too busy to be with her."

"Give me Carmeleta back."

"She'd be in the streets all day, until what happened to Serafí happens to her, because if you can't look after your husband, how could you look after a little girl?"

"Give her back to me!" the woman cries and raises her voice.

"With me she would be taken care of, and she'd have a family. I could bring her here once in a while, so you could see her, but she'd have a father and a mother."

"Bitch!" shouts Manuela, and the bark of a dog is heard from the street.

"If you don't sell her to me, I plan on coming back here one night and taking her." Now Enriqueta is standing up, no more disguises, her back well straight. "And I'll split your belly open from top to bottom like a piglet and leave you to bleed to death, and that will be the end of it."

Manuela screams unintelligible words, unable to comprehend how Cinta, that kind woman who took care of her during much of her pregnancy, could transform into a snake like this.

"Somebody's coming," warns Blackmouth, who sees that some neighbours are approaching because of the woman's screams.

Enriqueta throws the baby into the pot and walks out of the little house, with firm steps, towards the Model. Blackmouth stays for a moment, hypnotized by the image of Manuela pulling the reddening baby from the boiling broth, her hands scalded, and then he follows Enriqueta. The neighbours run towards the shack and no one pays attention to them, as if they didn't exist. Enriqueta, with her pinkie nail, picks a bit of celery out of her teeth, and she wonders if the soup, with the girl, tastes any different. And her mouth waters.

If my daughter is in jail it's because she's done things that no one could be proud of. And having said that, Pablo Martí banged his fist hard against the wooden kitchen table, eroded from all the banging that Enriqueta had made him do. The breadcrumbs from breakfast (mouldy tomato and fatback, a few glasses of warm wine) scattered from the impact, and some fell onto the dish of sour milk that fed the dozen cats that came and went oblivious to their owner's troubles. It's curious how the ties you establish as parents also serve to blindfold you. Look at how Pablo Martí acts, and you'll know what I'm talking about.

The farmhouse in Sant Feliu de Llobregat has only one human inhabitant, but he's never alone: cockroaches, flies and moths, rats as big as cats and a pair of field mice from the garden live in the pile of crap that Pablo Martí has accumulated over the years. You can barely smell the feline scent any longer, amid the stench of rotten vegetables, old meat and damp wood that inundates the two floors that once, long ago, tried to be a home.

Pablo Martí is a corpulent man, with white hair and a face etched by traces of childhood smallpox, his nose split as if by an axe blow and sunken eyes that can no longer see into the distance but which still fix on the person he's speaking to. He wears a shirt and trousers he hasn't taken off in months, not even to sleep, like a second skin. And very often, when he goes out in search of someone with a coin willing to treat him to some spirits, he layers himself with more articles of clothing, one over the other, it's never enough, until he looks like an overstuffed, Pantagruelian scarecrow.

The farmhouse is like a den, and Mr Martí the peevish, surly ferret that lives there, baring his teeth to whoever comes near. He talks through his teeth and you can scarcely understand him; he speaks little and vehemently, as if beating on each word before letting it through his lips. You can't make out what he says and he has no intention of speaking intelligibly. But, all modesty aside, I had no trouble striking up a conversation. Remember who I am. You think it's hard for me to get a few words out of someone? Never.

"She doesn't come to see me much. And I'm not saying that because she's locked up now, I understand that. She's very much her own girl, she's never needed anyone else except for material things. Don't misunderstand, it's not that I don't love her, she's my daughter, but even when her mother nursed her she'd make disgusted faces. It was impossible. And if you forced her, she'd bite."

Hoarse voice, ideas unravelling word to word, not taking any clear path.

"Those are women things, and I don't stick my nose in, never, ever, ever, but don't be surprised if it was her fault my wife left this world."

Mr Martí wasn't far off. After years of asthenia, the body of Enriqueta Ripollès shut down when her daughter was eleven. The girl's strong personality, her repulsive face—she was disobedient, taciturn and always distant—just ate away at her.

"Poor thing," said Pablo Martí, and he looked up towards the ceiling, where a long, blackened spider's web hung, with no spider to tend to it.

"When was the last time you saw her?" I asked him. He, half dozing, half absent. He lowered his head and looked at me with those two holes that hide his eyes.

"Here?"

"Anywhere."

"Here, here. I never leave, I never go down to Barcelona. I'm not missing anything in a city where everybody wants to rob you. Especially the politicians."

"When was the last time she came here?" I insisted.

"What is it now... August?"

"September."

"September... before the summer. In May, I think." Enriqueta hadn't visited her father since March, but that doesn't matter. "You probably already know she doesn't talk much. She came with that gimp she's with now, they spent the day here and the next morning they were gone. The gimp just complained, that it's so dirty, just burn it down, haven't I ever thought about selling it and going to the flat they have in Hostafrancs... but no, no, no, they are the way they are and I'd be there for a week, and when they found someone to sublet the hole to I'd be out on the street. And on the street, in Barcelona, everybody wants to rob you. You're from Barcelona, aren't you? I can see it in your bearing. Don't think I'm not watching you: if you try to take anything out of here I'll bash you with my cane. I don't like thieves. Don't like politicians either. They all steal from you. Especially if they're from Barcelona."

Without saying a word, I took a drag on the cigarette I had just lit. I savoured the tobacco on my palate and felt the smoke filling my lungs. Being human allows you these small privileges and vexations that I can only mimic. Arching my eyebrows, I asked him if he wanted one.

"No, no, smoke. My lungs can't take it."

I knew that, when I left, he would pick up the butt and smoke it. I put it out halfway through, so he could have a few decent puffs.

"What did you talk about?"

"Who?"

"You and your daughter."

"We don't talk. She almost never speaks, and I don't have much to tell her."

"She came and that was it."

"She came and that was it, yup."

"She didn't do anything."

Pablo Martí was suspicious. He stood up with difficulty and headed to the door that leads to the garden. He put a jacket on over his shirt, and on top of that another jacket that could barely fit over all the others. It wasn't cold. He went out and stood amid the tomato plants' orphaned stakes.

"You are a policeman, aren't you?"

"I get that a lot, but no."

"You want to know things about her."

"No. Just what she did."

"It's not about the money or the jewels."

"No."

"She brought two bags. The gimp carried them, but they were hers."

"What was inside?"

"I don't know."

He was lying.

"What did she do with them?"

"This year it will rain like it hasn't in years. Look at those clouds." There weren't any. "One time a bolt of lightning hit nearby and killed one of my father's sheep. It went through her like a sword: a hole here" he pointed to the nape of his neck—"and another in the belly. She smelt singed. Watch out for lightning."

"What did she do with them, Mr Martí?"

When was the last time someone called him Mister?

"She threw them into that well."

He is surprised to see I don't head over to it.

"You never took a look?"

"No."

"You're not curious?"

"She's my daughter. She's not a good person, but she's the only daughter I have."

We were silent. I knew what he would say: the conversation was over.

"It's getting late."

"It's cooling off." He huddled, the sleeves of his jackets pulled taut.

When I left, the cats hid from me, as always.

"We'll see each other again, surely?" It sounded like the cry for help of a lonely, scared man.

We always see each other one last time.

The Model Prison looks like a fortified island in the middle of nothing. The car transporting prisoners is trapped by a flock of sheep a few metres from the entrance. The shepherd doesn't do anything to clear up the ambush as if, in a gesture of complicity towards the prisoners, he wanted to give them a few more minutes of life outside the walls. Actually, the shepherd has been there long before the panopticon, and his attitude is nothing more than stubbornness, an autistic protest in the face of the changing times.

Enriqueta hadn't said anything since they'd fled the level-crossing guard's house. Blackmouth thought he could made out a few frightened drops tracing a path down her cheeks, as if she weren't as ironclad as he'd thought up to that point. As if deep down she were a coward incapable of facing up to anyone in the light of day, who needs company in case things go wrong so she can shift the blame onto them. And that was his role. But Blackmouth isn't clever enough to follow that chain of deductions and soon is back to fearing her, because he knows one thing for sure: whether he helps her or turns her in, the cards are stacked against him.

"You still haven't asked me," she says, and sits down in a doorway.

"Asked what?"

"Why I want the children."

He stammers.

"I… the other day…"

The dark girl with big crying eyes, the machete sinking into her flesh, the blood dripping into the bowl under the table.

"They are life, innocence, everything adults have lost and want to get back."

Blackmouth would rather not know anything, but he doesn't dare say that. She uncovers her basket, which she carries covered with a rag, and shows him what's inside: a jar filled with what looks like plum jelly. The girl's heart, marinated in honey and white wine, and a few sprigs of rosemary. He doesn't know, he can't even imagine.

"Are we waiting for someone?"

"Yes."

But no one comes out of the prison, just the car that has left the new inmates and is returning to the police station. An hour passes, the sky grows overcast and they remain sitting, without exchanging a word.

Now another car arrives, but this is a private one, somebody with money, thinks Blackmouth, with a chauffeur in a peaked cap and a metal angel on the hood. It stops in front of them. The driver comes out and opens the back door. Enriqueta gets in and when she sits down the leather crunches, brand new.

"The lad's not coming," says the slight man with sunken cheeks and prominent nose.

Enriqueta looks at the man and understands there is no room for negotiation. He closes the door and leaves Blackmouth on the street, alone, watching as the car starts and takes the woman up the street. Her bearing is that of a countess, or a baroness, or somebody with a lot of money. As if she weren't the same person he would have eagerly strangled that morning.

6

I N HIS ATTEMPTS TO AVOID HIS WIFE, Moisès Corvo got
used to spending the evenings in the printing press where his
brother Antoni works. First he went there to circumvent convers-
ing with Conxita or listening to her reproaches (I spend nights
alone, it's like I wasn't married, she tells him bitterly). But one
day his brother gave him a freshly bound book:

"Take this, since you're here, at least don't snooze in the chair,
it gives a bad impression."

"What is it?"

"Read it, see if you like it."

Corvo had learnt to read at seventeen, but he had never really
taken to it. The occasional dog-eared little novel during the Rif
War, criminology manuals in the police academy and not much
more. Now in his hands he holds *The Strange Case of Dr Jekyll and
Mr Hyde*, and he gradually works his way into it. Before his eyes
opens up a new, limitless world. After that one, Moisès asked for
more. *Carmilla* by Sheridan Le Fanu, Conan Doyle's Holmes
stories, *Frankenstein* by Mary Shelley and Stoker's vampire. Moisès
Corvo, secretly, at the press (when have you ever seen a copper
reading, Millán Astray often exclaims), became a devoted reader
of horror and detective fiction. You read too much, is Malsano's
typical barb, and Corvo has a clever reply prepared. The last

book Antoni provided him with is *The Phantom of the Opera*, by Gaston Leroux. A mysterious being murders from the shadows… Today Moisès Corvo is unable to read a single line. He needs distraction. And when he is preoccupied, he takes shelter at the Napoleón. Moisès Corvo is sitting beside Sebastián, who is working on the projector.

"Take off this crap." This crap is a film about a couple arguing in a park, she's got a pram and he's got some major-league exasperation.

"What do you want to watch?" replies Sebastián.

"Got anything with sex between vestal virgins with huge breasts?"

"Only with small breasts."

"Then forget it. What a crap selection the owner of this place has…"

"I have the one about the hotel."

"If there's no melons…" And he makes a gesture with his hand as if saying go ahead, set it up. "I'll pull a few strings to get some decent cinema"—quality here being inversely proportional to the use of clothing—"I know it's out there."

"Keep me posted, once we've got it we can really pull in the customers," says Sebastián, a cigarette swinging from his lips as he puts the roll of film into the projector.

"We can pull on something else, too."

On screen, the lobby of a hotel. The bellboy appears, along with a married couple. He is dressed as a ridiculous harlequin, she with loose clothes. The bellboy starts a machine in motion and all of a sudden the suitcases march on their own over to the elevator, they go up to the room and open themselves up. The man and woman arrive shortly after and while her hair and make-up are done by brushes that float through the air, he receives an expert shoeshine. Things move as if by magic, and the clients seem satisfied. Moisès Corvo doesn't look away from the film, which is no more than five minutes long, while the ash gains ground on his cigarette.

"Doesn't matter how many times I watch it, I don't know how they do it," he thinks out loud.

"The comb can't fly and the suitcases can't walk. It's a trick. They film the movement bit by bit as if they were photographs, and then they stick them together."

"It looks real."

See what I was saying? For Corvo, the more fantastic the fiction, the better.

"It's an illusion. The photographs are static, it's our brains that recreate the movement."

"Have you been reading Freud too?" he says. He knows Freud from the magazines and because he is one of the city's favourite conversation topics.

"What are you, barmy? I'm not saying anything that's not true."

"No, but every evening you sell lies."

Sebastián shrugs his shoulders.

"They're on screen, right? So it's no lie. It's happening or, at least, you believe it's happening."

"Two realities," says Moisès, putting on a deep voice. He can smell the pickled lupini beans and the sawdust, despite the odour of shag tobacco. "One that's true and one we imagine."

"You want to see the one with the acrobats?"

"The Chinese?"

"They're Japanese."

"I never say no to Japanese ladies. Not the real ones and not the imitations."

A bunch of actors dressed as Orientals swirl around and twist into impossible shapes, one atop the other, in a display of prodigious strength and agility. Moisès quickly catches on to the trick: the camera is hanging from the ceiling and frames the group dragging themselves along the floor, pretending they are standing.

"It's better with a pianist," Sebastián apologizes, needlessly.

But Moisès has already grabbed his jacket and is getting up. He doesn't say goodbye, he never says goodbye, and Sebastián is left alone, thinking that he still has a lot of sweeping up to do.

There is a wrought-iron dragon on the staircase of the police station on Conde del Asalto, one of those modern things he can't be bothered to try to understand. He greets the policeman at the door, a man who's been watching over the same stones for 300 years, and he ascends the stairs two by two. At this time of the day there is no movement. Juan Malsano hears him coming before he enters through the door.

"Hey, man without a shadow," calls out his somewhat dishevelled partner from his desk. "Looks like they pay a salary if you come and spend some time here."

"I was busy working, Juan. More or less like you, but without sitting around scratching my balls."

Malsano throws a pencil that Corvo doesn't dodge.

"Well, then it's my balls that had to listen to that bastard, Buenaventura."

"Congratulations, it's the first time in months they've had a visitor."

"Quit it, Moisès, he's been shown up again."

"What happened?"

"The damn gangsters, up to their old tricks."

"Don't they know to stay home, these guys, when it starts to get cold? Anybody dead?"

"No, unfortunately not. They were shooting each other up, but only one was wounded."

"And what does he want? Us to go and finish him off?"

"No. He wants us to go by the hospital and check in on him, ask him a few things and stay there to make sure nobody comes by to dispatch him."

"Oh, sorry, I missed the huge red cross on the station door when I came in: I was too loaded down with chamomile and linden tea for the needy."

"If you keep this up it'll be Buenaventura who goes to the hospital tomorrow to make sure I don't finish you off."

"Is there anything else?"

"In this city? More than you can shake a stick at. Let's see." He opens up the notebook and brings his index finger to his lips. "...Where'd I leave the pencil? Oh, yeah. A stabbing between neighbours on Flassaders Street, but that's all tied up; a hanging on Comtal Street, a crazy woman who tried to scald the baby of a level-crossing keeper by the Model, a—"

"Wait, stop. What was that about a baby?"

"Nothing. From what they told me, some old lady went barmy, argued with a friend of hers and threw the girl into the soup pot."

"Did they arrest her?"

"No, she ran off, and the mother isn't up for much explaining. They pumped her full of Agua del Carmen to control her hysterics."

"And the aggressor... do they know her identity?"

"It's not your kidnapping monster, Moisès. It's some crackpot who went too far."

"We should go and check it out."

"No way. It's not our district, and we have commitments, whether you like them or not."

"If we don't have the freedom to investigate, then tell me what we're doing here at all."

"Hierarchy. Every ship's got a captain. And if there are no reports of children disappearing it's because they're not just vanishing into thin air."

"Where there's smoke…"

Juan Malsano has the statement from the gunmen in his hands, and he shows it as if it were the ten tablets of the law.

"A bird in the hand…"

Moisès Corvo furrows his brow, fed up with the proverb contest, frustrated because time and again the higher-ups are clipping his wings: office bureaucrats, the closest they've got to working the streets is stooping to wipe horseshit off the soles of their loafers.

"Why are you getting so worked up about this?" asks Malsano in the following days, when Moisès Corvo goes to schools and stands around in front of their doors, waiting for a hairy ogre to show up and head back to his cave with one of the more trusting students in his mouth, for his next meal.

But the children always come out shouting, running, playing and beating on each other, happy to be free after an exhausting day of numbers and letters and endless lists of dead people, of dates that seem so far away and that smell of mothballs that's in every hall of every school. Their mothers take them by the hand, look both ways before crossing, Tomaset, and there are a few who look at the policeman suspiciously and talk to the caretaker and say who is that bloke, and the caretaker warns the municipal policeman who's having a coffee with brandy in a café near the school and shows up with his truncheon at the ready to mess up the strange guy ogling children on their way home. The detective pulls out his ID, half hidden under his jacket, so the circle of spying mothers about fifteen metres away doesn't see it. He asks a few questions, all very vague, so as not to cause alarm, because then the municipal will chat with the women and we'll have a kerfuffle on our hands. Every answer is either no or I don't think so.

"Forget about it. So two girls got lost. That's always happened, but you know how whores are: they spend their days crying and drinking, when they're not taking drugs." Malsano is the practical type, never going beyond the call of duty, working just the necessary, no more, no less. He doesn't understand how Corvo, his partner, can waste his time off duty trying to resolve this stupid matter that has no reliable basis. "They must have been sold to some perverted kid-fucker."

And thus Malsano achieves the opposite effect he was hoping for with his advice, and Corvo suggests that they go and look for Bernat the next day.

In a two-storey building on Tapioles Street, an old haberdashery that could fall down at any moment, hidden behind scaffolding abandoned God knows how long ago, lives Bernat Argensó, sixty years old, bearded and bald, scrawny, with very long, filthy fingernails and sulphur breath.

Moisès and Malsano come in at midnight, after having quickly taken care of the red tape that had accumulated at the station (reports, witness statements, copies for the files), and they scare Bernat Argensó when they shout out his name. He is alone, the house a nest of darkness, the silence broken by the beating of the wings of nightingales, budgies and goldfinches locked in dozens of cages on the ground floor, where the counter was, now awoken by the detectives' bellowing. Bernat is lying in a child's bed on the upper floor, his fingers clasping Elisa's blanket, surrounded by withered cardboard dolls, frayed rag bears and marionettes without strings.

"Good evening, Inspectors." It is a powerful voice that doesn't match the little man's image.

"The door was open."

"I don't like to sleep all locked up."

"You're welcome," says Malsano.

Bernat Argensó had been a model citizen, the owner of Argensó Notions, a well-known business that was beloved by the whole neighbourhood. Married and with a daughter, Bernat was sent to jail by Moisès Corvo. For years, the shopkeeper had been roaming around the Ronda de Sant Pere looking for children alone. When he found one, he would corral them up against a doorway, undo his belt and masturbate violently on them. He never went so far as to force himself on any of them, just as he never came, and he'd end up either crying or fleeing as fast as his little legs could carry him when caught red-handed. The same can't be said of Elisa, his daughter, whom Bernat had been raping from the age of three to the age of fourteen. One Friday, Elisa tied her favourite rag doll (a greenish bear called Moss) from the ceiling with one of the strings she sold every day in the shop, and then she hanged herself with the sheet on which her father had been taking her, where he threatened to tell her mother it was her fault, and told her she had turned out dirty and a liar, and that she only wished bad upon her family and their business. The years of prison had only served to muffle Bernat's violence, but it hadn't quenched his thirst.

"Whatever it is, I haven't done anything."

He's right, but not for lack of wanting to as much as for lack of ability.

"How do you make your living now?" Moisès asks him.

"I sell the birds downstairs."

"This is…" Malsano points to the blanket, and leaves the sentence hanging.

"Yes," he hugs it to his chest.

"We want to ask you some questions."

"Here or at the station?"

"Right here."

"What do you want to know?"

"You have an admirer." Moisès carries the weight of the conversation.

"What?"

"There is someone who is snatching kids."

Bernat lowers his gaze and takes a step forward. His lower lip trembles, a mix of cold and nerves.

"The vampire."

The detectives know they've hit pay dirt.

"What do you know about him?"

"The same as everybody."

"What does everybody know?"

"What you must know too: there's a vampire who seizes children and drinks their blood."

That's new. Up until then Moisès had ogres, devils and monsters, but not blood-sucking vampires.

"And what's the reality?"

"What do you mean?"

Some birds coo in the night.

"The theory that the Transylvanian aristocrat has moved to Barcelona for some nibbles isn't working for me. What's really going on?"

"I don't know. I already told you: a vampire."

"Vampires are creatures of the night, they turn into bats and fear crucifixes. Considering the number of churches on each street of this city, and that a beast with a two-metre wingspan flying around wouldn't be very discreet, let's rule out that theory. Let's imagine there's another Bernat Argensó, for example, who doesn't want to have to wander around the streets looking for young 'uns and so he takes them home."

"Are you accusing me, Inspector?"

"Is that what it looks like? Because if it looks to you like I'm accusing you of something, you might force me to do just that."

"I don't know anything. I didn't do anything. I love children. Whoever this beast is doesn't love them."

"Love? Is that what you call what you did to your daughter?"

"You're a rapscallion!"

Moisès Corvo smacks him in the face.

"First of all, speak to me with respect, you disgusting rat. Second, tell me where we should look or we'll arrest you."

Bernat has a hand to his cheek and is very angry. When he arrested him the last time, Moisès Corvo beat him badly. That was the beginning of a chain of beatings and humiliations that continued in the Model Prison and led to his being sodomized by a group of inmates who wanted to make clear the only two certainties behind those walls: everyone has a mother and children are innocents. Hours, days, weeks and months of frustrations brewed inside Bernat's mind and body, but he is too old now to release them and he is too afraid to challenge the policemen.

"Look, Bernat, you'd better talk or I can't be responsible for what he'll do." Malsano knew that he couldn't control his partner. If there were children involved, he became more rash, and he didn't even have any of his own.

"He eats them. He kills them, drinks their blood and eats their organs."

"Now we're on the right track." Corvo puts his arms in prayer position, and makes an innocent face. "Continue."

"That's what I've heard, that it keeps him alive."

"Who is he?"

"I don't know." He protects his face against a possible blow. "But I've heard he's been doing it for years, but that lately he's got more greedy, as if he needed more and more."

"Why would he need to drink blood?" Malsano is repulsed by the idea.

"Because children are life and they keep you forever young."

"Superstitions," declares Moisès.

"Really? I would be dead, if not for them. At my age, after my daughter died and my wife left me, all those years in prison, all the—"

"Don't come crying to us."

"If it wasn't for my contact with children, I'd already be on the other side. If not for sleeping in Elisa's bed, with her sheet that still gives off her perfume when I take a deep breath, I'd be pushing up daisies. They give you life, and that's what the vampire is doing: taking life from them. I'm incapable of hurting them, but this monster kills them."

"I don't feel the least bit sorry for you, Bernat." Moisès spits on the floor, as if to stress his words. "You deserve what you got."

"Elisa never understood me, neither did Mercedes. But I need to be close to children, give them love, make them love me. I'm not guilty of anything."

"Give us a name," demands Malsano.

"It could be anyone. It could be you."

"If I find out you have anything to do with this, even the slightest coincidence, I'll be back, Bernat," threatens Moisès, already on his way out. "And I'll strangle you with the same sheet she killed herself with."

I met Moisès Corvo six years ago. Conxita was seven months pregnant when I came for the baby inside her. I had to do it. I'm not proud of what I did, but I don't regret it either. Its time had come while it was just winding its watch. That was very hard on the couple, who were hoping to have a child when they were still young enough to raise it. A year later they tried again, and Conxita got pregnant once more. In her fourth month I came into their home and caressed the woman's feverish face. Moisès Corvo was sleeping by her side, after long, wakeful hours attending to her every need. She awoke haemorrhaging heavily, and the doctors said that the baby had destroyed her from inside and she'd never be able to have another. Moisès Corvo was grieving and in pain (he blamed himself for not being able to make good babies, for not being a whole man) and he distanced himself from Conxita. She needed him by her side, but she never found him there, and she too closed herself off into her own world. They shared a roof and little more, each sleeping in separate rooms. It wasn't so much that they had stopped loving each other (the love that accrues over time together) as that they'd buried their affection along with the foetus. The couple channelled any parental feelings towards Moisès's brother Antoni's son. Little Andreu Corvo is the boy they could never have, the over-indulged one of the family, the last link that binds them. And Moisès Corvo can't stand to see Andreu suffer or have anything bad happen to him, and he will stand up even to me if he has to.

He's got real balls on him, that copper.

In the next few days nothing happens worth mentioning. The city, in that parenthesis of stillness, fills with comments of this can't bode well, it's the calm before the storm, now comes some big trouble. Even the weather turns grey, the sky covered in clouds heavy with a rain that never falls. Moisès Corvo haunts school doors, knowing it's a waste of time. He goes to the Children's Hospital on Consell de Cent Street and talks to Sister Euclídia. Scarlet fever and tuberculosis are the main dangers, she says, maintaining she hasn't heard anything about anyone kidnapping children. There are always orphans and the penniless here, and the last time anyone tried to take one of them it was a stranger, must have been eleven years ago now, who said he had just as much right to be a father as anyone else. They stopped him before he got to Sicília Street, but I don't know any more. Nobody, not even the police, came about it and around here it was business as usual. Corvo wants to check the files from 1900, but the fire a few months earlier at the Palace of Justice makes it impossible to find anything there. He visits the Model and no one remembers any man who snatches youngsters.

Blackmouth hasn't seen the woman for days. It's as if, after the incident with the level-crossing keeper, she'd got scared and didn't want to show her face in public. Moisès Corvo had tried, in vain, to contact Manuela Bayona. The woman had taken her daughter, still wrapped in bandages from the burns, to Murcia, with some cousins. Blackmouth fears the moment when Enriqueta again demands he be by her side, but at the same time he is hugely curious.

The bullfight before Christmas at the Arenes ring would have been one of the most soporific of 1911 if it hadn't been for one of the bulls up against Vicente Pastor escaping out onto the street and sowing panic. It charges an omnibus and a few men try to cut it off and play the hero, meanwhile the municipals do their best to hide at a safe distance and a woman faints to get her suitor finally to take her in his arms. Some contraband officers take it down, making the front page of every newspaper the next morning. It is the only topic of conversation in Barcelona. People make circles in front of the cathedral, and the social gatherings in cafés mock the matador's talent that led to the animal's escape in the first place. Someone suddenly says out loud, without malice: the animals are restless because the beast is still here. The next day, the word on the street is that two children have disappeared. A day later they are three. On the seventeenth the victims of the creature from hell are up to nine.

It is unclear whether Moisès Corvo's wife can't stand her husband dyeing his grey because it leaves his hair looking like it's covered in shoe polish or because it mucks up the bathroom sink and there's no way to get it clean. It is he who can't stand the sight of her, and he takes advantage of the moments of calm, when she goes down to buy some beans and chat with the girl at the grocer's, to shave his moustache until it looks as if his lips have grown eyelashes, darken the mat of hair on his head and splash cologne in his crotch; he is on duty that night and plans to visit the new ladies in Portaferrissa. They say there are some exotic ones who do things the local girls can't even imagine.

You're such a romantic, Lord Byron, Malsano will say when he sees him. He sucks on a menthol and cocaine lozenge he bought at the pharmacy to cover his breath, which smells of tobacco and poor digestion, and he smiles at himself in the mirror.

When he arrives at the police station to say hello I'm here, see you tomorrow, he bumps into the guard at the door, who greets him with a resigned expression, tired of greeting everyone who's been parading in and out all day long.

"Boss is here, Inspector."

"Still?"

"He's been here all afternoon."

He swears under his breath, looks like today he's going to have to lie low. He finds Malsano on the staircase. He receives him with a sour face.

"They told me that—"

"Yeah, yeah, he's waiting for you." And he sighs heavily with his hand on his stomach, folded over.

"You're pale. Someone drain your blood?"

"No, this goddamn ulcer, it sees the holidays coming and starts setting up a manger scene."

"What the hell is Millán doing here, at this time of the day?"

They go up the stairs and a press photographer lets them through, hidden among the tripod, the camera, the plates, the suitcase and the sweat from having to carry it all around.

"This morning he met with the city's safety alderman and a group of dignitaries."

"Dignitaries? What are you, a barrister now?"

"Shut up and listen. They want to put the kibosh on these rumours about the disappearances. And this afternoon they had the newspapers come."

"Oh, yeah, makes perfect sense to call in the journalists when you want to put an end to the rumours," says Moisès Corvo sarcastically.

"Yes, I see you're having a bad day." He sucks his teeth. "Thing is they've been ordered to hush up any unsubstantiated news on the subject."

"Are they going to do it?"

"They'd better."

They reach the door to the office Barcelona's chief of police keeps in that station, and they knock on the glass. Come in, and José Millán Astray is waiting for them, standing stock still behind his desk. Sit down. There is no please, not in the orders given by that man.

"Has Inspector Malsano brought you up to date?"

"Yes, sir. He says they've recovered the Mona Lisa that was stolen in Paris last summer."

Millán Astray ignores the comment. If there were a firing squad in the office he would have given the order to shoot. He grits his teeth and continues:

"I want you to know that I have analysed the situation with City Hall and we have come to the conclusion that the stories about children being abducted in Barcelona, for the time being, are absolutely unfounded. There is no reason why the newspapers should report on them, nor why this police force should be investigating anything. We have much more important cases than the gossip of a few prostitutes. Our streets are filled with anarchists, for one thing."

"Sir, pardon me, but it's not just a—"

"There is nothing more to say, Inspector Corvo. Have there been any reported kidnappings in recent months?"

"No, reported, no, because they are afraid of—"

"They? If there is no report, Inspector, there is no investigation. It's a basic principle that I don't think you should have trouble understanding. And if there is no investigation, there's no case."

"I know the case of one disappearance in particular, sir."

"Children aren't civilized like adults are. They play in the street, they get into things they shouldn't, they're always getting themselves hurt. There are youngsters who fall into wells and are never found again."

"I understand what you mean, but…" Moisès Corvo can't finish his sentence. The police chief wants to leave and is in no mood to listen to his reasoning.

"You shouldn't understand anything: just obey. There is no bogeyman, so I suggest that from this moment on you forget all about it."

"Yes, sir." That's what you have to say, according to Corvo, when you don't agree but there's nothing more to be done.

Later, Corvo and Malsano discuss it while they make their rounds on horseback in the area around some of the city's aldermen's homes, as he'd sent them to do that night.

"That's why people trust the municipals more," reasons Corvo. "Maybe they don't do any more than us, but at least they don't have to play at being stupid bodyguards for politicians."

"He who pays the piper calls the tunes. Stay out of it."

"It annoys me to be a puppet."

Malsano brings his left hand to his ears, eyes and mouth, and with the other tightens the reins to stop the horse. Hear no evil, see no evil, speak no evil.

A cold, placid dawn breaks, the mist orangish around the streetlights and rosy on the cobblestones. All that is heard is the clip-clop of the horses' hooves and some distant muffled crying behind the panes of closed windows. Here and there, the light of a bakery, the policemen who stop in there and chat with the bakers. It's still three hours until the workers get up and head to the factories, which—like giant beings—also sleep, stuffed with metal and hierarchy.

"I'm going to Montjuïc," decides Moisès Corvo.

"What?"

"Come. Let's go and see Mr Camil."

"Are you crazy? Do you know what time it is?"

"Yes, a time no one will notice we've gone."

He turns tail and gets his horse trotting. Malsano follows him, half-heartedly, sick of his partner acting on whim.

On the seaside slope of the mountain of Montjuïc, before reaching Morrot, there is a camp of gypsies under the protection of Mr Camil, the patriarch. It is made up of at least a dozen shacks located on different levels, united by paths chopped through the weeds with a scythe, around an esplanade where there are carriages and a permanent watchman sheltered by a few shoddily nailed-together walls and a bonfire that can be seen from the sea. There are even those who say that more than one sailor has confused Mr Camil's gypsies' fire with the entrance to the port and run aground. There are those who go further and claim Mr Camil's gypsies can often be found selling the contents of the ship's hold the next day.

Corvo and Malsano arrive there amid the silence, crickets and stars, and stop at the entrance. The former learnt to ride in Africa during the war and the latter in the uprisings at the turn of the century, sabre in hand. He's always saying he's one of the policemen in the famous painting by Ramon Casas, but it's always a lie.

The watchman receives them with his blunderbuss in his hand, a weapon that's not very practical but quite a deterrent, and the policemen open their jackets just enough to reveal their revolvers.

"We want to talk to Mr Camil," states Corvo.

"Not at this hour," responds the gypsy, big and fleshy, with a calm voice and a bearing that seems to say just you try it, and see what a thrashing you'll get.

"Tell him we're here and let him decide."

"No need for that," a hoarse voice says from the largest shack. "Chacote, let the inspectors in."

Before they enter, three of Mr Camil's sons come out to meet them and watch them dismount and tie up their reins with the mules. They greet them with a nod and remain outside in case their father should need them. Mr Camil shakes his wife, make them some drinks, and smoothes his clothes. Grey hair, receding hairline and bushy eyebrows, he uses his fingers to slick down his moustache in the shape of an inverted U, and he receives the surprise visitors with a courtesy not typical of that time of day.

Malsano realizes that his partner is very trusting, but he keeps checking behind him. It's not only that they're among gypsies (he can't stand them), but they are in the patriarch's house, alone, nobody knows they're there, it's the middle of the night and they are disobeying a direct order from their superior officer. The next day they could as easily end up in the clink as chopped up and mixed in with the hash these riff-raff on the outskirts of civilization feed their pigs, damn them.

"Cognac?" asks Mr Camil, who is already filling his glass. He drinks it, savouring the taste. "A good midnight snack is important." And he looks at the empty glass with a glimmer in his eyes, amid the sleep, promising loyalty.

"No, coffee," requests Corvo, and Malsano leans back in silence.

"Fina!" he bellows, even though she's right beside him. "You heard the inspectors."

The woman, more sleepy than resigned, lights a little burner that serves as their stove to boil a pot of water. She grabs a sock from the table and fills it with ground coffee beans.

"I've haven't been by here in a while."

"Good sign: my boys are behaving as they should."

"Yes… or they are learning to be independent."

Mr Camil smiles, revealing a gold incisor and his best cynicism.

"You know you are always welcome. Fina, where's that coffee?" he mutters under his breath. "She's a good woman, a saint, but sometimes… what can I do for you?"

"I need names."

"Gypsies or gadje?"

"I don't know."

"Mmm…" He adopts a serious stance, pure front. "What is it about this time?"

"Have you heard talk about the disappeared children? About a…"—he hesitates about using the word—"monster?"

"Who hasn't?" He yawns.

"I want to know his name, face and address."

Mr Camil gets up from his armchair and, with his gaze, urges Fina to hurry up.

"Not a simple task. I can't give you what you want."

"You're out of coffee? What's your wife cooking up?"

"Fina, bollocks! You heard the man!"

"It's coming, it's coming." She carries the smoking cups, burning her fingers.

"I don't know who it is, but I've heard things."

"What things?"

"Ugly things. Buying and selling."

"Buying and selling?" Corvo knows what he's insinuating, but he wants to have as much information as possible.

"It's hard to reach conclusions, Mr Inspector. Now there's a child, now there isn't. And it's happening more and more often—with one constant that repeats."

"They are the children of prostitutes."

"Yes, but no. My boys spoke to a woman on Mata Street, a beggar who lives off the alms of the crowds on Marqués del Duero. About a year ago they stole her son, a few months old. She had left him in the care of another panhandler while she went to look for food at the poorhouse on Barberà Street."

"You didn't tell me about this."

"You didn't ask."

"What was the man like?"

"Lame. That's the only thing she remembers."

"And why didn't she report it?" asks Malsano.

"Are you joking?"

"You heard the chief today," says Corvo. "If they aren't visible, they don't exist. In a way, their children can't disappear because it's as if they'd never been real."

"Exactly." Mr Camil sits down again, places his glass on a chest of drawers and crosses his arms.

"So, the guy responsible is lame, and not a gypsy," reflects Malsano out loud. "We have to look at the anthropometric files, because that would reduce the range of suspects by—"

"Nothing," concludes Corvo.

"Don't bet on it," the patriarch warns them. "My boys—shit,

I can't drink this coffee like this"—a few drops of cognac—"my boys, I mean, they've heard a lot of things."

"They have good ears."

"As big as pockets, Mr Inspector. But we leave the work to professionals such as yourself." Another swig, rolled eyes, barks from dogs outside that Chacote solves with a stick. "There isn't just one."

Moisès Corvo is stunned.

"That's not possible." Malsano puts down his glass where he can, between porcelain figurines and rosaries of Majorcan pearls. "When there is more than one person involved in things like this, somebody ends up talking. Always. And where there's somebody talking, there's somebody else listening. And the news spreads very quickly."

Mr Camil leans forward in his armchair, like a hustler about to reveal a good hand created with cards hidden in his sleeve that appear at just the right moment.

"My boys, I'll say it again, they hear everything. But if the... news, as you would say, Mr Inspector, doesn't flow, it's because someone can silence it."

"What are you insinuating?" asks Corvo.

"That you aren't just looking for a monster. And not a handful of incompetent sons of bitches who rape children. That you are going after people with enough power to anaesthetize an entire city. People who will do whatever it takes to indulge in their disgusting vices, who have money, who have status and who have power. That is all I know."

Moisès Corvo walks in circles, brooding, knowing that the words of his informant could have more truth to them than he was expecting. A dangerous truth.

"Can I do anything for you?" offers the policeman.

"Look for the money and you'll find your monster. It won't be long before they blame us for all that. It is the first thing they do when the fear strikes. And that is bad for business."

"If you have any problems, you know what to do."

"We'll keep that in mind. If my boys find out anything important, we'll let you know."

"Thanks."

"Good luck. My wife—" He turns and finds her sleeping, with her head fallen onto her chest and snoring freely, in a chair. "My wife will pray for you, we'll see if it turns out better than the coffee."

7

I DON'T WANT EVER TO SEE that wicked whore again, says Maria Pujaló. She has no heart, no soul, no feelings. I haven't spoken to my brother in a long time, and the only thing I know is that he can't free himself from her. He tried to leave her when they came back from Majorca. He realized he was married to a shrew, that it didn't matter if they were in Barcelona or on the Islands, that hate was eating her up and that was why she was like that, niggardly, a bag of bones, without an ounce of fat on her, with those frighteningly sunken cheeks. You never know if she is looking at you or spying on you, and she's always plotting something sinful. But Juanitu still adores her, I can't explain it. That whore turned him against me.

Maria Pujaló lives in Vilassar de Dalt and works as a maid in the home of the parish priest. She finally has enough stability, being that she's a widow. She opened the door to me reluctantly, and eventually ended up opening her heart to me. She has a lot to say, and few people to talk to. I'm the perfect confessor.

When I lived with her and my brother in the little flat on Jocs Florals Street I left Pepitu, my little angel, in her care. I had to go to Cervera for a few days because my father was very ill and needed me to care for him. After two weeks the doctor told us that it was best we bring him to the city, keep him close, because he would need extreme unction any day now and we would have to be by his side.

As soon as we returned to Jocs Florals we found that neither Enriqueta, Juanitu nor Pepitu was there. Some other family was living there! Ay, you should have seen it! How upsetting! You can't imagine what it is to find that your house is no longer your house. I cried wretchedly all day, with my father, who could barely even speak any more, beside me like a wilted little bird. Ay!

I looked for a hospice for consumptives where they could take him in, because on the street, with me, he would wither like a little flower, but we didn't have the coin and without money you die on the street.

Maria Pujaló whimpers, pulls a handkerchief out of her cleavage and rubs her reddened eyes. She asks for my forgiveness and I brush it off with a hand gesture, because I understand. She has suffered, and I know it, but her suffering won't go on much longer. Enriqueta won't hurt her again. Naturally, I keep that to myself.

And one day I ran into her on the street, that wicked woman. She was dressed all in black, as if in mourning, and she had Pepitu by the hand, practically dragging him. I shouted: "Enriqueta! Enriqueta!" She looked at me as if she'd just seen me the afternoon before, and everything had been said.

"What do you want, Maria?"

I ran to cover Pepitu with kisses, he was filthy, snot everywhere, but she wouldn't let him go.

"My boy!"

"We are in a hurry."

She is cold. She's very cold. She is a very evil person, and she doesn't care.

"Where were you? When I came from Cervera with father I couldn't find you. I've been on the street for four days, sleeping in doorways!"

"Juanitu found a better flat than that hole we were living in, and we moved."

"But you didn't tell me anything!"

"We told the neighbours. They were supposed to let you know."

It was a lie: she hadn't even spoken to the neighbours.

That same afternoon we—father and I—moved in with them. I didn't want to take the matter any further because the important thing was that I was reunited with Pepitu, who is my life. The boy told me that she had been filling his head with strange ideas. She told him that now she was his new mother, that I wasn't coming back from Cervera because I didn't love him any more, that she would take care of him but that he had to call her Mama. I don't know why I believed her… I don't know why I ever believed her.

Shortly, a week after moving into the flat on Tallers Street, father died. Choked by a cough, alone, suffering, poor thing. We didn't even have the money to bury him, even though Juanitu beat on his chest and said that he would build him a pantheon in the new Cemetery of the East, that nothing was too good for his father. And we had to bury him in a mass grave, God keep him in His Glory.

They say ignorance is bliss but you see that it's not always true, because Maria Pujaló doesn't know much and she couldn't be more unhappy. She doesn't know, for example, that Enriqueta got sick of having her father-in-law in the house, always in the bed, coughing and doddering, he's going to give it to me, she thought, and she decided to get rid of him, the sooner the better.

Seeing that the man didn't pass away—there are many who seem about to die who never do—she waited until she was alone in the house with him. Her husband must have been getting drunk in some tavern and Maria had taken Pepitu out to run errands; she'd been keeping him close ever since the change of flat in her absence.

She had to screw up her courage and find a way to get rid of the sick old man. She wasn't doing anything bad, she thought, he'd have to meet his maker sooner or later. But the problem was how to do it without raising any suspicion. Stealing jewellery and money is one thing, killing someone quite another; and when you don't know how it's done, you have to roll up your sleeves and figure it out so you don't look like an amateur, Enriqueta.

The woman approached the bedroom where Mr Pujaló lay sleeping, his breathing jagged and so filled with whistles that it seemed she was entering the França railway station. She knelt down and opened his mouth with her long, skinny fingers, introducing them gradually. No. That would wake him up and he was still capable of screaming. She grabbed the pillow, disgusted to find it drenched in sweat. She folded it over the man's face and pressed hard, but she was in a bad position and when he tensed all the muscles in his body he made her fall to the floor on her ass. The victim sat up, his hair mussed, poorly shaven, his eyes bulging, as if he were now regaining the strength that had been slipping away from him in recent months. Seeing Enriqueta on the floor, he understood her intentions and got up as best he could with a crick crack creek of his joints to run (if that crippled, pathetic gait could be called running) towards the door. But when he tried to open it, the knob failed him. Enriqueta had locked it with two turns of the key she carried in her dress pocket. The man turned tail and headed down the hallway towards the dining room, where there was a large window overlooking the street and he could call for help.

Enriqueta appeared in the kitchen brandishing a bread knife. "Dear father-in-law, all this exertion isn't good for you."

The man wanted to scream, he wanted to call her a cynical bitch, but he could only get out a weak, unintelligible voice choked by anguish and exhaustion. He still had the pluck to challenge her and try to wrest the knife from her, but that just made Enriqueta laugh as she switched it to the other hand and sank it into his butt cheek.

Too much blood. Mr Pujaló shrieked and hastened his step towards the dining room, taking advantage of the fact that Enriqueta was hypnotized by the reddish reflection of the knife blade. Too much blood. She would have liked to lick it, but that was infected blood. She had to finish him off, but without making the place look like a slaughterhouse. She went towards the man, whose wound was gushing down his leg like uncontrollable diarrhoea, and strangled him with her hands from behind. He coughed, but kept breathing because she didn't have a good, strong hold on his neck. The smell of leather, coming through the window from the hide workshop on the lower level, excited her. The man extended his arms as if someone could see him and help him, and he thought he'd survive when she let him go. But a second later he felt a sharp, delicate pressure on his throat. Enriqueta had pulled off one of the curtain cords and tied it around his neck. He spat and turned blue as she pulled it taut. He tried to hit her in the face, the shoulders, the breasts, desperately, but Enriqueta wouldn't let her captive go until he was well dead, enjoying the moment, savouring the feeling of power, discovering a new pleasure, playful and more intense than any she'd known up until then.

She left the inert body near the window, face down, just as she had killed him, and she cleaned his legs with a damp sponge. Then she scrubbed the floor, calmly, as if she'd dropped the remains of lunch off plates, and she went back to check on the body. The wound had stopped gushing. She covered it with a clean rag and put some pyjama bottoms on him which the dead man never wore but would cover up the cut. Then she remained by his side for a few minutes, looking at him, revelling in what she had just done.

Finally, she got up and went to take a walk until around ten, when Maria received her in tears.

"Father is dead and I wasn't here. He tried to lean out of the window to ask for help and he died." Maria hadn't seen the wounds, and no one would. Who looks for signs of violence on a consumptive old man?

Enriqueta consoled her with a big hug.

The chauffeur who had driven her to the mansion and is now keeping a close eye on her is a man named Marcial but, from what Enriqueta has seen, he only responds to the voice of his master. He is sturdy and serious, with a bowler hat and his hands crossed over his belly. She notices a bump under his armpit that confirms he has other duties beyond the steering wheel. And for the moment, one of them is staying close to the healer that Mr Llardó has called for.

Enriqueta already knows the mansion in the Bonanova where they've brought her: she has been there a few times before. But that doesn't stop her from feeling envious of the luxury surrounding her. As she enters through the wall covered in vines, the well-kept garden of topiary animals, a fountain with two cherubs spitting water over a small lake filled with colourful fish, the porch with columns at the entrance, she is convinced that it was all built for her, that she is the one who deserves to live there. She has to wait in the vestibule, despite the fantasies that invade her, sitting on a chaise longue and escorted by the chauffeur, contemplating the velvet curtains, the pale sculptures of satyrs chasing nymphs, the carpet that looks to be several inches thick and the distant murmur of bustling in the kitchen.

A nearby bell tower rings some quarter-hour after twelve.

Mr Llardó comes through the door with a boy of seven, tall and chubbier than his father. They both enter laughing, but the little one loses his smile when he sees Enriqueta, who has stood to greet them. Mr Llardó smacks the boy's nape affectionately.

"Go to your room."

His son obeys and leaves running, phlegmatically, without losing sight of the woman who is also watching him out of the corner of her eye. With a hand gesture Mr Llardó dismisses the chauffeur, who disappears without a word.

"Sir." Enriqueta is so fawning when it comes to the wealthy that those who deal with her normally wouldn't recognize her. Even though she attempts to sound sweet, she fails.

Mr Josep Vincenç Llardó Romagosa made his fortune in the Indies before Spain lost Cuba and can afford peacefully to while away the rest of his days in Barcelona, where he is an alderman. That allows him to keep a hand in small business deals that maintain his good position, both economically and socially. He seems shorter than he is because he always walks hunched over, due to the dampness of the boat where he worked for fifteen years, he says, and he has a hollow-cheeked face from which an enormous hooked nose emerges. Bald on the crown of his head, he hides it by combing over a cow-lick like a spiral *ensaïmada*, a technique that works as long as the wind isn't blowing.

"I need more salve," he says as he accompanies her to the parlour.

"I told you it wouldn't be enough. That it has to be one for each full moon, Mr Llardó."

"I know, I know." The alderman seems baffled and even somewhat ashamed. "But I didn't want my wife to find it and start asking questions that… well, you know what I mean."

Mr Llardó's wife had gone to spend the days before Christmas in Caldes, to soak in some thermal springs on her doctor's advice, since lately she'd been feeling very weak of spirit and very feeble. Maybe it was completely unrelated, or maybe not, but Mr Llardó had caught a raging case of syphilis over the summer and, through a friend, was put in touch with Enriqueta, who is providing him with the balms that are meant to cure him. Mr Llardó is afraid to go to the doctor, and Enriqueta takes advantage of that.

"Right now I don't have any more salve."

"It's very urgent." He seems like a little boy about to pee himself.

"Let me see the affected area."

The man hesitates, but the need is pressing. He lowers his trousers and unfastens his underwear. Like a scarecrow, making sure his son doesn't appear on the stairs, that the servant girl doesn't appear through the kitchen door and that—rattled by his nerves, in short, with his arms extended. Enriqueta examines his genitals without touching them. The chancre on his penis has disappeared, but he is starting to show symptoms of mucous-membrane irritation.

"How does it look?"

"Not good."

"When can you have the salve?"

"I'll have to prepare it, but reckon on seven days."

"That's… next Wednesday?"

"Yes, right before the full moon. You're in luck. For the moment, make an infusion of rosemary and two heads of garlic and soak a pillow and some rags in it. Use the pillow, when it's dried, for sleeping. The rags will be for scrubbing down where you are having discomfort. And tomorrow morning drip candle wax on a drop of Agua del Carmen, mix well and add it to your bath water."

The alderman lifts up his trousers and smoothes his moustache as if nothing is going on, sweat drenching his forehead.

"What do I owe you?"

"Today's visit is 300 pesetas. The salve will be 1,000."

"A thousand?"

"The ingredients are difficult to come by, and the urgency makes them costlier. But think that if you heed my words, you will not only be cured but also protected from infecting those who come into contact with you. And I know that you have many lady friends that you don't want to let get away while the lady of the house isn't here."

Mr Llardó pays 400 pesetas. The extra is the price for silence.

"One week, without fail."

"I am a woman of my word."

The next day, Inspectors Corvo and Malsano are covering the beat between Conde del Asalto Street to Marqués del Duero, searching for the woman whose son was abducted by a lame man, as the gypsy patriarch had informed them. It is cold and the shelters are teeming, so it will surely be an unsuccessful undertaking, but this is the thread they have started to pull on. They have nothing else.

Mata Street is empty, and Moisès Corvo is feeling frustrated.

"We are looking for a goddamn ghost."

"I would let it go, Corvo. We've done all we can."

Marqués del Duero is all lit up: theatres, cafés, bars, dance halls. A few steps from the deserted street they've just left behind there is a throng of people lined up in queues, bundled up to their eyebrows, for the different cabaret, magic and variety shows. Raquel Meller draws the biggest crowds at the Teatre Arnau. The Petit Moulin Rouge, made to look like its Parisian older brother, attracts the curiosity of passers-by.

"What are you doing for Christmas?" asks Malsano.

"I still don't know. My brother asked us to sup with them at their house, they're going to roast a chicken, and my wife is excited at the prospect because she complains that she never sees her nephew."

"Andreu? How is he?"

"Big, I guess. Youngsters are always bigger than the last time you saw them. He's quite a clever lad."

"So, what will you do?"

"Work, I guess."

"Something's wrong with you, Corvo. Don't give the force an hour more than you have to, not a minute more. It's not worth it."

"I'm not doing it for the force." He furrows his brow, like a small child.

"If you don't mark the time for you, the force will take it all."

Moisès Corvo wants to find the son of a bitch who's snatching children. He feels like a vulture circling the scent of rotting flesh, but he can't quite find the corpse. He's obsessed. Each passing day brings them closer to the next disappearance. And while they're only the children of whores and indigents, they are just as defenceless as his nephew, Andreu, for example. And it enrages and frustrates him no end: after all these years of experience wading through the dung heap of criminals in that city, now he can't even find a goddamn cripple. It is his duty, not only professional, but moral. The last moral left to him, perhaps, but it's all he's got and he wants to hold on to it.

"We're not going to find beggars here, not today," he mutters.

"Let's go to the station, we have work backed up."

Silence, coloured lights on the fronts of buildings.

"Do you like magic?"

"Magic?"

Moisès Corvo crosses the street, dodging cars and drivers' insults. It looks like half the cars in Barcelona are jammed up there that night, and it's not even a weekend. Juan Malsano follows him to the entrance with the windmill, the former Pajarera Catalana, below a large illuminated sign announcing the performance of the Great Balshoi Makarov, master of the disappearing act and artist of the mind. He shows his police credentials to get in. His partner is already inside, through the curtains that lead to the vestibule and then on to the seats.

Darkness.

"Shit, Corvo…" he murmurs, but the inspector elbows him to be quiet.

The light from the crucibles tints the master of the disappearing act and artist of the mind's silhouette in pastel colours. He is standing beside a box some two metres tall, some sort of vertical coffin.

"I need a volunteer," he states, with an obvious Russian accent. No one responds. "It can even be a lady."

Nervous laughter, until a woman stands up, earning the audience's applause. She wears a hat and a long dress that reaches her ankles, and the Great Makarov receives her with a bow, as if she were a princess, removing her hat and making it disappear. A bit of small talk before introducing her into the box where he will eventually saw her in half; from a hole in the upper part we see her frightened face, and from another in the lower half some dancing feet. You know, the typical magic-act number. The audience bursts into applause and the Great Makarov nods in every direction to acknowledge the praise.

"This is a cock-up," Malsano says, taking advantage of the pause. "If anybody sees us here—"

"Shush."

The illusionist puts the volunteer back together and asks for another ovation for her. The act continues for a good hour. The Russian guesses with his eyes blindfolded what people in the audience are wearing, makes pigeons come out of the most unusual places and escapes from a locked and bolted safe before making a last triumphant appearance floating over the audience, handing out 100-peseta bills with his face on them.

The people leave happy—how does he do it, where's the trick—and gradually the theatre empties. The policeman stay in the penumbra, waiting, until the Great Makarov comes out of the door from the dressing rooms with the volunteer he had sawed in half at the start of the show. The girl starts to sweep the corridors with the skill of someone who does it mechanically every night, and Makarov is surprised to see that there are still two people at the back of the theatre.

"If you like it that much, come back tomorrow, there'll be more and even better," he calls out.

"It was quite good," responds Moisès Corvo, as he approaches him.

"Can I help you?" says the Russian, and the girl stops sweeping.

"Inspectors Corvo and Malsano." They extend their hands.

"Vladimir Makarov, at your service." He reveals his name and shakes hands without trying to hide his disappointed expression. "I thought you were producers interested in the show."

He turns and nods to his assistant, as if saying you can continue.

"How long have you been here?"

"Here where? In Spain?"

"No, at the Arnau."

"Oh, that here…" He thinks back. "About a year, not quite. At the end of this year my contract's up and I doubt they'll renew it."

"It seems you're quite a success."

"Appearances can be deceiving: this is Christmas, it's a good time of the year. In June there was nobody here. In fact, I doubt they'll let me premiere the performance I'm preparing." Theatrical stance, arms extended, gaze out on the horizon. "*Beneath the Wings of Death.*"

Vladimir Makarov seems more French than Russian. He is crammed into a burgundy silk vest over a linen shirt, all in all very bohemian, very Parisian.

"They'll renew: magic is in style."

The artist sucks his teeth.

"Illusionism. Magic is for crazy old men who wear goat horns on their heads and throw animal guts into pots of boiling broth."

"Illusionism," concedes Moisès Corvo, deferential but unconvinced.

"Everyday life is too grey; I help those who come to see me to escape it. Note the irony."

The policemen don't see the irony anywhere, but they use the conversation thread started by this Frenchified Russian.

"Speaking of seeing you…"

"Yes, of course, you are policemen, you haven't come to my dressing room to give me flowers."

"At what time do you usually arrive at the theatre?"

"At seven in the evening, more or less."

"And you don't leave again until?…"

"Well, I was heading home now."

"Do you have supper before or after the show?"

"Before, I have a loud stomach."

"Here inside?"

"Sometimes, but usually I go to a café nearby, where they make delicious sausages." He smoothes his pointy blond moustache, pensive. "I'll help you in any way I can, I envy your job, but… could you be more specific? I'm beginning to get uneasy."

"There's no need. We are looking for someone who sleeps near here, on the street, and we'd like to know if you've seen him."

"No need to beat around the bush then. Now, in the winter, there's no one around, as you've noticed. But during the summer there are a few guys who spend the night out here. Who are you looking for?"

"A lame man."

"Lame?"

"Lame."

"No…" He thinks, furrows his brow, rolls his eyes upward, quite the actor.

"A few months ago he snatched a woman's son just a few metres from the theatre."

"I'm sorry, but I don't usually lend my ear to gossip. I haven't heard anything about it."

He seems sincere, thinks Malsano. Moisès Corvo is silent, hesitant about saying what he is about to say:

"Have you heard talk of a monster?"

Malsano sighs loudly. Here we go again.

"Corvo, we've got to be going."

"No, no. What monster? The lame chap?" Makarov is getting interested.

"Corvo…" insists Malsano.

"Nothing. Forget it."

"I'm not in danger, am I?"

The girl keeps sweeping, now paying more attention to the conversation.

"Not at all," respond the policemen in unison, which produces the opposite effect in the illusionist.

"He's talking about the vampire," says the girl from the other end of the theatre. "The one that takes children without leaving a trace and eats them."

"There's no vampire," denies Malsano, raising his voice.

"Then why did your partner ask about the monster?"

Ask him about the Xalet del Moro.

"Do you know the Xalet del Moro?"

"What?" Now it is Makarov and Malsano who ask the question in chorus.

Have you ever gone there?

"Have you ever gone there?"

The Russian hesitates, confused.

"Yes, but… Goddamnitalltohell! The gimp, I do know him!"

"You know him?" Malsano can't believe it.

"Well, I know a man with a limp who hung around the theatre, but he doesn't sleep on the street. A fat, ugly bloke. I noticed him because in one week I saw him around the theatre and at the Xalet del Moro."

"The brothel?" asks Malsano.

"There they are ladies of the evening," qualifies Makarov.

"Whores with money," maintains Corvo, and asks, "How long ago was that?"

"I don't know… maybe the last time I saw him was in the summer, or September. But I don't go there very often, to the Xalet del Moro, don't get the wrong idea."

"Do you know his name?"

"No, I already told you I've only seen him, and it surprised me to see him there, because it doesn't exactly look like he has much money and they don't just let anyone into the Xalet." He smoothes his clothes, proud. "I also have to say that it didn't look like he was a client."

"What do you mean?"

"He didn't look at any of the girls. I saw him chatting with the madam, and then I stopped paying attention to him."

"Your mind was on other things."

"Exactly." He put on his Tyrolean hat, ready to go out to the street. "So, this guy is the one snatching children?"

"We didn't say that."

"But he snatches them."

"Around what time did you see him?"

"The gimp?"

"Yes."

"I don't know. Late afternoon maybe, I don't know."

"On a weekend?"

"No, during the week. On Saturdays and Sundays I do two shows, so I'm busy all afternoon and evening."

"You would recognize him if you saw him again." It's not so much a question as a statement.

"Yeah, I guess so…" He hesitates. "Yeah, yeah."

"OK. I'll go and look for him. I want you to come with me."

They say goodbye and the policemen go out to the street. The blades of the windmill are no longer spinning but the city is still throbbing.

"We should go to the station," recommends Malsano. "Who knows what's happened while we were in there. And besides, we have work to do, Millán Astray is going to kill us if we don't finish it."

"Let's go over there, Juan. If we had a photographic file like we should we could show it to that Makarov."

"But we don't."

"No."

They cross the avenue and enter into the dark, narrow streets of the Santa Madrona district.

"Where did that bit about the Xalet del Moro come from?" he asks, finally.

Moisès Corvo pleads a stroke of intuition, a response that doesn't satisfy his partner, but which he's just going to have to accept.

Maria Pujaló, crumpled handkerchief in her closed fist, pale knuckles and dried tears forming a map of desolation on her face, is a scared woman.

"What can you tell me about Angelina?" I take her by the hands, but she doesn't let me. She looks away.

"What do you want me to tell you?"

"When Enriqueta had Angelina was when you decided to leave Barcelona."

I know that it hurts her.

"I had just lost a baby," she says in a reedy voice.

Now I like you.

"What?"

"After my father's death, may God hold him in His Glory, I was glum for a while. I didn't have much energy and Pepitu really wore me out. Enriqueta was always taking him around with her, all over, and he'd become all quiet, always afraid and peeing in the bed at night. He didn't have anyone, you know. Juanitu is a scatterbrain I never saw, my son was like a stranger to me, and Enriqueta said that if I was going to live like a soul in torment anyway I might as well die, that I would be more helpful to my father on the other side, that all I was doing was bringing in evil spirits."

"Evil spirits?"

"Yes. She said that since I had one foot on this side and one on the other, since I ate like a bird and never left the house and I was a bag of bones and my skin was getting all wizened, I was like an open door to all sorts of ghosts and demons and who knows what other superstitions."

"But you don't believe in such things."

"No, but they still scare me. Enriqueta wasn't home much, but when she was she was always burning bundles of thyme in every corner and hanging rabbits' feet from the door lintels."

"Against you."

"She said I brought bad luck. That my condition brought only misfortune. She accused me of everything. If she lost clients at the herbalist's shop, it was my fault."

"What herbalist's shop?"

"The one Juanitu set up for her, by the house, with the few pennies my father left us."

"And she worked there?"

"I wouldn't exactly call it working. At first she did make some balms and syrups, and she seemed… I was about to say excited, but I've never seen Enriqueta show any real excitement. She was more like obsessed. But when she started to have problems with the police, she quickly grew tired of it. And she blamed me for it, that they arrested her all the time, and again with the amulets all around the flat and the strange prayers at every hour of the day and night. Then she opened the store only when she felt like it. The customers got tired of her, her odd ways and her bad humour, and she only went to the store when… well, she didn't go there much."

"No, go on, please."

"With what?"

"When did she go to the store?"

"No."

"No what?"

"I didn't mean to say it. I made a mistake. She didn't go there much and that's it."

"And why were they arresting her, the police?"

"For a million reasons. Once they came to the house, with Pepitu, asking me if the boy was mine. Turns out that someone had accused Enriqueta of panhandling with him. A few days later they brought me some other boy, saying that they had arrested her again for the same thing, and that I should keep an eye on my children. I told them that he wasn't mine, and it turned out his mother was a neighbourhood woman who regularly bought herbs from her for infusions, and it seems she was a bundle of nerves and she would leave her son in Enriqueta's care while she shopped for groceries at the Boqueria."

"But did Enriqueta need to beg?"

"No! Not at all. We always had money coming in, and she would buy dresses and jewellery she never even wore."

"Then I don't understand why she did it."

"Out of greed. Because she likes money, and she likes hood-winking people."

"And do you know where the money came from?"

"I spent all day lying in bed, eating gruel. You think I knew anything?"

She seems sincere, but she's not. She knows full well what that woman had her hands into. But she is incapable of admitting it. It's too painful for her. I have to ask her about Angelina again, before she changes the subject.

"The money coming in wasn't legal."

"She was wicked. It must have been money from her evil deeds."

"Before you said that Enriqueta had Angelina when you had just lost a child."

"Yes." Her voice trembles.

"But you are a widow."

She lowers her eyes again.

"Enriqueta told me that in order to get over that half-dead state I was in, the best thing to do would be to have another child. She told me that she knew people from good families who would be thrilled to knock me up."

"And she brought them to the house."

"For six months. Sometimes three or four in a single day, some-times weeks would pass without anybody showing up. Enriqueta would dress me up elegant, real pretty, with crêpe and bright colours, and she'd paint my face and put shiny earrings on me. I was like a doll. Today you have a visitor, she'd say, and she'd get me ready. Then the man, or men, would come in and—well, you can imagine. This way you'll have a child of good lineage, healthy and strong and with money on the horizon, she would repeat at the end of every visit. But I had my doubts, because I was so weak that I didn't get my periods, and I couldn't get pregnant. I felt dirty, fouled, like a whore, but I couldn't resist because I had no strength, and because Enriqueta frightened me more and more."

"Did she threaten you?"

"She would hit me. She would yell at me, saying she'd kill me if I didn't show more effort, she'd already had one of the men complain that doing it with me was like doing it with a corpse."

"But you got pregnant."

"Yes." Her eyes filled with tears. "But it went wrong from the very beginning. She forced me to stay at home, because in my fragile state I could lose the child at any moment. Luckily the visits stopped, but the following months were a nightmare. She had me tied up at home and she wouldn't let me see a doctor. I was alone, and Juanitu did his own thing, and I only had Enriqueta, who was the one who woke me up, fed me and took care of me when I had fever, vomits or dizziness, and I had a lot. I was like a dog, and Enriqueta said she wasn't sure, that the pregnancy was very complicated because there were too many evil spirits in that house And after a few weeks she got pregnant too."

"Enriqueta?"

"Yes. And I thought she wasn't able to, that that was why she always sought out others' children, because she was like a piece of dry land that had been sown with salt. She said that Juanitu had given her a child, and that we would have two babies in the house at the same time, that fortune was smiling on us. But you could see she didn't believe all that, that she was just lying so I would hold on to the baby and not lose it. She was afraid that I might make myself abort: she hid the parsley and knitting needles from me. She was controlling me. She had me locked up."

"And you lost the baby."

"No, not until the birth. Enriqueta gave me all kinds of drugs to have a quick delivery. But it was so painful that I lost consciousness. When I came to, Enriqueta sat by my side, her hands bloody. The room was silent and she stared at me. It was born dead, she said. The cord was wrapped around its neck and it came out bluish, not breathing, poor thing. My boy. My baby. Enriqueta had already buried him before I woke up. She assured me it was better that way, that in my state I couldn't stand the pain and I could die. But I already wanted to die. I wanted to die."

"You never saw him, the boy?"

"No. When I asked where she had buried him she told me that it was in a well in the flat on Tallers Street. I never had the courage to go over there."

"And Angelina?"

"Angelina was born a few weeks later."

Maria Pujaló has spent the last two years suspecting that the girl is her daughter. That Enriqueta tricked her about her pregnancy and the birth. When she looked at the baby's face, she saw her reflection. But something inside her has helped to keep up the lie, as if it were necessary to survive, as if she had to forget to go on living.

"And what did Enriqueta do?"

"What do you mean?"

"With Angelina, with Juanitu, with you. How did she act?"

"She blamed me for what happened. Said that if I hadn't been such a bad omen my boy would be alive now. That I wasn't as strong as she was, she who had a beautiful girl. And then she pushed me aside."

"How?"

"She ignored me. And she spoke ill of me to Juanitu, who would then come and give me a tongue-lashing because I was making Enriqueta nervous. He said that I had no consideration, that now that they were parents I was making their life impossible, that I was envious, that I was covetous. He went so far as to say that I shouldn't go near Angelina, that he was afraid I would hurt her. Me!"

"And you left."

"Yes. I left, far from them, with Pepitu. And I found a shelter here in Vilassar. And over time I met a good man, a widower as well, with three young 'uns, and he asked for my hand."

"And you haven't seen Enriqueta again."

"I don't want to know a thing about her. I already told you that I haven't spoken to my brother for some time."

Maria Pujaló squeezes her handkerchief hard when Pepitu comes running through the door, his face all dirty. She grabs him under the chin with one hand and spits into the handkerchief, which she uses to clean him. The boy looks at me and stares, as if hypnotized, as always happens with children when they see me.

"Pepitu, don't look at the man that way, it's rude."

In the nights, Maria dreams that Enriqueta enters her room, in the darkness, ties her to the bed and sucks the life out of her. When she wakes up, she is never sure it was just a nightmare.

But it's best she doesn't know that now Blackmouth, when he knocks on Enriqueta's door, finds Angelina opening it. Enormous eyes, very short, badly cut hair, with a fabric band around her head. Her little dress is in rags and she's barefoot.

"Your mama's not here?"

The girl shakes her head no.

Blackmouth doesn't hear any noise from inside the flat. Angelina turns and goes back to playing in her room.

The boy enters and closes the door with the bolt. He moves slowly, afraid he'll be caught, but also aroused. The kitchen is empty and orderly, with no sign that anyone cooks there. There is no smell of broth, or meat or fish or anything. He passes quickly through the room with burgundy velvet walls, expensive furnishings and mirrors on every wall, trying not to leave footprints in the thick carpet. Enriqueta's bedroom is empty, as is the walk-in closet where she hides the youngsters she collects off the streets, which locks with a sliding door. Angelina is sitting in her room, playing dolls with sticks. Blackmouth realizes that they are small bones, like tiny phalanges. They must have been boiled because there is no trace of flesh or tendons or blood.

"What are you playing?"

"Dead little brothers and sisters," she says, her focus still on her game.

"And how do you play?"

"This is my daughter." She lifts one of the bones. "And she plays with the other brothers and sisters."

"The other ones aren't your children?"

"No." She hits one against the other. "They are other people's children. And when she's hungry, she eats them."

Blackmouth is so scared that he gets an erection.

"Can I play?"

"No."

"You don't want to play with me?"

"No."

"Why not?"

"Because Mama says I shouldn't pay you no mind."

The boy caresses the girl's nape, and looks for the button to undo her clothes.

"And what do you think?"

The girl stops playing and looks outside the room, as if she had heard something. Blackmouth gets frightened and stops short, but he doesn't take his hand away. With the other, he touches himself inside his trousers, grabbing his member.

"Mama says you're repulsive."

Blackmouth has pulled his penis out and approaches Angelina, who is in her own world, drumming with the finger bones again.

"You and I could be good friends, you know?"

"And she told me that if I play with you she'll kill ya."

8

KEEPING WATCH over the Xalet del Moro isn't easy. In fact, it's not easy keeping watch over any place. It's a question of waiting and waiting and waiting some more, of not getting discouraged, of giving yourself a goal that you may never reach, always with the idea that you are exposed, that everyone can see you, because it is so obvious that you are watching, that the roles are switched and there you are, like a zoo animal munching on grass as rivers of visitors flow by.

I am Patience itself. I wait, I observe and I only act when intervention is necessary, with surgical precision. I'm not innocent, I don't need to tell you that. But neither am I guilty. I'm just another person and at the same time I'm everything, because, in the end, *everything* reverts to me.

Moisès Corvo has spent four afternoons on Escudellers Street, feeling that he was being watched when he was the one spying, alternating between the lamp posts, the doorways and the café in front of the brothel, which is the best spot for vigilance but also where you get identified as police the quickest. And he's sick of it.

He saw the girls enter punctually at six through a side door, covered in cloaks and protected by a huge man, as wide as he was tall, who was also waiting for them. Here everyone waits, everyone is on the lookout, but nothing happens. Not a trace of the gimp or the monster or their goddamn mother. It seems this is all just something out of the imagination of whores, another one of those rumours that get under the skin of the poor because they want to think somebody gives a fig for them, even if it's just a made-up creature from hell.

The Xalet del Moro is named for its arabesque architectural style, an exotic combination of mosaics, arches and filigree work on white stone. Even though it's known that the building serves as a knocking shop, or at least that's the popular suspicion, few people have entered. You should see how the clients begin to show up, in dribs and drabs, starting at nine in the evening, in carriages with windows hidden by curtains or in cars that stop right in front of the door. Moisès Corvo hasn't recognized anyone, because they enter too covered up and too quickly. They'll have plenty of time to shed their layers and take things slowly once they're inside.

I like you. I wouldn't want to be one of you, sorry; I didn't mean it that way. I like you because sometimes, notwithstanding all the years I've been with you, you still manage to surprise me. As I said before, I'm the one waiting for you. Occasionally, though, it happens the other way round, and it is one of you who receives me after a wait. Today, 20th December, I met the poet Joan Maragall. I knew you'd come, he told me. And we chatted for a while, since neither of us was in a rush. I enjoy coming for poets. They aren't so different from each other, they're always searching for the less common gaze, the hidden side of life, they are always observing, like me. Like everyone, sure, but they do it expressly, wilfully. And will is the part of your souls that I most envy. Maragall, who had been sick for months, if not years, had prepared himself for our meeting. He had accepted it with both lucidity and fear, and he had collected questions that he asked me one by one, with a serenity I appreciated. It's nice to find that, among millions and millions of "why mes", there is someone who asks me "why you". Please, when I come to meet you, don't ask me why it's your turn. It's like questioning the queue at the market stall, and no one does that. Listen to his verses and tell me they're not thrilling, if only I were capable of being thrilled:

> *But I'm so jealous of the eyes, and the face,*
> *and the body that you gave me, Lord, and the heart*
> *that's always moving inside… and I so fear death!*

I was very sorry not to be able to answer all the poet's questions, but I don't have answers, merely some consolations.

The day I met Joan Maragall, Moisès Corvo had gone to see Makarov. The inspector needs to go into the brothel right now, he's been waiting too long, he's choked with urgency, the sense of an imminent attack from his particular monster. And he's not too far off, because Enriqueta is about to kill another child.

It's not that there hasn't been work recently, anyhow. There have been steady, violent deaths in Barcelona, almost every day. It's just that Moisès Corvo and Juan Malsano (but especially the former) haven't really worried too much about them. There are suicides every single day, too: workers who stay in the factory when it closes and hang themselves from one of the beams; a spurned banker threw himself from the terrace of the Hotel Colón; more than one person—more than two or three—unable to rebound from despondency have let themselves be decapitated by the train, lying down on the tracks… and like that there is a long list of etceteras. But both for the police and for me, we don't fool ourselves, it's routine, a series of procedures in single file that must be completed: the removal of the cadaver, the identification, the autopsy report and the case file. Red tape. I don't even look at them, poor people, in such a rush to the finish line as if there were anything better on the other side. Or as if there were anything at all. In the case of the banker, the chief pressured them a bit, as usually happens when the dead person is important or wealthy (or both), but he didn't take them off the case that was really weighing them down.

Malsano had been questioning the nightwatchmen of the district. If anyone knows who is active at night it's them. But this time he had no luck there either. There are dozens of gimps in the neighbourhood, but none of the watchmen had seen any of them with children.

"You're looking for the bogeyman," says Severiano, one of the most veteran. His face is marked by smallpox and his eyes are so sunken they look like two black holes.

Malsano nods and releases the smoke from his lungs slowly. A cigarette burns down between his fingers.

"You aren't the only one," continues Severiano. He grabs his bunch of keys and lifts them to the height of his face; they are on an iron ring with all the keys hanging from the lower end. "You'll have to hurry up and find him, because if the others find him first"—he starts to lift keys, one by one, three by three—"you'll have to pick him up in pieces." Now all the keys are on the upper part, gathered in a ball by the watchman's big, scaly hand.

"What do people know about him?"

"Same as you. And they're livid. They don't trust the police."

"We're doing all we can."

"You don't have to tell me. But people think that what you aren't doing, they have to do themselves."

On the way to Escudellers Street, Vladimir Makarov doesn't hide like the rest of the Xalet del Moro clients. The Tyrolean hat, the bison coat and a lacquered cane with a handle in the shape of an ant head isn't the best outfit for passing incognito.

Moisès Corvo doesn't get why they let the illusionist into the elite bordello, even though his claim that he's a distant relative of the tsars has opened a lot of doors for him. That must be why he doesn't hide: he likes to be seen going in, for people to think he has possibilities, that he's a dandy, a moneyed bohemian, and he makes himself as noticeable as a turkey surrounded by ducks.

"Now, when you go in, don't make me look bad. The Xalet del Moro is different from all the other brothels. The girls are prettier and have more sophisticated vices."

"What do you want me to say? I've been in more brothels than a confessor."

"I can assure you that what you'll see inside here, though, you've never tried."

"Mr Makarov… I've seen too much deviance to be surprised now."

"Man, I wouldn't call it deviance exactly…"

They chat animatedly as they cross the Rambla in the darkness. A pickpocket recognizes the inspector and greets him with a false smile that Corvo doesn't return.

"Once destroyed pots started showing up on the street."

"Pots?"

"Yes, with geraniums and flowers. All the pots of every plant on the lower storeys…"

"Lower storeys in your lower stories, you're being redundant."

"Yeah, yeah." Corvo was discovering that Makarov is a bit scattered, and that he has trouble following a conversation without putting in his two cents' worth. "…The pots on Ample Street were broken first thing in the morning. If it wasn't the wind, it must have been someone with a terrible botanical phobia who went around breaking them at night."

"A difficult case, no doubt."

The policeman pulls a face, and here we go again.

"We decided to wait. Around midnight a guy showed up, about your height, dark skin, not badly dressed, not particularly well dressed, walking down Serra Street."

"Dragging his balls through the dirt."

"Are you a magician or a comedian?"

"A master of the vanishing act and an artist of the mind."

"Do you want to hear this or not?"

"Yes, sorry. Go on, please, I wouldn't want to get in the way of police work."

"It was obvious he was guilty. He was scouting around, suspiciously, and looking at the geraniums that were still standing in a… libidinous way."

"Is it possible to look at a geranium in a libidinous way?"

"Just like you can cover a mouth with homicidal intent. If you want me to demonstrate, just ask."

"And what happened?"

"The bloke pulled out his willy and stuck it into the soil."

"What?"

"Yup. And he moved his hips around to penetrate it. Pretty well, actually, you could tell he had experience."

"And you arrested him."

"No! It was too amusing to interrupt. We let him do it, and he got more and more excited. By the fourth screw he had his trousers at his ankles, and his legs covered in dirt and leaves.

When he tired of one, he threw it to the floor and went for the next. He left the street filled with crap."

"People are sick."

"I told you. We called him the geranium-fucker. We scared him a little and he took off. We haven't seen him since."

"He wasn't a gimp?"

"If only."

"Inspector, take this card." The magician gives him a two of coins. "When they show you the king of clubs, hold it up."

Makarov advances and knocks on the door with his cane. The policeman fears that the doorman who opens it will recognize him from the last few days, but he breathes a sigh of relief when he sees that his eyes are too close together and his head too small to fit even a little brain in there. The bouncer has them enter a small arabesque foyer and begins the ceremony. He shows him a seven of swords and the magician doesn't even move. Then he lifts up the king of swords, and his response comes in the form of an ace of coins. The small man moves aside and opens a door of fine wood. For a few seconds the scent of cinnamon seeps between Moisès Corvo and the hellhound. Like an automaton, he shows him a king of cups, and Corvo holds back his desire to lift his card. He feels stupid, but he consoles himself thinking that the other chap doesn't feel stupid: he is stupid. In his eyes, however, he sees distrust, which has never had a falling-out with stupidity, they more often go hand in hand. The doorman puts the card away in a cigarette case he carries in the inner pocket of his jacket and pulls out the king of clubs. Now Corvo proudly shows his two of coins and is invited inside.

He opens his eyes like a little boy discovering the magic of Christmas. Makarov stands waiting for him in a covered patio lit by oil lamps and with a fountain in the centre protected by thirsty stone lions. The ground around it is white marble sliced through with rosy tones, and the ceiling is a labyrinth of ornamental borders and whimsical geometric figures, half in the penumbra of the oil lamps that hang from the pillars coming up on either side. At the back, an arch opens onto the vestibules; to the sides, three staircases ascend to the upper floors.

"What do you think?" asks Makarov, as if it were his house.

"No geraniums here."

They cross the patio and once they are in the vestibule they are received by a woman wrapped in a single piece of sky-blue silk, the whites of her eyes like two sea urchins split in half, and her generous breasts free beneath the fabric.

"Good evening, Mr M." She lowers her eyes. A real professional, the madam.

"Good evening." Makarov bows.

She turns towards the inspector, and Corvo kisses the back of her hand, gallantly.

"You brought company!" She is pleased, or it seems like it. "What an honour, such a handsome boy."

It had been years since anyone had called him a boy. Son of a bitch, sure, bastard, as well: crap copper, more often. But boy, lately, no.

"The honour is mine, ma'am." He deepens his voice, pretending he knows how to act in this setting, but it's clear he's out of place.

"Miss… You can call me Miss Lulú." She looks him up and down. "You're not related to?…"

The king, as usual.

"No, no, ma'am… Miss Lulú."

"Well, you're like two peas in a pod."

"In this case we'd be like two pearls."

"I'll tell Alfonso, when I see him, that he has a double, and that his name is…"

"Lestrade, at your service."

"French?"

"On my grandparents' side."

"We french very well here, Mr Lestrade. I hope you enjoy yourself to the utmost."

"I haven't the slightest doubt I will."

"Where are the girls?" Makarov is growing impatient, he's no longer the centre of attention and he doesn't like it.

"I'll have them come in right now. Sit down, please."

The woman disappears behind some curtains and Moisès Corvo realizes that there is soft music playing but he can't identify it. A gramophone out of sight grinds out notes by Ravel and Debussy.

"Above all be discreet," requests Makarov. "I like this place and I want to come back."

From the curtain where Madame Lulú vanished emerge six girls in disciplined formation. In silence, without even looking at each other, they make a wall in front of the two clients, who are now lying on two sofas with baroque upholstery. A Botticelli, an Ingres, two Romero de Torres, a small Gauguin and a lovely Negress no one ever dared to paint.

"Marianne, Monique, Rosa, María, Adriana and Eram," lists Madame Lulú. "If the gentlemen don't find what they are looking for, I can show you more…"

But the harlot is playing it safe, because she knows that the redhead drives Makarov wild, and she sensed quickly that Corvo (because it's his first time, and because of his gaze and tone of voice) will choose the Oriental, as he does. The woman puts one hand over the other and lets a gold incisor show between her lips, which tense into the smile of a fox.

Electric light, heat, running water and a Tahitian named Adriana are the main luxuries Moisès Corvo finds when he closes the door to the suite. The girl led him up some stairs from the main patio, and he allowed himself to be hypnotized by the small but hard and round ass that swayed on each step and hadn't been broadened by any babies. The whores Corvo usually visits lost that firmness years ago. And, obviously, that, the exoticism, the mystery of the playing cards at the door and the discretion of not passing anyone (even though moans and screams of pleasure can be heard through the walls) comes at a price. And what a price. A policeman's salary couldn't cover the layout of 150 pesetas the service would cost him, but the inspector came with his pockets filled with money. When a robber is arrested and carries part of his spoils on him, you can always negotiate a small fee in exchange for talking to the judge about his repentance. Golem and Babyface, who are the ones that do most of the bank-robber chasing during the day shift, turn a blind eye when Corvo chats with one of their clients. In the end, the inspector has done them quite a few (a lot of) favours, so they can be delicate about the money. If the bank's already lost it, they won't miss it much. Moisès Corvo has saved up some cash from that percentage he gets off the detainees and the full sum he gets off the dead that die at home (the easiest, quickest way to make a little extra), and now he can pay the Tahitian in advance, as she settles onto the softest mattress he's ever felt in his life.

The girl, who doesn't say a word, unbuttons his shirt and caresses his chest, without taking her eyes off his, to lick his nipples softly, as if she planned to melt them with her tongue like a candy. Wow, thinks Moisès Corvo, and he goes along with it, because he'll question her better once he's shot his wad. She, obliging, kisses his belly and undoes his trousers, and takes out the policeman's member, erect, pink and about to explode, places it in her mouth immediately and fellates him like the hookers he's used to screwing never have.

I could tell you how she kept Corvo from discharging right away, parcelling it out, taking the lead (unheard of!), guessing at each moment what he wanted and satisfying it. But there's no need for me to get into descriptions that don't move the story along. Moisès Corvo stayed in the bed, dozing lightly, he still had enough time, while she kept stroking him affectionately as if she were really in love. He rolls a cigarette and lets the ash drop gradually onto his chest. He could do this for ever. Every once in a while he looks at her, she smiles but stays silent.

"Adriana."

She responds agreeably, like a dog anxious to please its master. If she had a tail, she'd be wagging it.

"You've got a great tongue, but you don't loosen it much, do you?"

"Mr handsome." She has a wisp of a voice, with a strange accent.

"How old are you?"

She seems only to understand the things she understands, because she starts slowly to approach the policeman's crotch again.

"Handsome."

"No, no, no." He moves the girl's head aside, she is now looking somewhat annoyed. "I'm too old to recover that quickly, sweetie. Old, you understand me?"

"No?"

"No, no, and don't look at me like that… Look, I…" He opens his hand and mimes counting on his fingers. "Forty-three years old." He points to her with his finger. "And you?"

She imitates him, and now she does understand.

"Twennon."

"Twenty-one."

"Yes, twennon."

"Yeah. That's what they told you to say. Have you been here long? You, here?" He raises his tone of voice and gesticulates exaggeratedly.

She laughs, angelic, and Moisès Corvo realizes that Adriana is no older than sixteen and he's not going to get a word out of her.

"Mister like Adriana?"

"Yes, baby, yes, I like you a lot, but you're too dear and not much of a conversationalist." Now he doesn't shout, because he fears someone in the hallway might hear him asking questions.

Adriana laughs again, and the inspector can't (nor does he want to) help getting another erection, and it doesn't escape the prostitute's notice. It seems she's pleased about it, because she applauds and says something I didn't catch and all of a sudden she's got her mouth full and stops talking but keeps looking him up and down.

"You're a doll, Adriana, you're an angel from heaven."

When the time's up, Madame Lulú receives them again on the patio. On the way Moisès passes three clients emerging from a small room where there must be Turkish baths, towels at their hips and wrapped around three girls he hadn't seen before. He doesn't recognize any of the men but his attitude awakens complicity in one of them, who takes off his towel and, using it like a lash, whips one of the whores' butts while winking at the policeman. Cream of the crop! he bellows.

"I hope it was to your liking," says Lulú, expectantly.

"It was quite an experience," and looks around him.

"Your companion asked me to tell you that you can leave on your own, that he is planning to stay with us a while longer. I hope you will return very soon, Mr Lestrade."

"Undoubtedly, but I'd like to ask you a small favour."

"Your whims are our commands."

"Adriana is a wonder."

"She is one of our best ladies. We can reserve her for when you return."

"Yes, yeah, but… I'd like to know… would it be possible to get one that's more innocent?"

"They're all as innocent as you desire, Mr Lestrade."

"Yes, but I meant, don't misunderstand… younger."

"I think I understand." Madame Lulú hesitates. "You aren't with the police, are you?"

"Do I look like a policeman to you?"

She decides that no, he doesn't.

"Here we don't deal in younger girls."

"I understood that if I asked for the service expressly…" Moisès Corvo has set out the bait and crosses his fingers that she'll bite.

She grabs him by an elbow and takes him aside.

"You realize that girls bring more problems, and the price isn't the same."

"I'm prepared to pay whatever it takes."

"If I find out that you're a policeman and this is a trap, I'll send Hugo to cut off your balls and I'll fry them up for my breakfast." The warning comes out as sweetly as the rest of the conversation. Madame Lulú is quite the actress and the man who opened the door for them only has to hear his name from the doorway and he perks right up. Now he really looks like a circus gorilla, dressed up ridiculously like a human.

"It's not easy for me to ask for certain things, you know it's not well looked upon."

"You do realize that what I am doing is an exceptional favour."

"And I appreciate it from the bottom of my heart." And from his heart he pulls out a wad of bills, 100 pesetas more.

"I don't have any here, and I won't bring one to you. The risk is too high, but I can put you in touch with someone who can provide you with what you're looking for. Wait here." And she goes into an adjoining office, where she makes a call. "No problem. Go to the Casino de l'Arrabassada and ask for André Gireau. Tell him I sent you."

"I'll tell my cousin that you treated me as he said you would, Madame."

"You're a devil." It's obvious she doesn't really believe that he is related to Alfons XIII, and he didn't say it seriously either, but with these things you never know.

"And you, my redemption."

Sunday, at midday, the Ciutadella Park is a concert of children shrieking. Blackmouth walks among the little tables where couples sip vermouth. A feline on the hunt, searching for a solitary victim. The roller coaster of Saturno Park thunders along its path, as if the open mouth of the monstrous devil face that is the first car were roaring. Parents wave at their children every time the coaster turns near the group of tables, and they respond with shouts and laughter, not daring to release the grip of their hands.

Blackmouth was born an adult. He was never a child, he never played in the streets with other boys and girls his age. Not ball, not tag, not hopscotch, nothing. He begged for food, the police would catch him, they'd take him to the poorhouse and he'd escape. No friends, just cohorts in mischief. No affection, just cold institutional protection. Really, Blackmouth could have been in a Dickens novel, and nobody would have batted an eyelash. And I'm not trying to justify him by saying that. Not every orphan who grew up on the street turned half wild with necrophilic and paedophilic tendencies. And in Barcelona at the turn of the twentieth century, the prosperous Barcelona of the world fairs, there are many of them: some end up dead from tuberculosis, others run over by the tramcar, most of them become thieves until a bad thrashing kills them, and there are a few who start families. Blackmouth feels bad when he does something really wicked; he blames himself and hates himself and wants to kill himself. But while he's doing it, as he acts, he is a real son of a bitch.

Enriqueta forced him to shower, or more accurately she showered him herself. She soaped him up with a scratchy sponge and threw a bucket of water over him.

"You have to be presentable or women will be afraid of you. And a scared woman keeps her children under her skirt. There are too many rumours going around, and that doesn't help us at all."

Only the nuns in the reformatory on Aribau Street had treated him like that. Blackmouth fears Enriqueta, but at the same time finds in her a protector. He feels like one of those mice at risk of being devoured by their mother at birth, if she sees it as a threat.

He meanders through the attractions, acting casual, observing the nursemaids to find one who is distracted.

A boy about four years old is in a crowd of people, with a lost gaze. Blackmouth spies on him for a while. He watches him wander, his eyes brimming with tears. He tries to find his parents or whoever might also be looking for him, but there is no one. Blackmouth's bones are still aching from the test Enriqueta subjected him to in the café and he doesn't want to get another thrashing for choosing the wrong moment. The demoniacal convoy passes again screeching very close by, as if it were the devil pushing the boy to take the definitive step.

"What's your name, cutie?" says Blackmouth, squatting, with the sweetest tone he is capable of.

"Antoni," he responds without looking him in the eye. He is searching for a face he knows. Actually, they are both afraid.

"Your parents left and they told me to take you home."

The boy does look at him now, but he remains mute. Like the entire park, which seems like a desert of sounds. As if everyone could hear each word that Blackmouth says.

"Come with me, I'll take you to your parents." His voice trembles.

The lad doesn't dare, he is rooted to the spot. Blackmouth pulls out a sweet that Enriqueta had given him and offers it to the boy. For the way, he says. It works, because Antoni extends his arm and grabs the sweet, not without reluctance, and Blackmouth uses the gesture to take him by the hand and stand up. Let's go.

Blackmouth feels that everyone is watching him. That the men in straw hats and the women in their Sunday best have turned to watch him leave with the boy. That they are following him with their gaze as they leave the park. That the attractions have suddenly stopped, the laughter silenced, the prams empty, the stream of water in the fountains frozen and a cry of alarm hatches in the throats of the parents of the boy he is abducting.

But none of that happens, and when he reaches Indústria Avenue, before heading down Fusina Street, the world regains its normality.

Antoni is about to cry when they pass by Santa Maria del Mar and the people just coming out of Mass, but a timely slap across the mouth, hidden among the doorways of Agullers Street, nips the tears in the bud.

9

JUAN MALSANO reaches the Hospital of Sant Pau about dusk. Even though it's Sunday and he doesn't have to work, Moisès Corvo had come looking for him because that afternoon a man was beaten for, it seems, giving out sweets to children at the Saturno Park in the Ciutadella.

"A four-year-old boy has disappeared: Antoni Sadurní," he told him when he came by his flat. "I talked to his parents and they didn't see a thing. Seems they lost him at the pergola near the lake, and they haven't seen him since. They heard someone say they'd seen a man taking a lad who fits Antoni's description, but there are no reliable witnesses. From what I've been able to gather, the kidnapper didn't walk with a limp. Later in the afternoon someone reported seeing a guy talking to another boy in the Born and they beat him up. He's at the Hospital of Sant Pau, but you'll have to go there alone, I have another job tonight." And he shows him a photograph of the boy dressed as a sailor, with a perfect parting in his hair.

Malsano doesn't go alone. He is accompanied by Doctor Manuel Saforcada, the city's forensic doctor, who is also a specialist in psychiatric disorders. He asked for his help in determining whether the subject they will find there (they don't yet know in what condition) could be the monster they are looking for. And if he is, they'll have to get little Antoni's location out of him.

The large main entrance embraces them as they enter, beneath the watchful gaze of the spire that pokes through the December mist. The Hospital of Sant Pau looks like a fairy-tale castle on the outskirts of the city, Hansel and Gretel's gingerbread house in mad dimensions.

A nun asks them whom they've come to see and makes them wait a while, until a tiny man appears who looks like he's been soaking for a good long time. He extends his hand.

"Doctor Saforcada, I'm Doctor Martín. It's a pleasure to have you here. I was your student five years back."

"I remember." It was the first year of students the forensic doctor had taught. "I see I passed you."

The small doctor looks all smug and gestures for them to follow him. Since he is nervous about their visit, he can't control his tic of opening and closing his eyes as if trying to catch flies with his lashes.

"Anyhow, the pleasure is mine," he continues. "It's a joy working in this building."

"Well, on the outside it's very original, but inside it's not much different from the rest."

"You must not have been by the Clínic lately. It's as new as this one, but much dirtier and darker. Have you seen the autopsy room?" The other man shakes his head. "It's like a latrine. And I ask them to please clean up, but it seems that only the dead dare enter there. And they're busy enough with staying dead."

"Superstition is still an obstacle to progress…" the doctor laments, turning down another hallway.

"Lack of hygiene is an even bigger one," stresses the forensic doctor.

When they reach the pavilion, they have to wait for one of the nuns to finish washing the patient.

"I doubt you'll be able to reason with him much."

"What is it he has?"

"General contusions, nothing serious. But he's not playing with a full deck."

"Has he said his name?" asks Malsano.

Doctor Martín wrinkles his nose, hesitating before responding, and then scrunches it up three or four more times as a side effect of the tic. He decides to answer.

"Yes: Jesus Christ."

"You talk to him first," offers the forensic doctor to the policeman.

The man lying down is corpulent but not very tall, and the first thing that draws your attention is that his arms are tied to the bed with strips of torn sheets. The upper part of his body that's visible has bruises and he has some bandages on his shoulder. He moves his head with relative calm, like a spinning top about to stop. The inspector calculates he must be about thirty or thirty-five. He is thirty-three.

"Good evening," begins Malsano, managing to get the man to focus his eyes on him. He has the kind of gaze that emits fear.

"I'm Inspector Malsano, of the police, and we're here to ask you a few questions." The man opens his eyes wide. "Do you understand me when I speak to you?"

"Yes." His is a reedy voice that is lost in the murmurs of the other patients.

"What's your name?"

"Yes."

"I told you he's not well." Doctor Martín puts in his two cents' worth.

"What is your name?" Malsano says slowly.

The man looks for the nun, as if she were the only person who could understand him.

"I'm Juan. And you?"

The man being questioned is restless.

"He spoke, before, right?" asks Doctor Saforcada.

"Yes. Incoherently, but he spoke."

"To whom?"

"I was there."

"And he spoke to you directly?"

He hesitates, his face tenses and relaxes several times. Malsano looks at the man on the hospital bed because Doctor Martin is starting to make him nervous.

"No…"

"And?" The policeman is growing impatient.

"Conxita, I mean Sister Concepció was there."

"Is she the one who was bathing him before?" asks Malsano.

"Yes."

"And would you mind calling her over again, please?"

The doctor asks around for Conxita, until he finds her and she returns to the side of the bed. It seems that the nameless man calms down.

"Ask him his name," enquires Doctor Saforcada.

The nun obeys.

"Jesús."

"Jesús what?" Malsano looks at the man, but speaks loudly so that Sister Concepció realizes he's including her. She once again acts as a bridge.

"Jesús of Nazareth."

Malsano snorts and turns towards Doctor Saforcada who, lifting his eyebrows, instructs him to continue.

"Ask him what happened this afternoon."

I'll spare you the transcription of Sister Concepció's repetitions.

"I am the son of God, and I was sent here to save humanity. I am a martyr and those envious of me wanted to kill me. But the son of God cannot die."

"No, he's not well," is the spot-on diagnosis of Doctor Martín.

"But why did they try to kill you?" Malsano furrows his brow.

"I can't die, I'm immortal, I already warned Archangel Gabriel when he appeared to my mother, the Virgin Mary…" Blah, blah, blah, continues Jesus Christ. He'd been so quiet when the investigators arrived and now it turns out he's a chatterbox.

"Why did they try to kill you?"

"…If you do not obey the divine mandate and you act like Pharisees, I will be your punishment…"

"How old are you?" It's Doctor Saforcada's turn. When Sister Concepció repeats the question, the man stops short his diatribe.

"Thirty-three."

"And when are they going to hang you on the cross?"

Jesus Christ seems confused, and Malsano takes the opportunity to show him the photo of Antoni.

"Do you know him?"

Jesus Christ looks at him for a while, and for the first time responds directly to the inspector.

"Aren't all children the same?"

"Do you know him?"

"I am me. You are you. We all are."

"Did you take him this morning, from the Ciutadella?" He uses a severe tone.

"He is the branch of a tree where another will be born. He is the love of God made flesh."

"What did you do with him?"

"Let the children come to me!"

"Where is he?" Malsano stands up and gets just inches from Jesus Christ's face.

"I don't know."

"Did you kill him?"

"No." He is about to break. He is not the same as a few seconds earlier.

"You killed him!"

"No… no. Jesus is love. Jesus is the son of God."

"It's not him," ventures Doctor Saforcada. "This man suffers from schizophrenia."

"Premature dementia?"

Doctor Martín still employs old terms. The Swiss psychiatrist Eugen Bleuler had coined the name schizophrenia to specify a phenomenon that wasn't so much an early deterioration of the mental faculties as a disease in which outbreaks produce a rupture with reality. If I have to be frank, though, the break is imprecise, as you will now see.

"The subject has delusions and a persecution complex. He doesn't present symptoms of alcoholic intoxication and he should be kept under observation to determine if this episode was brought on by medicines or drugs," diagnoses Saforcada.

"But could he be the one we're looking for?" asks Malsano.

"If it's him, which I doubt, it's impossible to know that now. We have to wait until he recovers consciousness, and interrogate him again."

"Go! Go!" shouts Jesus Christ, and Sister Concepció places a hand on his forehead to calm him. But he pulls the sheets tied to his forearms taut and shakes the bed forcefully. "Go!"

"What happened to him?" asks Inspector Malsano, puzzled.

"Inject him with novocaine," orders Saforcada, and Doctor Martín runs out, partly to search for a syringe and partly afraid that the messiah will escape his constraints.

"Get him out of here!" he bellows, looking me up and down, spitting drool and his face reddening. "The son of God demands that you take him out of here! I don't want to see him! I don't want to see him here!"

I told you. You know, but the people gathered around the bed (Inspector Malsano, Doctor Saforcada and Sister Concepció) wonder whom he is referring to. I get him to quieten down by putting my index finger over my lips and Jesus Christ, who is actually named Pere Torralba and is from Sant Andreu de Palomar, grows silent. Just in time for the injection and the deep sleep.

"This man is incapable of planning anything or hiding anyone without giving himself away," the forensic doctor reflects aloud. "He is not the person we are looking for."

If there is one widespread pastime in Barcelona, it's starting trouble and getting worked up when people are on edge. Not long ago, around June, a car ran over a pedestrian on Gran de Gràcia Street. The enraged crowd turned over the vehicle and set it aflame in an act of urban justice that satisfied everyone except the pedestrian, who had a femur up in the air, and the driver, who had to run for his life.

"Another closed door," laments Malsano. "I hope Moisès has some luck tonight."

*

Luck is too dangerous a noun to employ with a vengeance. Sometimes, a dose of good luck can push us towards places we wanted to go, but which lead to a terrible end. Sometimes bad luck, like not achieving what we've set out to, puts us out of harm's way. Now that a Swiss patent clerk is finishing up writing what will be one of the most influential scientific postulates of the century, I will remind you that, in the end, everything is relative.

But Moisès Corvo doesn't even consider that, as he heads up the Arrabassada highway in the dark in the tramcar that goes from Craywinckel Street to the casino. The route takes forty-five minutes and costs sixty cents and a raging head cold. Luck is something else, and he is about to try it in the form of roulettes, cards and tombolas.

The Arrabassada Casino has been open for five months, since July of this year, and is destined to be a European landmark, or at least that was the intention of the project's investors. Crowded in front are cars, private carriages and the tramcar that comes from the city, in a constant bustle of visitors who are dazzled by the large metal entrance, an imposing iron hoop that reads 'La Rabassada Casino Attractions' and is flanked by two Art Nouveau towers with neo-arabesque touches (it seems that's very popular among well-to-do Barcelonian society). The towers are crowned by a dome with flags limp from lack of wind. Men in tuxedos beneath their coats escort their beloveds, showing off the jewels they keep hidden in flats during the week, secret nests not so much of love as of sex. There are many Frenchmen and Germans, and some British, Spaniards who've made their fortune in the Indies and owners of textile factories who've made some money out of army uniforms.

And there is Moisès Corvo, who gets out of the tramcar, huddled beneath his duster coat, protected by a wide-brimmed hat that hides his face in shadow, with the cold permeating his bones. He pays the fifty-cent entrance fee that includes one attraction, as if he cared, and goes up to the large balcony with two staircases, one leading to the casino and the other to the restaurant.

He notices that everyone is laughing naturally, as if that were paradise, the happiest place in the world. There are people everywhere, going in and out of the buildings with drinks in their hands, getting lost among the hedges or walking along the little path that leads to the attractions as if they were children. And Moisès Corvo understands that that's exactly why he is here, because that human desire to hold on to childhood is what makes people cross certain borders at any price. The inspector is disgusted and enraged, and he touches his revolver hanging from his belt, beneath his coat, as a way to relax. He doesn't like shooting, he never has, but there are moments when you have to act despite what you might like, and he accepts that.

What he finds harder to accept is having to change 100 pesetas into two fifty-peseta chips to be able to play (he's almost out of money) and mix with the moneyed people who pack the place. Anyhow, you can tell from miles away that he doesn't belong in that atmosphere, from his clothes, the way he walks and the fact that *they* all know each other. The casino is well lit, filled with lamps in every hallway, with large windows that now, at night, reflect like mirrors what is happening inside, giving the impression that there are more people than there actually are. Also, the Christmas decoration is quite baroque and fills the building with colourful glass balls, banners and other aesthetic blights.

The policeman walks among the tables, where various games of chance are being played. Most of them, though, are playing baccarat. The players challenge each other at a round table. And within baccarat, the *chemin-de-fer* version is the most popular, in which the bank lands on a different player each round. The policeman observes in silence, and watches how it is the men who play and the women who drive up the bets. On another table they shoot craps, and on some others further on there are French roulette wheels. After a while wandering around, Moisès Corvo realizes that they are already watching him: there are at least two men in charge of security who challenge him with their eyes from different corners of the place, brazenly. Perhaps they've mistaken him for an anarchist. The best thing, then, is to sit down and participate in some game before the suspicions turn into action. He chooses the roulette wheel he likes best, one with little figures of horses and riders that mimics a race when it spins, and he decisively places one of the fifty-peseta chips on black eleven.

"Are you sure, sir?" I ask him.

He looks at me, thinking of a reply. All of a sudden he squints his eyes and bites his lips.

"Yes," he decides.

"The game is closed."

I turn the roulette wheel and the ball runs fiendishly faster than the horses. Moisès Corvo can't take his eyes off me. But he is distracted when the ball staggers and falls onto black eleven.

"Good choice," I say, sweeping the chips towards him. Now he has some 300 pesetas and a croupier with little eyeglasses and bow tie on his side.

One of the ladies applauds in amusement and the bellboy, a boy about Blackmouth's age but significantly cleaner and more polite, approaches the policeman.

"Would you like me to take your coat, sir?" he offers.

"No," says Moisès Corvo curtly.

"Place your bets, ladies and gentlemen, place your bets." I look the policeman up and down. "Would you like to try your luck again, sir?"

The inspector takes the bait. He's only ever played twenty-one and for pocket change. This is as seductive for him as it is new. The lady who applauded approves his decision to try again.

"Red thirty-two." He moves three chips, 150 pesetas.

The bets are closed and I turn the wheel again. It should have been a black twenty-six, but—these things happen—the little ball jumps strangely and lands on red thirty-two. Moisès Corvo can't believe it. Two wins on two bets. The public goes oooh, the bellboy again offers (now more insistently) to put away his outerwear, and the lady who applauds approaches the inspector (like the roulette ball).

"You're very lucky," she says, leaning over a bit, enough to make her neckline ooze flesh and promise.

"Now that you are by my side, I guess I am," he responds, not forgetting that now, more than ever, the two security guards are keeping a close eye on him. Maybe not an anarchist, but he is looking a lot like someone with something up his sleeve.

I help him and make him lose the next two rounds. Well, more than help, I don't interfere, and the ball falls where it will, and the bank wins, and it seems that everything goes back to normal. Two hundred pesetas less make the woman insist they go for a stroll, but 150 less make her lose interest and look around for another winner.

Moisès Corvo finds that it's the moment to leave the tables and do what he came there to do. Now he has 250 pesetas, which is a lot more than he had when he came in, and he gives me twenty-five as a tip, which I thank him for. When he hands me the chip, though, he grabs my hand and gives me a penetrating look:

"Do we know each other?"

"I hope not, or we'd have a problem."

"Pardon me?"

"If we knew each other, I couldn't be your croupier."

"But I've seen you somewhere, haven't I?"

"This is a very small city."

Moisès Corvo thinks of all the people he's ever arrested or questioned, but he can't place me. He can't even imagine I'm the one who took his two children, and the one who was beside him the day he was shot, when he was expecting to cross over.

I can't deny that it excites me, though, when I'm recognized. Especially because the face of this emaciated, yellowish croupier isn't my face, or it is, but only circumstantially, and he was able to see past the skin, behind the disguise. He is much more perceptive than people think, and his contact with my trail every night has given him a deeper vision of reality. And darker, obviously. I've said it before, forgive me for repeating myself, but I like Moisès Corvo. We could be good friends, if I could have any.

The policeman addresses one of the security guards, the heftier one, and sees out of the corner of his eye how the other (a weakling who must be a relative of the owner because he doesn't offer much security) rushes over.

"Sir," he says in a serious tone, and then he turns towards the one who has just come over. "Miss."

"We don't like troublemakers," warns the big one.

"Neither do I," answers Corvo. "I'd like to see Mr André Gireau."

The guards hesitate and look the inspector over again. He doesn't look like Monsieur Gireau's typical client.

"We don't know any André Gireau."

"I think you do." Reluctantly, Moisès Corvo places a fifty-peseta token into the man's pocket. "And so does this."

"We can ask," he concedes, but not without a fight. "But we need a name."

"Madame Lulú."

The scrawny one laughs under his breath. That dead ringer for King Alfons XIII doesn't look like his name is Madame Lulú.

"Wait on the belvedere," concludes the one with the marmoreal bearing.

The belvedere is the chic way to say large balcony, and even though Moisès Corvo doesn't understand at first, he deduces that he has to go outside because the Milksop grabs him by an elbow and escorts him there.

"Let me go if you ever want to eat solid food again."

The threat does its job and the guard runs his hand through his hair to smoothe it, let's not fight. The policeman is a head taller than he: the Milksop is scared stiff.

At the balustrade, Moisès Corvo lights a cigarette and distracts himself watching the amusement park that extends along the mountain's slope. One highlight is the "scenic railway", which according to a sign is the name of the impressive roller coaster two and half kilometres long. The cars whip around those brave enough to ride it, in exchange for hair-raising screams. Further downhill, an attraction remains closed: it's too cold for the water chute, boats that go up and down, to run. The queues at the booths for Alleys Bowling and the Palace of Laughter are long enough to discourage those more sensitive to the cold. Moisès Corvo buttons up his duster coat and pulls his hat down even further over his ears.

"Choose one." A voice from behind him, unmistakable French accent. "You get a ride included in the price of admission."

The inspector turns and finds himself face to face with a Mephistophelean presence, a very slender individual dressed all in black, with blond, almost platinum hair and beard, and skin so pale that the bluish veins on his nostrils and temples can be seen, like tiny dark streams.

"I didn't come here to play," responds the policeman.

"That's not what Mr Roure told me." He points to the stocky guard. Yes, his name is quite fitting, as it means oak tree.

"I came to win."

The diabolical character (his fingernails long like guitar picks) acknowledges his wit and extends his hand.

"André Gireau."

"Tobias Lestrade." He shakes his hand.

"Like?…"

"Yes."

"It must be strange having the same name as a fictional character."

"You get used to it."

"*Êtes-vous français?*"

It's a bad sign when the other guy is asking the questions.

"My grandfather," he lies, as he has been for a good while. "And you, what brought you to Barcelona?"

"Oh, I'm surprised you ask me that. I figured you must already know, if Madame Lulú sent you to me."

"Ah, so you aren't going to put me in the uncomfortable position of having to ask you for what you already know I've come for."

"No, don't worry about that. I understand the difficulties expressing out loud our most private desires. I'll save you the awkwardness."

"I appreciate that. It's my first time and I'm pretty nervous."

"Then allow me to buy you a drink. We like our special clients to feel comfortable."

André Gireau leads Moisès Corvo to the restaurant, which now has the tables and chairs removed and they are setting it up as a dance floor for after midnight, when the rides close. With a sweep of his hand he orders the barman to serve them two cocktails, the regular, and he sits with the policeman at a reserved table.

"How is Madame Lulú?"

"Radiant."

"It's been a while since I've seen her."

"I'll give her your greetings next time I see her."

"Thank you. We both love the night, we don't like the sun, and we live locked up in our luxurious cages. We have few opportunities for socializing, beyond our clients."

"Do you have many dealings with them?"

"The clients? You're getting a taste of it. I like to chat a bit, find out their tastes, their inclinations, and suggest what I think will be best for them."

"And what do you think is my inclination?"

André Gireau runs his fingers through his thick beard and scratches his cheek, making the sound of toasted bread breaking.

"I think you are an imposter."

Moisès Corvo has to hide his surprise.

"I beg your pardon?"

"I think that this is a disguise, that you aren't who you say you are."

"You offend me."

"No, you offend me with a cheap trick. Do you really think I can't tell the difference between classy people and a poor wretch like yourself? Mr Lestrade…" He leans over the table, as if about to share a secret. He is completely relaxed, without a trace of anger in his expression or voice. "I have a gift. I strip people bare. In every sense of the word. I know how to look into people's souls, I can read everyone with a single glance. And I see that you are not who you say you are."

"And who am I, then?"

"I don't know. Will you tell me? Why have you come?"

"A man told me about Madame Lulú, and she told me about you. You already know why I've come."

"A man?"

"The gimp."

"A lame man told you that here we could get what you desire."

"More or less. I trust Madame Lulú and she trusts you."

"Madame Lulú trusts everyone. She's a whore who's come up in the world. A good woman, but too innocent. She trusted you, which was obviously a mistake."

"I know that you have what I'm looking for here."

"Yes. We have it. But not for you. Mr Lestrade, I'll say it more clearly, because it seems you don't understand: you are not looking for that. You are looking for me, and you will understand that I'm not going to make it that easy for you."

The waiter brings a tray with two yellowish drinks.

"What is this?" asks the policeman, keeping his gaze fixed on the blond man's eyes.

"Gimlet. Gin and lime. Delicious."

"Bring me a whisky."

The waiter silently asks André Gireau for his authorization and he grants it.

Moisès Corvo decides to reveal his cards.

"I want to know who's your provider."

"Ah!" Histrionic, Gireau opens his arms as if he's had an epiphany. "Now I like you, Mr Lestrade. You are starting to show yourself as you really are."

"And I can be even better, but you won't want to see it."

"I love this tough act. Yes, this is the real you. I sensed it the minute you walked through the door, Mr Lestrade."

The inspector, who is leaning against the back of the reserved table's armchair, ever so casually lets the sides of his duster fall to each side. His revolver is clearly visible to Gireau.

"I didn't come alone."

"I see that. But it's a shame, because your little friend should keep quiet during this conversation between two gentlemen, don't you think?"

"That depends on you. It's getting impatient with your arrogance."

"Hmmm." His index fingers on his lips, thinking it over. "I already told you that I can read people's souls, and it's not arrogant to admit that. Did you notice the skinny guard, the one who looks like he could be blown away by a strong wind?"

"Don't tell me you hired him because he's a good cocksucker."

"*Touché*... No, he has other skills. He is one of the best marksmen in Barcelona, and right now he must be aiming directly at your head from outside. No, no, don't bother looking for him: there is so much light here, you won't be able to see him, but I can assure you he can see us. Well, you."

"And if I were to decide that you are going to accompany me on a stroll tonight?"

"Do you know you're not fooling anyone by pretending you're not police? I mean, apart from the fact that you're a terrible actor, it's practically written on your face and in the way you walk. I know of what I speak, I've known a few in my time."

"I can introduce you to as many as you want."

"It seems you aren't understanding me, Mr Lestrade. I'll be frank with you: gambling has been banned for twenty years, but in Barcelona there are more casinos than in any other European city. This"—he taps his finger on the table, just as the barman brings over the glass of whisky—"this is one of the most important, and it has government protection. We have policemen, your colleagues, Mr Lestrade, covering our activities."

"I don't care about gambling. I want to know where the children come from."

"I'll make you an offer. I'll hire you to work for us. I can't deny feeling a certain sympathy for you, for this lone cowboy attitude of yours. You'll make much more than you're making now, and you'll move among people who'd never give you a second glance in your current line of work. It's a good offer."

"Mr Gireau, I'll admit you're good at bribery. Surely you get everything you want with your golden tongue. Even the support of your favourite marksman"—he waves with a very false smile at the large windows, dedicated to Mr Milksop. "But you are wrong. You can gamble, you can manipulate people, you can steal all the money you want, but I will not allow you to hand over children to the depraved."

"OK. I think I'll have to explain it to you in more detail. Drink up your whisky, or grab the glass and come with me."

André Gireau and Moisès Corvo leave the restaurant and return to the belvedere. He can see his breath, he hadn't realized how warm they were inside.

"Look at the scenic railway. And look at the crowd queuing up. Why do you think they're there, with this ball-busting cold?"

"Because they paid."

"Wrong answer. Don't try to think like them. You aren't one of them and it won't work for you. Their mattresses aren't filled with feathers, they're filled with 500-peseta bills."

"In prison they won't have either of those, Mr Gireau."

"Don't ruin it, Mr Lestrade, please. Answer."

"Because they're like little children with a toy."

"Not bad, not bad. They have fun, and why? Because they have everything anyone could have, except for strong emotions. They can wake up and bathe in water from the Nile and breakfast on caviar and French wine. OK, I wouldn't recommend it, but they could. But none of them wakes up feeling death close, or risk, or transgression. That's what they've come here for."

"A roller coaster, or a roulette wheel, is one thing, but fucking children is quite another."

"There's no need to be so crude, *monsieur*. I don't like that expression. Fucking children."

"You don't like it because it's reality, and I see that you live with your back to that reality."

"Let's go to the casino, my fingers are freezing." They enter the game room, where there are considerably more people than before. "Someone has to provide consumers with what they are looking for. Someone has to give them danger. It's as licit as selling bread or meat. We humans need it to live, because otherwise we'd die of boredom. And I sell it. I give my clients what they want."

"There are limits."

"What are they? My clientele doesn't know them. The law? Laws can change. In fact, my clients devote themselves to changing them when it suits them."

"Ethics, morality."

"Don't try to lecture me, Mr Lestrade. You are a policeman,

and the police are the last people who should lecture on ethics and morality. When you beat somebody up to get a confession out of them, is that ethical? When you grab money off a thief, because after all it's stolen money, are you thinking about morality? I've never shot anyone, Mr Lestrade."

"No, you have people to do that for you."

"Men shoot each other. The rest is circumstances. Let me show you something."

They walk among the gamblers, who form little groups. Many are chatting or closing business deals.

"I think you're not going to show me what I came to see."

"Look, that's the French consul"—he points to a circle—"and that one, Mr Membrado, the shipbuilder. And those ones talking to that woman in the hat with veils are German brothers who work in… what was it… something to do with the arms industry."

Moisès Corvo looks at the woman, but doesn't recognize Enriqueta Martí. He's seen her around the neighbourhood, he's passed her more than once, but since she always looked like a beggar woman, she was invisible to him until today. Another one, he would say to himself. She is very changed, very elegant, very majestic, but at the same time just as pale and giving off the same dangerous air. He looks at her for a few seconds, as if he'd known her all his life but forgotten about her. André Gireau has them open a door behind which there are stairs going down. How close he was, and he has no idea.

They cross a hallway with a door on either side from which emerge men's voices, shouting loudly. No, it's not what you think, says Gireau, and he stands in front of one covered in a greenish colour. One I visit quite often. When open, all the walls and the floor of the room are white ceramic, even a ledge that serves as a chair. At the back, a smaller door opens onto a hallway that leads to the mountainside, but Moisès Corvo doesn't know that.

"As I told you, I'm a vendor. I provide all the things no one else sells. Sometimes it's so risky that fortunes are lost. You can't even imagine how a millionaire suffers when he loses it all. The only thing he's got left is life, and he wants to lose that too."

"And you also offer that service."

"We are a very well-rounded company."

"How? You give them a pistol, leave them there and they shoot themselves? It's that simple?"

"You don't disappoint me, Mr Lestrade."

"And I suppose the walls are like this because they're easier to clean."

"Exactly. So, as you can understand, our business is too large and at the same time painstaking to worry about ethical or moral details. What we don't give them, someone else will, and at a higher price. And we can't allow that."

"What's keeping me from shooting you in the stomach right now and leaving you to die in there? Your queer sniper can't see us."

"Yes, that's true. But he wouldn't like seeing you come through that door alone."

"And if you come with me, under arrest?"

"I wouldn't go there. We have very strict rules about possession of weapons inside the casino, and you haven't identified yourself as a policeman at any point."

"But I could come back."

"Yes, but you won't."

"Is that a threat?"

"No, it's a piece of advice. You can't touch us, Mr Lestrade."

"To bury a corpse you don't need to touch it."

"Now I'd appreciate it if you left. I think that we talked too much for today."

The next day, Moisès Corvo was scheduled to meet up with Quim Morgades, the journalist from *La Vanguardia* with whom he sometimes exchanged information. Well, the term "exchange information" is imprecise, because usually it's the policeman who goes on and on, and Quim who jots everything down in his pad, his only contribution a bottle of anise. Of course, Corvo only says what it's in his interests to say.

The inspector debates now between speaking and not speaking. Letting it all out or keeping the investigation silent until he reaches conclusions with evidence, which is when the journalist can help him. They are meeting at the Gambrinus pub, number twenty-nine on the Rambla Santa Mònica, and Corvo arrives late and with a pounding headache. Too much pressure for him, and it's starting to take its toll.

"You have to explain to me what the hell is going on, Moisès. It's been a month now where nobody's talking about anything else, but fucking Millán Astray silences it and says nothing's going on. Yesterday another lad disappeared, and we found out that you arrested a suspect in the evening, but nobody knows who it is."

Should he tell him? What does he have to lose? He still hasn't talked to Malsano about it, but he fears that the guy who got beaten up isn't the guy they're looking for. Surely his partner wouldn't have hesitated to tell, and last night he wasn't visited by anyone except Morpheus. He's going crazy, this is too much for him, he feels nauseated and a stabbing in his temples. It's like a permanent hangover, and almost without getting drunk. Almost. He sips on his nice, cool, blond beer.

"He's at the Hospital of Sant Pau, but it's not worth your time visiting him. It was popular hysteria that accused him."

"But there is a kidnapper, right?"

Yes, there is someone who is kidnapping children and making them vanish off the face of the earth. Someone who selects from among the children who already don't exist, but who made a mistake this time because this wasn't the son of a whore, but of a middle-class family, without means, but from a visible stratum. And if he doesn't hurry, another one will disappear, and another, and another, and another, until who knows when, because now it is very clear that the monster won't stop unless he traps him, because it seems nobody else wants to do it, because the chief of police avoids problems and there's a child-prostitution business set up and they are each mutually covering each other's asses, as unfortunate a choice of words as it is in this case.

"They're isolated events," he lies, like everyone, but he does it to keep panic in check and maintain the slight thread holding the investigation together taut.

"Just isolated?"

"Coincidences."

"And what do I say in the paper?"

"Whatever you want, but don't talk about monsters."

Quim Morgades gathers his notebook and puts it in his bag. He finishes his glass of beer and asks the waiter for the bill. He addresses Corvo in a confidential tone.

"Are you going to catch 'im?"

"I'm trying as hard as I can."

Moisès Corvo reaches the conclusion, in that moment, that he needs more help than he thought. And, in his desperation, his memory comes up with a name.

If you are easily upset or have a sensitive stomach, I recommend you skip to the next chapter. Avoid the paragraph where I explain an example of the evil woman's madness. If you aren't apprehensive, stay and a corner of your mind will be revealed to you.

Enriqueta uses a very sharp knife to take out little Antoni's eyes. First she makes an affectionate slice around the eyeball and rips off the skin like pieces of a mask. She introduces the point and levers, bit by bit, delicately but decisively, making sure they don't burst and soil everything and get ruined. Now they are soft, because eyes, when life has abandoned them, gradually deflate and turn into something like gelatinous water. That's why it's so hard to trick me and pass yourself off as dead: the sunken, grey, liquid eyes always tell the truth. Antoni is still warm and Enriqueta can smell the gases leaving him through his mouth, in lifeless burps, the stench of decomposition.

All of a sudden, like in a miscarriage, out comes the whitish ball, flippity floppity, until she cuts the optic nerve. Blood doesn't flow from the socket, everything is so clean that the next one is easier to remove.

She brings them to her lips and kisses them, she sucks them and she chews them up. A gasp at the explosion of salt, which her saliva sweeps down her throat.

Enriqueta feels immortal.

10

"I DEMAND AN EXPLANATION."

José Millán Astray demands an explanation.

Moisès Corvo and Juan Malsano are sitting in front of the police chief, a bit tense because it's not normal that he waits around until their shift, their night shift, to call them into a meeting. Bad news, for sure.

"About what?" asks Moisès Corvo, who isn't going to make it easy for him, no way.

"I've got complaints from up high." As devout as Millán Astray may be, Corvo knows he's not referring to the Lord Our God. "It seems you two have been sticking your noses where they don't belong."

"Is that what working is called these days…"

"What you do isn't working. On your free weekend you don't work."

"I don't understand, boss." Moisès Corvo leans forward. "Are you accusing us of working too hard?"

"I'm accusing you of meddling too much. Instead of being at home, with your families, you're going about hassling people you shouldn't be hassling."

"Hassling people is usually what they pay us for," interjects Malsano.

"Then you'd rather we did nothing?" stresses Corvo.

"Let's take it step by step." Wham, a fly down, against the chair. "Inspector Corvo."

"Yes."

"What did I suggest you do a few days ago?"

"That I forget about the subject."

"Exactly. And what did you do?"

"I forgot about it."

"That's not what I've heard. You've been asking questions."

"Yeah, I was asking questions because I couldn't remember."

"Keep playing the jester, Inspector Corvo, and I'll have you shot."

"That wasn't my intention, sir, I apologize."

"Am I speaking Chinese, or what? Gentlemen: there is no case. There are no missing children, there is no investigation. What the hell were you doing at the casino last night?"

"I was trying to increase my income."

"You were pestering people. And you were pestering good people. How do you think it makes me look when the mayor calls me this morning and asks me what orders I've been giving my inspectors?

"Bad."

"Exactly. Very bad. If I tell you to shut your mouths and go after anarchists, shut your mouths and go after anarchists, that's what we're here for, bloody hell."

"A lad disappeared yesterday." Malsano puts in his two cents' worth.

"And?"

"You said that without missing children there's no case. So now there should be a case."

"Closed, Inspector Malsano. And I have a question for you in this matter as well. Since when is this your business? The abduction yesterday was under the jurisdiction of the inspectors on duty, not you. What the hell were you doing in the hospital interrogating the guilty party?"

"That's what I wanted to mention: I'm not so sure he's the guilty party…"

"I'll show you that you are wrong. The boy's parents have identified him this morning as the man who took their son."

"But they didn't see it!" exclaims Malsano.

"They were too nervous and confused yesterday. Today they fingered him without the slightest hesitation. That lunatic was sent to the Model this very afternoon."

"So, has Antoni shown up?" questions Corvo.

"We are waiting for him to confess where he has him hidden or buried."

"But don't you see that it doesn't fit together at all? He abducts a lad in the morning, they see him talking to another at midday and beat the crap out of him. He checks into hospital and it turns out that he's already killed and hidden or buried the lad—"

"That's right, Inspector Malsano. Case closed. And you, Inspector Corvo, stay out of it or I will have to take serious disciplinary measures."

A slight parenthesis is needed here: when Mayor Sostres met that morning with the police chief and revealed his displeasure over one of his inspectors showing up in uncomfortable places, he also gave him a message from the prefect. The rumours about these disappearances must be silenced, by any means possible. So, when he accompanied Antoni's parents to identify the supposed kidnapper, he advised them that the best thing for them would be to put an end to this drama as soon as possible. The advice, in the form of an envelope with bills inside, came along with the warning that, if they broke this pact, Antoni's disappearance wouldn't be the only one in the family. What could they have done, poor people?

Later, at Lolo's tavern, Inspectors Corvo and Malsano use alcohol to wash down the reproof.

"At least tell me that you found something out at the casino, Buffalo Bill," probes Juan Malsano.

"Yes. That it's more of a tangle than we thought, and that there are too many people mixed up in it, and too much money."

"It breaks the golden rule: if he has a knife, bloody hands or a corpse at his feet, he's guilty. Reality is usually very simple, but this time there's a lot of knives and no corpses."

"Not necessarily. The fact that he's covered up doesn't mean that our man doesn't exist. And if he exists, we can find him."

"They keep sticking spokes in our wheels. I'm not sure of anything any more."

"Those Negroes we arrested, the ones who killed One Eye…"

"Yeah."

"I don't think they did it."

"That doesn't matter. They weren't good people, that you saw. And they're in the clink."

"Blackmouth was lying. And I haven't seen him anywhere, lately."

"It's a very big city."

"It's very big and has a lot of people. In the casino they are prostituting children and we can't do anything about it. The son of a bitch I talked to was screwing with me."

"You want us to go there? Rain on their parade?"

"We won't even get through the door. They are ironclad, and you've already seen they've got friends in high places. If we want to take apart their business, we have to start from the bottom and that means finding the monster."

"And the casino can't be the only place children are getting fucked."

"No, but it's the most prestigious. The madam at the Xalet del Moro must be hopping mad. No doubt it's already reached her that she screwed up by giving me a name and address. We know that our gimp has been through there, but she's just the intermediary. We have to find out who else he could have supplied children to."

"We're groping around in the dark, Corvo. We're looking for a man and we don't know what he looks like, where he's going, or how he lives."

"But we know someone who can help us. What do we owe you, Lolo?"

To which side is the balance shifting in the city? Will fear keep the Barcelonians at home at night, or will they celebrate Christmas just like every other year? Ferran Street is packed with families taking advantage of the holidays to do their last bit of shopping, or taking the children for a stroll and pushing back bedtime. No one would say that the city is tense and the people worked up, seeing this behaviour. Agustí Massana's bakery has the longest queues, and lively conversations crop up everywhere, always on the same subject: the vampire. And the conclusions don't vary much from conversation to conversation: that the police are incompetent, that the new mayor is turning a blind eye, that the government in Madrid has left us in the hands of God, that all this comes out of the war with the Moors, which has only ever brought us misfortune. If one stops to study the attitude of the masses individually, obviously, signs of paranoia crop up. The children play, and no adult that isn't their mother stops to muss their hair or stroke their faces, or even return the ball to them when it goes out of bounds. Their fathers keep one eye on them at all times and are suspicious of anyone who approaches. The news of the abduction last Sunday being an isolated incident hasn't convinced anyone. Anybody could be the ogre.

The inspectors dodge bicycles and tricycles to enter Raurich Street. The pong of piss grows very intense. They knock on the door and Doctor von Baumgarten is slow to open it for them.

"Happy Christmas," Moisès Corvo wishes him, with the manner of an undertaker.

A little while later, sitting in armchairs, Malsano's gaze is lost in the horrible green wallpaper. Three cups of coffee steam and Doctor von Baumgarten asks the question, "Have you reconsidered my offer?"

Inspector Corvo has trouble taking other people's help, but he has no choice.

"What you told me about looking for the monster. How would you go about it?"

"Actually it's not that different from hunting a wolf, a bear or any other beast of the forest. The animals leave a trail you can follow, if you are a good observer. Some, a few metres behind them, others, kilometres away, but everyone leaves a trail."

"The killer always leaves behind or takes away something from the scene of the crime," declares Malsano. "It's another golden rule."

"Yes, that's it, but in a wider sense. What do hunters follow?"

"Tracks."

"For example. Has your monster left any footprints?"

"I'm afraid I don't understand," says Corvo, furrowing his brow. He takes a sip from the cup.

"Not literally, obviously. But has he left any belongings there where the children disappeared? A coin purse, a shoe, a hat?"

"If he had, we'd have already solved the case, doctor. We don't even know where the kidnappings took place."

"Perfect." But he doesn't think it's perfect. "Then, we'll look for other signs. The snatchings often aren't seen directly. Sometimes, if the animal is wounded, there are vultures that fly over it and show us its location. At other times, the silence in the middle of the forest alerts us to its presence."

"Where are you going with this?"

"Witnesses."

"We don't have any," says Malsano. "Nobody's seen anything."

"The gypsy did," qualifies Corvo.

"What gypsy?" Von Baumgarten's taken an interest.

"The one who saw a lame man trying to make off with a boy, on Marqués del Duero."

The doctor claps his hands and spills coffee on the floor, but he doesn't care.

"Fantastic! And what else do we know about this lame man?"

"That he was seen going into a brothel, one of the dear ones."

"We're making progress."

"No, we're not making progress. This line of investigation doesn't lead anywhere. We followed it and they've closed every door on us."

"No, not every one. Look at what we have: a man, with a physical defect, and seen in two places… are they very far from each other?"

"About a fifteen-minute walk."

"So we can place him."

"Don't get your hopes up. If you go out on the street and start counting, you'll find dozens of gimps."

"And if you go to the port," adds Malsano, "there are countless more, with all the ones arriving from Africa."

"Are there any more witnesses?"

"The mother of one of the girls believes it was a demon," answers Corvo.

"Believes. We already discussed it the last time you were here, Inspector. Belief is one thing and empiricism another entirely. There are no more witnesses, then."

"The madam of the Xalet del Moro, but she won't open her mouth."

"And can't you bring her in to the station to interrogate her or whatever it is you do?"

"We wouldn't be here, doctor, if what we do was working for us. Continue."

"Would you like more coffee?"

"Yes, please." Corvo offers his cup, and Malsano shakes his head; his stomach is upset and another sip could be dangerous.

Doctor von Baumgarten stands up and heads over to the coffee pot. He is uneasy, I'm about to catch a good one, he thinks, a museum piece, the cornerstone of his study.

"How many kidnappings have there been?"

"We don't know. For sure, we have two, but from what we've heard there could be at least nine."

"In how long a period of time?"

"A year?"

"You don't sound very convinced."

"There are too many legends surrounding it all, and so much fear that in the end it's hard to know what to trust," says Malsano, still intrigued by the doctor's words.

"That works in our favour."

"Yes, now everything's much easier. We're going to arrest Hans Christian Andersen," says Corvo sarcastically.

"He'd probably be helpful, actually… but think carefully about it. You guys have known pederasts"—the policemen nod. "And they act compulsively, unable to control themselves, right? They don't plan, they don't think, they can't stop themselves. And how long does it take you to catch them?"

"Depends on the case, but… they fall fast."

"Exactly. And I suppose you've gone through the archives, to see if any of them is out of prison, on the loose."

"Here we have a problem." Malsano sucks his teeth.

"We talked to one of them, but he's not the one."

"Are you sure?"

"I'm sure," responds Malsano. "And about the archives… they burned down."

"They burned down," repeats von Baumgarten, incredulous.

"You heard me. We've been putting together a fingerprint file, with the prints we have from people we've arrested. It's still in the initial stages, and not very useful. We checked it and didn't find anything of interest. The files in the Palace of Justice burned down after the summer; they were piling up in a basement until one of the guards fell asleep with a cigarette in his hand."

"And at the Model?"

"Impossible. If there's one thing you can say about that prison, it's no model for anything."

"OK, let's get back on track here. We have a man, lame, who has been seen in a specific area…" He raises his eyebrows.

"Marqués del Duero and Escudellers Street."

"Bloody hell, here, right nearby. And we know that he can control his impulses, that he's cold and astute enough to keep himself from being seen."

"Great, now we can also arrest Emiliano Zapata."

"He's a predator, Inspectors."

"Predators don't sell their victims."

"What?"

"We believe that he's taking the children to give them to people who can pay for them."

"Yes, yes, that's feasible, but… something doesn't fit."

"What?" Malsano gets up and places his hands on his lumbars, stretching. The dampness is killing him.

"His persistence."

"He treats it like a job," reasons Corvo.

"Nobody does their job with such dedication and over such a long period of time. You know that. And it's not easy to keep up the tension."

"You're suggesting that he doesn't only sell them, that he also wants them for himself."

"No. If he wanted them for himself, he would be like any other paedophile. He doesn't need them sexually."

"If he doesn't want to screw them and the sales aren't his only objective, what else is there?"

"I think that here we've reached the core of the matter. If we know what else he wants them for, we can catch him."

They go over the possibilities again and again, but they can't come up with anything. Plus, they're tired. The policemen have been carrying around this tension for too many days, and their thoughts get stuck in their throats.

"Let me think it over," pleads Doctor von Baumgarten, as he walks them to the door.

"Van Helsing," says Malsano in parting. "Thank you."

He goes by the name of Shadow and he doesn't have much of a story. Son of peasants who left the countryside to pile up in the capital, who suffered illnesses they hadn't even imagined existed, who starved to death and had to sell their son at the age of fifteen, to a good house, only to end up dying a year later when the shanty town where they scraped by burned down. Shadow wasn't adopted as a son, he was too old when they acquired him, but rather to be trained as a guard dog. An investment in the future: today he's a lad, tomorrow he'll be an insurance policy. Shadow knows what he has to know, which is only what he has to say and that's it. He is strong, he spent the last fifteen years punching first sheep and calves, then defaulters and back-stabbers. Shadow is a pair of fists and iron skin, and now he waits for the woman he has to deliver a message to.

He breathes slowly, through his mouth, like a canine snore, as he sits by the door in the penumbra. In the room in the hallway, the one with the sliding door, he left Angelina gagged. She had screamed her lungs out, but no one in the building had said anything because they are already sick of the sounds that are always coming out of Enriqueta's flat. And they are afraid of her. One day she threatened a lady neighbour with a hatchet and ever since then she leaves turds on her landing and hides broken glass in the dirt of her geraniums. Angelina was half choked with tears and the handkerchief tightened around her mouth, and the struggling left her unconscious.

On a chair, no need to tie him up, lies the slack body of Salvador Vaquer. Shadow had pushed his way into the flat and thrashed him good and proper, without giving any explanation—none was necessary. He didn't want anything from Vaquer, so he left him alive enough not to kill him, but dead enough so that he doesn't look alive. Enriqueta's lover's face is swollen (more than normal, that is) from the blows and his nose filled with dried blood. Shadow ripped off one of his nipples, for no reason other than that he had got on his knees begging for forgiveness with the first punch. It seemed that with each breath Salvador deflated.

The sound of keys, yellowish light fanning out from the hall-way, the creak of wood and Enriqueta's silhouette, stopped short because she realizes that something's afoot. Shadow tenses and Enriqueta doesn't see him, but can make out Salvador's body curled up in a foetal position.

"What happened?" She closes the door, turns on a bulb in the middle of the dining room. "Salvador!"

"Good evening." Shadow speaks.

"Who are you?" she says when she locates the origin of the voice.

Shadow sees that she is ready to pounce, she is dangerous, he knows how to read gestures and he can sense that she is no average woman.

"I'm here to give you a message."

Enriqueta doesn't know where the shots are coming from. It's Wednesday, and she's just come from the mansion of Mr Llardó, in the Bonanova, from bringing him the salve they'd agreed on, the one she made with the tallow from Ferran Agudín. Who is this man?

"Who are you?"

"That doesn't matter. I'm nobody and you shouldn't be either. But it seems you don't have that clear. Up until this point, the gentlemen haven't had any complaints with your work, you've been discreet and efficient."

"The gentlemen?" Enriqueta tightens her thin lips until they blanch, and Shadow takes note. He remains seated, but expectant.

"You're getting careless. The police have seen Mr Vaquer and they are asking too many questions. And the gentlemen don't like them asking questions."

"Get out of my house this instant." Without moving an inch, she challenges him.

"Disappear. Vanish. The gentlemen can forget about you for a while, the police have to forget you as well."

"I was given to understand that the police wouldn't be a problem."

"They aren't if you don't give them reason to be. And now you have. If the police ask more questions, we'll have to squeal on you. And you can understand that we don't want to have to do that."

"You dare to threaten me in my own house?"

"It's a warning, Mrs Martí."

"Allow me to warn you as well. Give a message to the gentlemen"—there couldn't be more hatred in the pronunciation of that word—"tell them that, if I want to, I can sink them. I have all their information, their names, their vices. That I keep a list where they are clearly identified, all of them. That if I fall, they fall with me."

"Your word against theirs, Mrs Martí. You have all the right in the world to behave this way, but you know full well it won't get you anywhere. Not even to trial."

"Get out of my house."

Shadow gets up and heads towards the door, his hands in his pockets, gripping two brass knuckles with spikes, ready to act. She doesn't move, just challenges him with her gaze.

"We'll take care of the police," says Shadow in parting. "But you disappear."

And he leaves.

Popular wisdom swears that people who carry a weapon end up having a special character, transfixed by the power it bestows, the ability to decide between life and death, ascendancy and ruin. It is even believed that it is not the man who decides to use, for example, a pistol, but rather the pistol itself that finds the perfect moment to make its appearance. An armed man is a fearsome thing, and the more cowardly and puny and whingey he is, the more serious the consequences.

But popular wisdom is more superstitious than empirical. And in this case, quite off the mark.

Let's take Moisès Corvo, a man who's seen it all, whose balls are rubbed raw from scrapping with the *crème de la crème* of society. A copper with his revolver in his belt. Inspector Corvo isn't used to using his piece unless the situation requires it, and that's happened very few times. He shows it when necessary, he pulls it out as a threat when he knows its presence will be intimidating enough, he uses it as a calling card, sure—but shooting, pulling the trigger and releasing a bullet, only in exceptional cases. No one remembers that time when, as he was heading up the stairs of a building on Sant Gil Street to find out which flat a sixteen-year-old girl had just thrown herself out of, ending up a muddle among the horse manure and straw—no one remembers, I say, the pub employee who chose that day (that day, with Corvo muttering because the steps are very narrow and his knees creak and crack) to go barmy and start shooting at whoever passed by, with a hunting shotgun his brother had lent him to keep it out of the curious hands of a boy in the touch-everything phase. No one remembers... well, the brother of the deceased, yes, he was never able to recoup his shotgun or say goodbye beyond an empty wake filled with the boy's cries. No one remembers the extraordinary aim the policeman displayed on that occasion, blowing a hole in a door, a banister, a groin and a piece of ceiling plaster, in that order.

An armed man walks differently, not because of the power of the revolver but because of its weight. With each motion he is aware that the rod is scratching against his ribs, or his hips, or his leg, depending on where he carries it, and that gives him a forced, almost orthopaedic, gait, challenging to an outside observer. Moisès Corvo feels the Euskaro near him, a Smith & Wesson model 1884-type revolver, a burden that weighs a kilo and looks like an antique, and that gives him enough confidence not to need to use it. Almost ever.

It's the 25th of December, *fum fum fum* as the song goes, and Moisès's wife has left first thing in the morning for his brother's house, on Petritxol Street, to help her sister-in-law prepare the chicken for dinner. You'll come when you feel like it, she'd said when they parted, and Corvo had nodded as if she could see him through the closing door. The policeman had dozed until his body said *enough*, out of sync, as always, and he woke up with his head murky. He can't stop going over it in his mind, as hard as he tries. He is obsessed with the kidnappings, and he fears that today, Christmas day, *fum fum fum*, there could be another while he is dining with his family. As if he could do anything about it. The best thing is a drink to cure his sluggishness, so he dresses, combs his hair, grabs his revolver, with its pearl barrel and wooden butt, and takes a good look at himself in the mirror. He looks older, pale, puffy-eyed, the image of the monster he thinks he's chasing.

On Balmes Street he runs into families, fathers, mothers, sons and daughters, filled with illusion, desserts and wines, one of the best days of the year because everyone pulls out the few coins they'd been saving up and spends them on a nice meal. There are beggars at the church doors. Today their hats are filled with banknotes, because everyone knows that Christmas generosity is, more than a virtue, a tradition. The sun is beating down, forcing Moisès Corvo to squint his eyes, and that keeps him from seeing the man who's following him.

The tavern is half empty, only the four stalwarts who were born with bottles of beer in their hands. The policeman leans on the bar and orders an anise. A moment later in walks a well-dressed man, in suit and tie and with a bump under his jacket that doesn't escape the inspector's notice. He sits beside him and asks for a glass of water.

"Inspector Corvo."

Moisès turns his head and takes in his features: grey hair doused in cologne and a moustache that hides his lips, eyes like slits and cheeks like ceramic, as if they were a poreless mask. Burnt. No: he still has his eyebrows and facial hair. He asks himself where this gentleman came from, why he's armed and how he knows his name.

"Who's looking for him?"

"Asking questions is one of your favourite pastimes, eh?"

"I get that a lot, lately."

"Asking questions is good. You learn a lot. But sometimes, we don't need to learn so much and we should just stick to what we know. Have you ever thought about taking up some other pastime instead?"

"It just so happens that what I enjoy is, also, what I'm paid to do."

"I understand." The man with the strange face turns 180 degrees and leans back against the bar, subtly enough not to seem aggressive, while being aggressive. "What is it you enjoy most?"

"Drinking in peace."

The man moves his moustache and decides that the best thing to do is smile. Behave ourselves, for the moment.

"That's a good leisure pursuit." He pulls out a wad of notes and addresses the waiter. "My treat."

"Give me three more," says Corvo to the barman. "And the bill, it's his treat."

"What would you say if they paid you to keep up this 'hobby', as the English say?"

Moisès Corvo has stopped looking at him, but out of the corner of his eye he hasn't lost sight of the bump under his jacket.

"I don't know what a 'hobby', as the English say, is."

"What would you say if for coming down here, having a couple of drinks and keeping your mouth shut, we were to pay you royally."

"That is very elegant to use the word 'hobby' when what you mean is bribe."

"You asked too many questions, Inspector Corvo." He shows

an open envelope, with some 100-peseta bills inside, and he puts it into the pocket of the policeman's jacket. "You bothered people you shouldn't have bothered."

"I don't like receiving money from someone who hasn't introduced himself."

"Accept it as a sign of goodwill. There are people who are very displeased with you. People you lied to. They want to settle things with you."

"Madame Lulú."

The man gets uncomfortable, Corvo has spoken too loudly, but he covers it up well enough. He offers him a hand to shake and the policeman thinks it over.

"Keep the money. It doesn't bring happiness, but it'll help you forget your worries."

Moisès Corvo feels wounded, humiliated. It wouldn't be hard for him to accept the envelope, but a stab inside him (very, very deep inside) forces him to pull it out of his pocket and place it in the man's hand. It's not easy, not easy at all, but he feels better when he's got rid of that burden.

"You take it. Give it to Adriana, Madame Lulú's Filipina, and you'll see that she knows how to make you happy."

The man's expression has changed and he looks like an automaton.

"You asked for it." He turns to leave the tavern.

The inspector knows how this works. It would have been so easy. To just not do anything, let himself be carried along, look the other way. Easy and dirty. And now he'll have to struggle. Climb the mountain while the wind and snow blow and rocks fall from the peak. He cocks his revolver. Yes, Inspector Corvo already knows how this works. He rolls a cigarette to control the trembling in his hands, lights it and brings it to his lips. A bell tower rings out twelve noon on 25th December 1911, and Moisès Corvo goes out onto the street.

The elegant man is on the facing pavement, still, waiting for him, and their gazes cross as if they were the two sides of a mirror. Moisès Corvo's reflection unbuttons his jacket and reveals his revolver, in its sheath, hanging from his belt, the man's two arms tense on either side of him. Corvo repeats the ritual. There are a dozen metres between them but they seem millimetres and kilometres at the same time. There is no traffic on Balmes Street, and few people around. The sound of some window frame as it closes, the blind lowering, a distant tramcar is all that stands between the policeman and the man who challenges him. And for a while nothing happens, they are both still, dancing without moving. Corvo's fingers tremble, they want to pull out the weapon and shoot, they need it. It's not the revolver that wants out, but the person who chooses the moment.

And suddenly something metal sticks into his ribs. He realizes that he wasn't watching his back and now he has another man there. He can't see him, but he can hear his breathing and smell his rotten breath.

"Don't move," he whispers sibilantly.

Corvo thinks he has a knife or a razor sinking its tip into his flesh. It's not a firearm, so he still has some possibility. And he waits, waits for someone to make a move.

The man in the suit pulls out his weapon and quickly points it at Moisès, who takes advantage of the pressure from the man holding him to grab on his forearm and pull, and uses him as a shield from the shot that resounds throughout the entire street. The bullet hits the man with the rotten breath's back, but doesn't go through it, and when Moisès Corvo manages to free himself of the wounded body and pull out his revolver, the elegant man shoots again. The policeman notices a burning in his left arm, but it's not quite pain, because his heart is beating furiously and he has no time to feel anything. He opens fire on the elegant man once, twice, three times, perforating his abdomen and shoulder, and manages to bring him down.

There are screams and running around, and whistles alerting the police, who will show up soon. Moisès Corvo checks that the guy with the rotten breath is dead and crosses the street to the elegant one with the slanty eyes. He leaves a trickle of drops of blood, which slip down his arm to the ground, and mix with the dust and make curds. He kneels beside the man he has wounded and sees that he's not breathing. He tries to take his pulse but he can't move his left arm and his right is still paralysed, gripping the revolver. The man is dead.

Moisès Corvo sits down and takes a deep breath. Now the pain rolls in on unbearable waves, and tears come to his eyes. He only just has time to take the envelope filled with banknotes off him and stick it in his own pocket before he loses consciousness.

I collect the two souls left stretched out on the road.

11

T HE PLATE OF CHOPS with beans is piping hot, and Anastàsia
thanks me for it with a growl of her stomach. We are at one
of the common tables of the first dining room of the Maternitat,
a house for fallen women on Peu de la Creu Street, beneath gothic
arches, with three other women and their children dressed in
rags. The children, who should be making a royal racket, behave
like the elderly, as if they were aware that they can't take away
a freshly cooked meal every day. Anastàsia chews slowly, tasting
the beans, leaving the meat for last, and sometimes she shoots me
quick glances like a starving dog, beneath the mask of make-up
she hides her face with.

"Enriqueta is a coward."

Anastàsia had been perfecting the art of making an impression
with words throughout her long career. She was a fortune-teller on
Baesa Street, which disappeared with the Urban Reform. Later
she went to live in Hostafrancs, renting a room from Enriqueta,
and she had to quit the tarot when a rabid mastiff bit off her right
hand. She survives by doing chiromancy, in one of those delicious
ironies: a one-handed woman reading palms.

"She always was, and that's why she's dangerous."

I want her to continue, I arch my eyebrows, she doesn't make
me beg.

"This is good," she says, her mouth full, meat between her teeth. "You learn a lot about someone when you live with them, and I spent some stretches with her. When she was running away, particularly. Because she was always running away."

"From whom?"

"In a way, from herself, because she is the main cause of her misfortunes. When the police were looking for her, she would hide in the little flat in Hostafrancs. When someone she had swindled was looking for her, there she was again. When somebody threatened her... well, as you can see, she was always hiding out."

That Christmas of 1911 Enriqueta Martí had heeded Shadow's advice and disappeared. She no longer had the flat she had once rented to Anastàsia, so she sought refuge in Sant Feliu, with her father, Pablo. She hides at the country house that the town knows as El Lindo, in obvious sarcasm, and she stays out of sight. She left without saying a word, not even to Salvador, Joan or Blackmouth.

"She's a loner, and she doesn't like to carry baggage," continues the fortune-teller. "She won't hesitate to leave you to your fate if she can run off in the opposite direction. She will use you for whatever she likes or whatever she needs, and then she'll dump you."

"She married Joan Pujaló. And then she got mixed up with Salvador Vaquer..."

"Selfishness, selfishness, selfishness," she rambles on. "Pujaló was handsome, as a young man, with eyes so blue he looked like a baron. I would have kept him for myself, but that woman has a hypnotic effect on men that leaves them stupefied, and once they fall into her web they are no longer men, they are puppets at her command. She uses them like a shield, to keep her skirt clean, you get my drift?"

"Perfectly."

"Pujaló was alone, his entire family killed in Cervera by some poisonous mushrooms, Enriqueta told me. They had married seventeen years ago and they were never a happy couple. She even, when Joan wasn't around, used a kitchen knife to dig around in his piggy bank, where he kept some money he'd picked up here and there."

"His sister was alive."

"Beg your pardon?"

"Maria Pujaló, she lived with them."

"Yeah, yeah, of course. His sister was alive, but not the rest of the family." Anastàsia rolls her eyes and takes a deep breath. "Oof Maria, the things I could tell you."

"What?"

"Didn't you want to know about their marriage? What do you prefer?"

"Continue about Joan and then tell me about Maria."

"But I didn't say a word, eh?"

"No."

"They weren't a happy couple. Enriqueta separated from Joan about six times, until the final one, about five years back."

"When they had Angelina."

"Yes, but don't interrupt."

"Pardon me."

"He held on to her with all the tools he had—as I said, he was well smitten. She has that power over men, from when she was a whore. Once she even faked a panic attack to make him feel guilty. Ay, ay, ay, I'm dying, she yelled, and so on and so forth. I'm dying because you don't understand me. He thought he had taken her off the street, but somehow she always found her way back there. If not as a whore, which she never actually enjoyed, as a madam. She knew all the tricks of the trade and she charged a very high percentage to the young women who worked for her. But they rose up against her and she disappeared again. Joan saw the opportunity and took her to Majorca. And, as always, it didn't work. During the months they were on the island, she not only had more lovers than in Barcelona, but she also discovered it was easier to manipulate a girl than a young lady, and she could always charge more for the former. A profitable business. When she returned to the city, she didn't hesitate for even a second."

"She was prostituting little girls."

"And boys. She didn't care." She doesn't mince words, there is nobody around who can hear us, but the woman speaks freely. "They arrested her two or three times for corruption of minors."

"So it was pretty well known what she was doing."

"No. Enriqueta always bragged about her clients. She never told me the names, but she would always come out with a few papers. This list is pure gold, Anastàsia, pure gold! I remember it as if it were just yesterday. And every time they arrested her, the next day she was free and there was no trial or anything, and she would say: me? I'm not guilty of anything. What she is is cynical, not guilty."

"She didn't suggest you get into the business."

"Who do you take me for? I read the tarot, I was very good at it. Now I read palms. If you'd like, show me yours, and you'll see how I can tell you a lot of things."

"But she told you everything. How can such a selfish woman confide in you?"

"She wasn't confiding. She was bragging. If there's one sin that stands out among the many that Enriqueta commits, it's vanity.

She can't hold her tongue when she thinks she's done something praiseworthy, no matter what it is. She wants to be flattered, and she wants to be feared. That's how she is."

"What happened with Maria Pujaló?"

"Yes." She looks at the empty plate and asks for another. "Suddenly Enriqueta said she wanted to be a mother. But not out of the instinct we women have, no. Because that way nobody would suspect her. How can a mother use her children at her convenience? Since she couldn't, as hard as she tried, and she tried hard, and not only with Joan—I would have given him a son, you can bet on that—she decided to keep her sister-in-law's. Are you following me?"

"She took Maria's daughter."

"Angelina. She had Maria under her control during the pregnancy, and when she gave birth she told her the baby'd been born dead. Actually, she had left her with me, there in Hostafrancs, to take care of for a few days. What a sweet girl, Angelina. Her name is very fitting, she's a little angel. I didn't see Enriqueta until she came to snatch her out of my hands... of my hand, you know what I mean. I had been taking care of her, bathing her, feeding her. Do you know I even nursed her? Without being pregnant, I had milk for the girl. It was as if that baby had to be mine. But she wasn't."

"And Pujaló didn't know that Angelina couldn't be Enriqueta's daughter?"

"What was there to know? All Joan knows how to do is talk and hoodwink people, but he has no idea how things work. Enriqueta told him they were going to be parents, well fantastic, great news. But Joan tired of the girl very quickly, and the arguing was so bad that he rented a flat on Ponent Street, a bit further up, number forty-nine. He opened up a painting studio on the lower level. He's a horrible painter."

"And they haven't lived together since?"

"Soon after, she met Salvador, and he was already 'pulling his weight' with her," she smiles, through her teeth, amused by the pun because Vaquer is fat. "And Joan tried to get back with her, but it was already too late."

"But they still kept seeing each other."

"Yes, that's what I understand, but she kicked me out of the flat in Hostafranes. Now I live in a pension on Cid Street, and when I run into her on the street she doesn't look me in the eye, because she knows I know all that and it's as if she's ashamed."

"And you don't know anything more."

"I don't want to. Would you like me to read your palms now?"

Since I'm curious, I offer her my hands. She turns white. There are no lines, no ridges, no scars, no signs of anything, my palms are as flat as two sheets of paper. I smile and wink, and before ten seconds have passed she's forgotten whom she was talking to.

In mid January, it seems that souls around the city are a bit calmer. That year had ended with the news of Pere Torralba's arrest, the supposed kidnapper of little Antoni Sadurní, and despite the fact that the cadaver wasn't found, rumour has it that he threw it into the sea and when the rains come (if they ever do) the body will show up on the beach. So the beginnings of popular hysteria were snuffed out, and most everybody felt stupid for having thought that dozens of children were disappearing daily in the city when, really, there was no proof and the only known case had been solved in a heartbeat.

But Moisès Corvo had been temporarily removed from the force.

"Why?" asks Giselle, curled up under the sheets, her hair messy, her skin white as a glass of milk.

The inspector shows her his hand again. He still has it bandaged and it looks as if it belongs to one of the mannequins in El Siglo department store.

"Let's just say they've given me some time off. To get well. To clear the path for investigating those anarchists who tried to kill me."

"Did they know you're police?"

Moisès Corvo is following the official version: some gunmen attacked him as he left a tavern on Christmas day—there's no respect any more, not even for the most sacred—and they tried to murder him. The most ordinary thing in the world; it's not the first time it's happened and it won't be the last. After all, what motive does he have for explaining what really happened? There's no need to alarm Giselle, or his wife, or his brother, no one really, it's best if they think it's an isolated event. Now that it seems the monster is resting, now that he hasn't shown his face in over two weeks.

"If they didn't know it, my friend told them." His revolver is on the table, in its sheath.

But the policeman hasn't been at a standstill. He went looking for Madame Lulú, but it was just as he was expecting: there was no trace of her. The bouncer at the door was still there, but he didn't see Madame Lulú enter or leave at any point. When Corvo tried to get into the Xalet del Moro, the doorman wouldn't allow it. And that was after he'd shown him the entire deck of cards, with thirty pesetas clearly visible between them. Corvo was seen in the Equestrian Circle Club, the Principal Palace Theatre, the Liceu Opera and the Artistic Circle. More than once he had to deal with the security guards. He couldn't identify himself as police without getting himself into serious problems, but he didn't let them intimidate him.

"Now I'm calmer," says Giselle. "Now that it's all over, I'm not afraid for my Tonet any more."

Corvo looks at her and winks. His head is elsewhere and he doesn't want to listen to her.

"I have to go." And he pays religiously.

He had held back his desire to tell her not to be too trusting, not to let the boy out on the street alone, that he knows how the whores are, forgetting all else while they work. But if he had done that, Giselle would have put two and two together and would spread the word again, and that wouldn't be good at all. In a certain way, it's better that everyone thinks that the worst is over, because then he can investigate more calmly.

I will qualify a comment I made earlier, when I said I have no friends. It's not that it's not true, but I could be more precise. I often have quite a bit of company, what you know as cadaveric fauna. Decomposing bodies give off gases and smells that attract the attention of a certain type of fly, the *Sarcophagidae* (a fairly explicit name, for that matter), which come from kilometres away to lay their eggs beneath the skin of a corpse. It's incredible the speed with which they move; sometimes they are even faster than yours truly. These flies aren't the typical summer pests. They are quite large, like a fat kernel of corn, but of darkest black, with round heads and monstrously hairy abdomens. Their larvae feed on the cadaver's rotting flesh until they are enormous and turn into flies. They stuff themselves so much that they get lazy, and they don't fly much because they get exhausted so quickly. As it turns out on Saturday morning they found the quite rotten body of a man in a flat on Riera Baixa Street. And someone thought to bring its clothes to the police station to take their time searching for any kind of identification the man might have been carrying on him, because the neighbours in the building didn't know who he was. Along with the clothes, without realizing, they also picked up cadaveric remains, particularly adipose substances filled with larvae. When the flesh flies appeared and the police on duty realized where they had come from, it was already too late. Not even throwing the clothes into the rubbish bins on the street worked to keep the offices from filling up with my little friends, who stick to the walls, desks and windows waiting for someone to kill them.

So, the scene Moisès Corvo finds himself in at the station on Conde del Asalto Street is pathetically comic. Malsano is smashing flies with rolled-up reports, while Golem and Babyface are telling him where there are more.

"Have you taken up tennis?" he asks.

"Goddamnitohell, Corvo. We've got the fucking station filled with these bugs." Sweaty and with his hair dishevelled, a rare sight in Juan Malsano.

Moisès greets Golem and Babyface, who are laughing hysterically. Hello, poof, responds the former.

Do you recall Corvo's run-in with the Apaches? Golem and Babyface are the two policemen who took him to the hospital. So in a way, they are responsible for his continued existence. And Moisès Corvo doesn't forget a thing like that.

An inseparable pair who work robbery cases in almost every district of Barcelona, Golem and Babyface have been a team for many years. Golem's nickname is because he is big and imposing, like the mud homunculus of Jewish tradition Gustav Meyrink captured in his novel. With small eyes and a considerable nose, Golem doesn't talk much but always says enough. Babyface barely needs describing. Malsano gave him that name the first day he laid eyes on him. Unlike his partner, he is much more expansive, chatty, and he likes to brag about all the robbers he's sent to the clink. And he's got reason to brag.

Moisès Corvo made sure that no one knows about this clandestine meeting at the police station. If Millán Astray, or Buenaventura, or some bigmouth found out, he'd be done for. Rest is a euphemism for don't show your face around here for a while.

"Do you have anything useful or have you just been playing around the whole time?"

Golem pulls out the file, one of the most complete of the corps, and which few people know even exists. The records of the most common offenders and the most dangerous are well organized into five boxes, according to criminal methods and alphabetically. They are used by Golem and Babyface, and they usually end up being much more useful than the official archives, which are disorganized and filled with dampness and lost files. Doctor Oloriz, from Madrid, tried to introduce dactyloscopy into the police force, with prints from those arrested carefully classified, but it seems that Millán Astray isn't up to the task.

"Juan gave us a quick overview of what you're looking for, and we have a few candidates." Babyface's tone of voice is shrill and nasal.

"But don't think we do this for just anybody," laughs Golem sarcastically.

"Only when you're sexually attracted to the person who asks you." Corvo swats away a fly passing by his nose.

"Exactly."

"Let's see what you've got."

"Ten men who walk with a limp, with priors for receiving stolen goods, robbery with use of force and fraud. All ten of them are jabberers, the kind who can't stand not bragging about what they've done."

"Not bad."

"Wait, wait," says Malsano, who's got his eye on another fly, stopped beneath a lamp. "Crap bugs... Buenaventura had to bring in the goddamn clothes with rotten, decomposed flesh on them."

"Also known as rancid mortis."

"Listen: of these, there are three that have also been arrested for corruption of minors. Your typical model citizen, basically."

Golem hands over the files, which have no photographs and are typed up on card stock, with handwritten annotations and additions regarding later arrests, aliases, consorts and all kinds of details.

Moisès Corvo reads out loud.

"Gerard Serrano, Albert Gené and Salvador Vaquer."

One of my little friends lands on the back. Corvo smacks it hard, leaving the record stained with blood, the fly like an exploded sultana. I love these coincidences, but I take no part in them, believe me.

"We are looking for a vampire," states Isaac von Baumgarten.

Malsano walks between the empty bunks of the doctor's parlour, and he makes horns with his fingers to touch his head and ward off the evil eye. Corvo hides his hands with gloves, because he doesn't want to give the Austrian doctor any more explanations than strictly necessary. He fears that, since he's helping them, soon he'll start asking for things, like everybody does. Quid pro quo, as they say.

"Unfortunately, I didn't bring any stakes, doctor."

"I've been thinking it over, these days. We are looking for a vampire who doesn't know he is one."

"I don't understand," admits Corvo.

"Vampirism has existed for years. Stoker didn't invent it, he's more of an apostle. Perhaps that's an unfortunate choice of words, but I say it that way so you'll understand where I'm going with this. For centuries vampires have been persecuted and hunted around the world, but few have ever been studied, and when they have the conclusions have been strikingly similar."

"Which are?…"

"One of the most famous cases on record is what's called the vampire fever, on the border between Serbia and Romania, in the late eighteenth century. A good bunch of peasants and ranchers suffered all kinds of disorders, accompanied by nausea and fevers. At night, they went to the cemeteries and dug up the most recent cadavers to drink their blood. It was said that they had been bitten and infected by vampires, and fear spread through the region. It was so spectacular that a Hungarian doctor, Georg Tallar, showed up to study the phenomenon."

"More or less like you here in Barcelona."

Von Baumgarten blushes, and continues. "He examined them over months, long enough to reach some quite interesting deductions. The winter in that area is hard on the shepherds. They live in isolation on the mountainside and most of them only have contact with the rest of the community when they attend Mass. The Orthodox Church is quite strict, and imposes very severe fasts on the faithful. This lack of nourishment, along with the conditions of cold and loneliness in the mountains, made them sick and gave them hallucinations, which would explain both the digging-up of cadavers and the consumption of blood."

"There were no vampires."

"Yes there were. They were, but they didn't know it. Like in a vicious circle."

"Then the man we are searching for is ill," Malsano thinks out loud. "But here we don't have extreme conditions like on the border between... where did you say it was?"

"Serbia and Romania."

"Yes, that. We live in the West, and in a city full of people."

"You're forgetting that typhus, tuberculosis, syphilis and other illnesses still manage just fine in this city. I'm not saying that our man is ill. At least not in the sense of Doctor Tallar's vampirism. I am saying that he is a predator who chooses his victims not only for their defencelessness, but also for the qualities of their blood."

"The qualities?" asks Malsano as he fiddles with what looks like an operating saw.

"The blood of children is fresher and more vital than the tired blood of an older person. The older one gets, the more contaminated and diseased the blood. The younger and more innocent, the more healing properties it has, the more pure."

"What attraction could this man have to drinking it? What led him to behave this way?"

"*Blut is ein ganz besonderer Saft*," recites von Baumgarten in German, and then he translates. "Blood is a very special juice. Mephistopheles says it to Faust, in Goethe's play. For years, blood has been considered an almost magical element, the bearer of Good and Evil, as coveted as gold, or perhaps more. In the Middle Ages it was believed to cure nervous diseases and illnesses of the joints, but it also contained the evils and that was why it was extracted in bleedings, which most times ended up weakening the patient to the point of killing him. Let's return to Stoker and his Dracula. There is a passage in which Lucy is half dead from a vampire bite. But when she drinks her lover's blood, she revives, she seems to recover."

"Our man is a real hard drinker," jokes Corvo, but he is actually very absorbed in the doctor's explanation.

"Yes, but he also knows the mysteries of haematology. He is an expert in transforming the liquid into remedies. He takes life and gives it at the same time."

"The vampire we're looking for is a druggist?" asks Malsano.

"The vampire we are looking for is methodical, cold and manipulating. He can surround himself with people who do certain tasks for him so he remains unexposed. He has two faces: the inner one and the one he offers the world; the dirty one and the elegant one. And he not only lives off sucking blood, but he also sells it. The vampire we are looking for has to be a doctor, a quacksalver or a healer, although I'm leaning more towards this last option, because our vampire has contact with popular culture, surely. He isn't a scientist, he comes at it from oral tradition."

Little did Blackmouth imagine that, when he knocked on Doctor von Baumgarten's door, he would find there the two policemen he'd duped with the story of the Negroes and One Eye. Since the lady hadn't shown any signs of life recently, and he's hungry, he went to visit the doctor who gave work to his consort, to see if he'd toss him a bone.

"Blackmouth." Moisès Corvo acts as if he's pleased, and the boy almost loses control of his sphincter. "You knew someone who made unguents and pomades and things like that, didn't you?"

*

The next evening, Blackmouth leads them to the house of León Domènech, the blind guitar teacher who makes remedies for all sorts of ailments. When he'd run into the police, he hadn't had any other way out. He won't rat on the lady, and León is guilty enough to be charged with fraud and innocent enough not to be linked to Enriqueta's activities. Von Baumgarten had asked to come along, but the inspectors had refused. The doctor isn't a man of action. He breaks down, he gets nervous and he doesn't know how to react in situations that are beyond him. But the vampire hunt, the fact of having him so close, almost in reach, is more powerful than any of his fears. He wants to move from study to praxis, from fruitless dissection to empirical application. He yearns to be face to face with one of these monsters he's been pursuing for years.

The building number twenty-two on Lluna Street is tall and narrow like a ravine, with stairs too small for the policemen's feet. Blackmouth takes the steps several at a time. Stop here, boy, we're in no rush, reprimands Corvo. They are in the dark and the only light slips from beneath the doors to the flats. The stench of urine surrounds them.

León Domènech opens the door completely nude. Lad, is it you? And Blackmouth invites Corvo and Malsano in.

"I bring company, León."

"The policemen."

"Cover yourself up," advises Corvo, curtly.

"Why? I like to air myself out."

The flat is dark as a dungeon, and when León turns and goes back inside, they see that he knows it very well. Not a sound, not one bump into a chair. Blackmouth lights a couple of candles, which tinge the air with melancholy. The blind man sits in an armchair, with his eyes closed as if he were sleeping, his legs spread and his arms at either side. If he isn't the monster they're looking for, he's surely one the Brothers Grimm would have liked to meet, thinks Corvo.

"Mr Domènech. This is Inspector Corvo and I am Inspector Malsano."

"The lad already told me you'd be coming. How can I help you?"

"You are a quacksalver, is that right?"

"Man, quacksalver is a very ugly word."

"But that's what you do."

"It's not my main activity. I don't have any real profession. Usually I teach guitar classes."

"Pardon me?"

León laughs in silence.

"The lad told you I'm blind."

"Yes." In unison.

"And you wonder how I can teach guitar."

"Please," Malsano invites him to explain.

"I haven't always been this way, you know? As a young man I lived some years in Paris. I lived the good life there, those were some days. I was a real artiste. I was good with my hands"— he lifts them up, now soft with fallen skin—"I played the guitar, I sculpted, I painted, I fondled the loveliest women…"

"And you went blind from touching yourself so much," says Moisès Corvo, and Malsano shoots him an admonishing look.

"I went blind from an accident. If it were an illness, believe me I would have cured it. It was in my workshop, I made wax figures for a living. A bucketful of hot wax fell into my face. It didn't only leave me without eyes, but it also left me with this face like a mask."

León Domènech has a white beard, thick in patches. Now he opens his eyes, colourless like two moons.

"And you became a quacksalver."

"I don't like that word. Natural remedies is much better. And no, it wasn't immediate. Remember, I'm talking about a long time ago. Obviously, I gave up the arts. Not only were they good for nothing, but they were trying to kill me."

Moisès Corvo looks at the naked man, a pathetic sight, and wonders if he is the vampire. It doesn't seem like it, but you never know.

"Have you tried to cure yourself?" he questions.

"I already told you that it was an accident. There is no possible cure."

"None at all."

"None at all."

"As strange as it might be."

León Domènech is blind but not dumb.

"Are you insinuating that I've committed some crime, Inspector?"

"No, I'm not insinuating. I'm asking."

"Well you can rest easy, because the answer is no. My fondness for natural remedies comes from a woman I met in Montauban, in the south of France. Have you been there?"

"No."

"Well you should go. It has a square with arcades that's magnificent. Obviously I felt it, I didn't see it, but I know how to recognize beauty."

"You said a woman taught you."

"Who else? We men are simple apprentices of witchcraft. The ones who hold the mystery, who really keep nature's secrets, are women. Confidentially, don't ever trust a male healer if there's the option of a woman." He laughs again, more for himself than his audience. "I'm shooting myself in the foot!"

"How do you make your remedies?"

"Oh, that I can't tell you. It's the secret house recipe."

"We are policemen, Mr Domènech, not the competition," Corvo reminds him.

"Yes. In fact, there are no big secrets. I remember the recipes of tallows, herbs and liquors that woman taught me."

"And do you have many customers?"

"A few. The ones I've always had. Neighbours who ask for home-made cures for flu and rheumatism."

"No one else?"

"Sporadically, some traveller they send over from a couple of pensions where they know me."

"And where do you get the raw material for your mixtures?"

"There is a rag shop in Hostafrancs that also manufactures tallows."

"On what street?" Malsano would jot it down in his notebook if he could see anything.

Blackmouth remains standing through the entire conversation, in the shadows, nervous. If he were bold, he would kill the policemen right there.

"Jocs Florals, I don't remember the house number. The owner is named Ferran Agudín."

January ends gradually, without news. It's as if the previous year didn't let the monster through, thinks Malsano. Every investigation leads them to a dead end. Two weeks ago they were watching over the homes of the three men that Golem and Babyface gave them. Two of them lead apparently normal lives, married, with stable jobs where they spend most of their time. The third, Salvador Vaquer, they haven't even seen. He hasn't come near his flat on Muntaner Street. They give up their vigilance there, day in day out, on the corner—he might even be dead and they just don't know it. Maybe he moved to another city. They don't know that Salvador lives at number twenty-nine Ponent Street, but he doesn't want to give up his old flat because he fears Enriqueta could kick him out of the house at any point.

On Jocs Florals Street, Ferran Agudín is beating a rug when he sees them arrive. Calling that rubbish depository a workshop is generous.

"Good day," he greets them, and at first glance it's clear he is a man without secrets.

"Mr Agudín?"

"That's me." He stops thrashing the rug and wrinkles his nose beneath thick glasses, curious. He wears a handkerchief tied on his head, covered in sweat, and a short-sleeved shirt open to the navel.

The policemen are all buttoned up, a freezing wind is blowing, despite a splendid day with a crackling sun.

"Mr León Domènech told us that you provide him with the raw materials for his unguents and pomades."

Ferran Agudín puts down the beater on a small table completely covered with tools and scrap iron, and it falls to the floor. He doesn't bother to pick it up.

"That's not exactly true."

"No?" Malsano acts surprised.

"No. I make the mixtures for him. He practically has them all finished when he brings them to me."

"The mixtures," repeats Corvo.

"Yes. Surely he's explained the story of the Frenchwoman to you, right? He goes on about that, the poor wretch. If I went blind, I'd cling to my memories too, obviously. But I've known him for some time now and that woman must be dead and buried, eh, but he keeps polishing that damn memory of his."

"You say that you make the mixtures for him," insists Moisès Corvo.

"Yes, the ones he asks me for. A few things here and again, cod-liver-oil capsules, or shark, unguents of pork fat with fungi— home-made remedies for small ailments."

"Where do you get the material to make them?"

"Here and there. I'm a rag-and-bone man. Today you were lucky to find me here, because I'm often going about the city, stopping at the markets, looking in the rubbish, I have contacts—" The man stops short. "Are you police?" Corvo and Malsano nod. "I have no problem with the police. I'm not doing anything wrong, I don't steal, everything I have I'm given or pay a good price for."

"Don't worry," Malsano assures him. This search is turning out to be entirely frustrating. The investigation path suggested by von Baumgarten seems as if it has to die out at any moment.

"We're particularly interested in where you get the tallows," interjects Moisès Corvo.

"Ah, the tallows. They used to give them to me in the Boqueria market, but the municipals cracked down and said there were no hygiene measures and... well, you can imagine. They wanted me to pay for them so City Hall would pocket their part in taxes, and they were just leaving them for me on the street."

"And do you pay for them now?"

"Yes. But I get a very good price, honestly. A married couple who do slaughtering in town bring them for me every once in a while. He is a very lively chap, very sharp, a nice bloke. But if you talk to her, you'll see she's harder to swallow than old bread without cheese."

"Do you know their names?"

Ferran Agudín thinks hard.

"Not hers. She's never told me. He's named Joan, but I don't know his last name."

"And where are they from?"

The rag man searches in drawers, pulls out papers, makes a mess of the mess.

"Wait, I have it written down here, with the address and everything. Joan, you see, yes, he's named Joan, Joan Pujaló, forty-nine Ponent Street."

12

ALL STORIES COME TO AN END, and the end of this one is approaching. It's never a full stop, but rather the abrupt break chosen by the narrator. The surrounding world keeps on spinning, more or less influenced by the events told, always moved forward by reality's momentum. But in our story the time has come, even though it doesn't seem like it because it's been some days since the city turned its back on the rumours of disappeared children and focused on something it knows how to do better: sterile political gatherings, eagerly following the incipient King's Cup that Barcelona Football Club is taking seriously, or robbing the drunk foreign sailors on the streets of the Marina district. Barcelona is as quick to love as it is to forget, as quick to hate as it is to fall asleep, and what's today an insurmountable fear will tomorrow crumble like a lump of damp sugar amid the newspaper pages.

Reality isn't very given to narrative climaxes. Fiction does that much better, as it's usually more structured and prepared for easy digestion. I could be accused of manipulating events at whim, I won't deny it, but I wanted to be precise with the strange dissolution of the events surrounding the end of Enriqueta Martí.

Moisès Corvo—cross, with his left hand useless and no work to keep him occupied—stops pestering the enclaves where he believes the monster sells the children to focus on the line opened by Doctor von Baumgarten. There are different worlds in the city, classes so separate they don't touch, borders impossible to cross without suffering the consequences. He dreams that he is shot again, and he wakes up in the middle of the night soaked in sweat. If he can, he stays confined to his flat, all alone. He had his wife go stay with his brother and nephew, because he doesn't want them to get hurt or be used against him. He looks out of the window onto the street before leaving the house, and he never takes the same route twice. He makes sure no one is following him every two paces. He is reminded of those nights in Morocco, when he waited for an attack that never came. The silence of the desert, comparable now with the silence of the city's leaders. The clear sky, filled with reeling stars, that died abruptly over the white sand, almost sparkling beneath the moonlight. Nights of watch around embers, warming the scorpions that climbed into their rucksacks, conversations interrupted by the whistling wind, by a strange noise, the Moors always on the horizon like a ghost, like a monster, like the threat that muddies the policeman's mind now, in silent Barcelona.

The neighbours of Joan Pujaló say they see him often, but almost never at home. He is a carefree man, very extravagant and reserved at the same time, and they never know what to make of him. Corvo and Malsano haven't found him in his flat or in his studio, and when asking for him all they got in return was pulled faces and closed doors. It's not Joan I'm afraid of, it's her. Her? They say she was his wife, but they're never been seen holding hands. What's her name? We don't know, and we don't want to know.

Saturday, late January, they kill a pig and break out the wine, preparing a big party around the slaughter. In the city there are buildings with interior courtyards where they bleed the pig and slit it open, and shortly after there'll be nice cuts of meat and sausages. The police are at the door of Joan Pujaló's flat, but they don't know that he is twenty numbers further down, alone with Angelina.

"Thank goodness I don't have children," says Moisès Corvo.

"How's your wife handling it?" Malsano tries the doorknob: it's weak and will give in with the first blow.

"She's anxious. Poor thing cries all day."

"You gave me a good scare, Cervantes. When they told us you'd been taken to hospital, that they'd shot you, goddamn."

"It's starting to be a tradition. I thought I was done for."

"Was there an angel taking you to the other side?"

"No. No angel or lights or heavenly court. Just an implacable darkness, and the absence of pain. It's strange that it didn't hurt, since my arm was torn to shreds."

"Then dying's not worth it, Corvo. Don't get in the habit of it."

"Tell that to her," and he pats his revolver.

"I thought they'd taken it away from you."

"And they did. But this one is mine. And now I have a special affection for it."

"What is it?"

"A hammerless." He struggles to pronounce it elegantly, like the owner of the gunsmith's had.

"It looks pretty new."

"I hope it stays that way."

"Was it dear?"

"A hundred and twenty-five pesetas… I came into some money after the shooting…"

Malsano smiles, and smoothes his moustache. They both pull out their revolvers.

"OK, shall we go inside?"

Moisès Corvo kicks in the door and enters the darkness of the flat. It is narrow and dark and not a soul is heard, but you can't trust that. They go through the vestibule and check that the kitchen and the two rooms are empty, until they reach the dining room, which opens onto an interior courtyard where there is a shack with the toilet. Moisès Corvo approaches and opens the door. It's also empty.

"This is too clean," he says out loud, so his partner can hear him.

"And too tidy, except for a couple of dirty dishes in the sink."

The neighbours lean out of their windows to see them, curious. Moisès Corvo feels their eyes like needles on his nape, but he is pretty used to it.

"A married couple doesn't live here."

"Did the rag man lie to us?"

"No, I don't think so. But only a single man lives here, and only every so often. Look at it all, this isn't somewhere somebody lives day in day out."

"You think it's a hidey-hole?"

"I don't know. But it gives me a bad feeling."

The sound of footsteps on the stairs alerts the policemen. The door is ajar. They lift their revolvers and aim at whoever is pushing it open, slowly.

"If you're looking for Joan," says the thin voice of an old woman when she comes in, and suddenly sees the weapons, "—ay, don't point those things at me."

They lower their guard.

"Who are you?" asks Corvo.

"The owner of the building, Emília Bernaus, at your service. I was saying that if you're looking for Joan, you've come to the wrong place."

"He doesn't live here?"

"He doesn't come here much, only when he wants to sell some of his paintings, or make a racket and get drunk, and the municipals have to come and give him a warning."

"And where does he normally live?"

"I don't think he lives far, because I see him on the street very often. Who I don't see as much is his little girl, poor thing, they've always got her locked away."

The woman doesn't know that Pujaló is often a few metres down, in the flat that Enriqueta has on the same street. But nor does she know that he could just as well be there as sleeping in a tavern, or whiling away the hours in a brothel. Joan Pujaló is a slouch who spends his time wherever he's likely to find fewer headaches. But Malsano is focused on her comment about the little girl.

"They've got her?"

"The woman he's separated from and he have a little girl. Maybe I've seen her twice in a handful of years. She must be with her."

"And she lives close by?"

"I already told you I don't know where they are."

"Do you live in the building?" asks Malsano.

"Yes."

"Look, do us a favour. Can you let me know, at the Conde del Asalto police station, the day that Mr Pujaló shows up at the flat?"

Emília thinks it over, running her fingers through her grey moustache.

"But I don't walk fast. By the time I let you know he might already be gone."

"Doesn't matter. I'm Inspector Malsano. Ask for me."

"Inspector Malsano. And your partner?"

"I'll come along with him, don't worry," stresses Corvo.

"Inspector Malsano," and she tries to inscribe the name inside a dried-up brain where not much fits any more.

Doctor von Baumgarten is as nervous as a little lad. He badly wants to find his specimen, which he has been searching for for so long and which is now so close at hand, but he fears the policemen won't allow him to study him as he would like. He fears that they will arrest him, take him to the clink, and that his specimen will rot there before he can get a chance to examine him. He would like to get ahead of the inspectors, but he doesn't have enough information to find him, nor enough courage to face up to him. Now he contemplates the leather case opened on the table, with tools unbefitting for a doctor, and he wonders if he'll also be able to study the monster once he's dead. He imagines killing him and dissecting him, finding the secret mechanism that leads a human being to behave like a beast. He yearns for scientific recognition after years of making do with clandestine autopsies, stolen cadavers and erroneous conclusions. Blackmouth has offered to bring him more bodies, but he refused. He is too focused on the vampire of Barcelona to keep wasting his time. In front of him, carefully organized on the case, are saws, dissection knives and scalpels, but also a crucifix and a stake. Isaac von Baumgarten believes that he is more than a doctor: he believes himself to be an envoy, a chosen one, a vampire hunter. And the flash of the silver beneath the oil lamp muddles his brain, he buys into his own fantasies and laughs like a madman, like the man they locked up in a psychiatric hospital in Linz for twenty years. When he got out he had to go into exile and create his own delusional world to survive and he ended up in Barcelona. Isaac von Baumgarten, the phrenologist who isn't one, the fake doctor who was a patient; the man who will kill the monster because he hates himself.

Joan Pujaló jumps when he hears the door slam. He is in Enriqueta's flat, on twenty nine Ponent Street.

"Who is it?"

"What are you doing here?" It's Enriqueta's voice, very hoarse, from the darkness.

"I'm taking care of the girl."

The painter has spent some days in his ex-wife's house, basically because she has enough food in the pantry so he doesn't have to buy any out of his own pocket. He's spent the idle time playing cards with Salvador Vaquer. Even though they can't stand the sight of each other, they're too lazy to express it. Vaquer doesn't leave the house much, although he did just go down to the winery to buy alcohol, because he's still scared and hurting from the beating Shadow gave him.

"Get out of here," she orders, and Pujaló grabs his jacket and his tobacco and he leaves, without even asking how are you, what have you been doing, or anything. He sees she's not in the mood.

Enriqueta heads to Angelina's room and turns on the light. The girl is curled up in a corner, her hair shoddily cut, skinny and pale, her lips dry. Mama, she whines, Mama.

"Ay, girl." She is acting, poorly, without any emotion in her voice. "Are these men not treating you well?…"

Mama.

Angelina feels Enriqueta's frozen embrace like a mauling. The woman sniffs her hair and runs the tip of her tongue over her soft, tender neck and then kisses her on the cheeks.

"You haven't eaten anything."

The girl shakes her head. She eats what she can find when she's hungry, but only when Salvador isn't around. She doesn't like Salvador, among other reasons because when she eats he sits her on his lap and kisses her all over, and the girl can't stand it. Joan just gives her sweets. Angelina has been locked in her room for most of the day and night.

"Mama will bring you food."

Enriqueta Martí is tired of fighting with her father, and she left Sant Feliu. She thinks enough time has already passed since Shadow threatened her, and she's been needing to recoup her strength for a few days now. She has to feed again, she is growing weaker with each passing day and at this rate she'll waste away in the blink of an eye. She believes her blood is thickening in her veins and not flowing. She has to replace it with some that's fresher, younger.

And she has to do it right away.

When Joan Pujaló walks the fifty metres of Ponent Street separating his flat from hers, he passes by Emília Bernaus and says good evening, and she wastes no time in heading to the police station, where she asks for Inspector Malsano.

The policeman runs out, no need to let Moisès know because Pujaló might have disappeared before he even gets there. In less than twenty minutes he is knocking on the painter's door.

"Who is it?"

"Police, open up."

There is a silence of waiting, and Juan Malsano has the feeling that all of this is looking awfully bad. Finally the door opens and Pujaló receives him, clearly disconcerted.

"Is there a problem?"

"No, I'd just like to ask you a few questions."

"Yes, yes, of course. For the police, whatever you need."

"May I come in?"

Whatever you need, he says, but now he hesitates about allowing him in or not. Pujaló covers it up very badly.

"Come on in…"

They both sit in the dining room, the oil lamps creating quivering shadows on the walls. Malsano listens carefully but doesn't hear any noises in the flat. They are alone.

"Are you Joan Pujaló?"

"Yes."

"Married?"

"Separated."

"What is your wife's name?" Malsano opens his notebook and pulls out a pencil.

"Enriqueta Martí Ripollès." His voice trembles, he trusts the policeman didn't notice. He stands up.

"Where are you going?"

"To light the brazier. I just came in and the flat is very cold."

"Where were you?"

"Around."

"In Barcelona or away?"

"Has something happened?"

"No, we have some information we want to confirm."

"I'll confirm whatever you like, Officer…"

"Inspector."

"Inspector. But you're worrying me."

"I already told you that there's nothing to worry about. Sit, sit, please, don't stand up."

"I've been in Cervera, these days after Christmas, I have family there."

"Your parents?"

"No, they're dead. Cousins."

"What do you do for a living?"

"Ah!"—this is a good subject for bragging—"I'm a painter. I have my studio here below, if you'd like I can show you some of my work. I'm quite good, and I'm successful, I can't complain. Now I'm finishing up a portrait of Mr Lerroux that—"

"Do you sell tallows, salves, oils, pomades?" He cuts him off.

Silence is the first response, the orangish light licking Malsano's and Pujaló's faces.

"No."

It was the least convincing in the history of "no"s, the policeman will later explain to Moisès Corvo, even less than the three from Saint Peter.

"I'd been led to believe that you do."

"No. Well, I don't sell them," Pujaló gets up again, this time without a clear objective. "I'm the middleman."

"What do you mean?"

"I get them from the slaughterhouses, under the table, and I resell them at a good price." He had done that a few times, but years ago, so it's not exactly a lie. "I don't make much, but it's enough to get by. You won't arrest me for that will you?"

"What slaughterhouses?"

"None in particular."

"And your wife?"

"What?"

"She in the same business?"

"Oof." Quick, quick, quick, think quick, Juanitu! "It's just that I haven't seen Enriqueta in a while."

"Where does she live?"

"Nearby, but she doesn't do that any more. She's more fickle. I set her up with a herbalist's shop and it didn't last long."

"Do you two have knowledge of natural medicines?"

"Yes, yes, that we do. She knows a ton, about making up those mixtures."

"And where did you say she lives?"

Juan Malsano knows, somehow, that his spade has hit the coffin. The first spadeful is always the worst, but the last few are exhaustingly exciting.

"Picalquers Street, three A," he lies.

Joan Pujaló breathes deeply. They won't find her there. She only goes there when she wants to get rid of bones and clothes and little shoes, and she hides it all in a secret compartment in the wall over the stove, which her father build some years earlier. But no one will look there. No one will ever suspect Joan Pujaló and Enriqueta Martí.

"Does your daughter live there, too, on Picalquers?"

"Beg your pardon?"

"You have a daughter."

"Yes." He almost chokes.

"And she lives there, too?"

"She's very pretty. Lovely. A little angel. That's why we named her Angelina."

"And she lives with her mother?"

"Yes. Yes. I haven't seen them in some time, but yes."

"Thank you, Mr Pujaló."

Juan Malsano can't wait to speak to his partner.

For those who are looking for some sort of message in every story, here you have it: there are always mistakes made, and they are paid for dearly.

Enriqueta's pressing desire is so irresistible, so much larger than she, that she throws caution to the wind. She becomes too visible as a starved predator, and obsession pushes her to lose her discipline.

The night of 10th February, after several days in bed with sweats, palpitations and tremors typical of withdrawal, Enriqueta Martí goes out on the hunt. Alone. Fragile. And she makes a mistake.

Her legs are wobbly, her knees knock against each other and she doesn't feel capable of going very far. She turns down Ferlandina and finds the street empty, but when she reaches Sant Vicenç she stops: a woman chats in a doorway with someone she can't see, while her daughter jumps about absent-mindedly a few metres on.

Enriqueta is aware that she is taking a risk, but she doesn't care. She is covered in a black cape, the one she wears when she goes to the Liceu, or to the orgies Mr Carner organizes at the chalet in Collserola, and the hood covers part of her face. She breathes deeply, excited, and gets the girl's attention with sweet words. The little one looks at her with some reluctance but Enriqueta smiles in the shadows and invites her to come closer. The girl does.

Five years old, too skinny, in a little white dress with reddish trim and a headband keeping her hair out of her face. Her large eyes wait for Enriqueta to say something.

"What's your name?" Sweet, almost musical voice.

"Teresina."

"Do you like presents, Teresina?"

Her mother keeps talking, not looking at her daughter. The girl nods her head.

"Do you want a little present?" seduces Enriqueta, and Teresina looks at her mother as if asking for permission, but she finds her with her back turned. "You can show her afterwards." Don't yell, don't yell, don't yell. "You'll see, she'll love it too."

"What is it?" she asks.

"It's a surprise. Come." She holds out her hand. Teresina takes it and goes to the corner with her.

Then Enriqueta Martí covers her mouth with her skeletal claws and picks her up in a swoop and places her on her hips. Teresina tries to scream and kick but she's just a slight little thing.

"If you don't stop I'll break your neck," whispers Enriqueta Martí, all sweetness and light.

When she gets home, twenty-nine Ponent, she locks Teresina in the room with the sliding door. She gags her and strips her clothes off, and tells her that if she tries to escape she'll kill her. She studies her carefully, and curses under her breath: she's a bag of bones, with no nourishing fat or flesh. If she drank her blood right now, it would be as if she hadn't had anything. Best to keep her there at home, fatten her up so she can get more benefit out of her. Besides, now that she has her in the pantry, she can better control the need that sent her out on the street. She grabs some scissors and with a few stabs cuts her hair, black as Enriqueta's soul, to boil up later with garlic and thyme and drink the broth. While she's fattening her up she can trim her nails, grind them up well and make some mush, or scrub her and use the dried skin she gets off to make some infusions. Yes, she'll keep her at home for a few days, she'll take care of her like she takes care of Angelina, she'll feed her... Enriqueta licks her lips, eager.

Two days later, for Santa Eulàlia, the city's annual festival has a dark edge to it. The Guitarts' daughter has been snatched, and word has spread. The monster is back and has taken away little Teresina. In the processions people ask the priests to please bless their children, they don't want the devil to drag them down to hell one night. In the parties, few people dance and the rumours grow to a widespread protest. The Guitarts are a modest family but well loved on their street, they have the poultry shop where Teresina always played with her older brother, Lluïset, and they've been searching door to door for the girl since Saturday night.

When Buenaventura Sánchez took over the investigation, by express order of José Millán Astray, he headed to the port with a group of agents and municipals to make sure that no one could bundle the girl onto a ship and take her far away.

"That's how the foreigners usually do it," he reasoned with the mother. "They abduct girls to sell them in their countries. The best way to find her is to keep a close watch on all the city's points of exit, especially by sea."

But the police don't have an easy job, because as much as they show people the picture of the disappeared little girl, the only answers they get are angry shouts. You knew that this would happen sooner or later and you did nothing. It's all your fault, you've been lying to us. You're only good for stifling demonstrations and controlling meetings, but where were you, eh? Where were you when they snatched little Teresina?

*

"This imposter lies more than he talks," curses Malsano.

"But we haven't got anything on him."

They haven't got an answer any of the times they've gone to the flat on Picalquers. They have definitely ruled out the possibility that anyone is living in the abandoned flat on Muntaner Street, the property of Salvador Vaquer.

They have been watching Joan Pujaló. He has settled back into his flat. He leads an apparently normal life, since the idle lifestyle is normal for him. The police have followed up on it, but they haven't found any indication that he is linked to the kidnapping, or any suspicious movements. Joan Pujaló hasn't gone to Enriqueta's flat while they've been keeping an eye on him. Now that she's got the girl in her house, and the whole neighbourhood is talking about it and searching for her, she's afraid, she doesn't want to get caught with her. It's one thing to take a child no one will miss and quite another to make off with one who is very beloved in the area where you live. Joan Pujaló doesn't want to talk to the police again, he had a bad enough time the other day and has no desire for them to come asking after Teresina.

Juan Malsano managed to get a photograph of the girl because José Asens, the staff sergeant of the Hospital district with whom he has a good relationship, gave him his. The police chief didn't want Malsano involved in the investigation in any way, you guys have already given me too many headaches, can't have you spreading unfounded rumours and getting people all scared and worked up. Keep Corvo out of this or I'll have you put on leave too, Inspector.

Please don't be upset that I've taken so long to inform you of the fact that Doctor Isaac von Baumgarten is not only not a doctor, but he's also insane. After all, I'm sure you noticed his behaviour was at least peculiar, with ups and downs and a certain tendency to surround himself with dismembered bodies. Everything he knows about medicine he learnt from the doctor who treated him and the copious readings on vampires that were all the rage during the years he spent locked up in the Linz bedlam. His reasoning hasn't been that off track.

"He can't control his impulses," says the Austrian.

"But you told us that he could, that he was cold, and he knew how to pace himself," responds Corvo.

"For some reason he's been… hibernating. He must have felt threatened, or pursued, or perhaps someone discovered him, even though it's unlikely. He's been in hiding or repressing his nature."

"And he's been building up a containment wall," Malsano continues the logic.

"Which has finally burst," underscores von Baumgarten.

All three are drinking together, at the Aigua d'Or, while the barman, Miquel, cleans a glass with a rag, his gaze lost in the distance. Corvo feels a stab in his right forearm where the bullet hit, and he grimaces with pain. Malsano continues, "And now it's a runaway river."

"Exactly. Our vampire will act compulsively, until he can restrain himself again. We have to seize the moment, because this is when he will slip up and leave a trail. It is an open door into his soul, and we have to find the way in."

"Has he…"—Malsano hesitates over the right words—"killed the girl?"

"It's very likely. He would have to have a very high level of self-control not to." He scrubs the damp wood of the table with the fleshy tips of his fingers, absent-mindedly. "There are still two possibilities."

"Which are?"

"One, that he's killed her and he's… devoured her. In that case I'm almost positive that his desire will grow, and he'll need to up the dose to satisfy himself. That means he'll have to act more often, and we will catch him if we keep a closer watch on the area where the disappearances are taking place. He can't live far from the last victim."

Pujaló, think the policemen, but he's clean.

"The official investigation is taking other paths," reflects Corvo. "We can't count on the force, only on favours we're owed. What's the other possibility?"

"That of self-control. That he hasn't killed Teresina and he's keeping her alive. That would denote a strong, dominating personality."

"We'll never find the girl at this rate."

"This type of character is usually tied to a certain egocentricity. They are so powerful that they feel they need to show it. Up until now he's stayed silent, but perhaps if we provoke him we can make him come out of his lair."

"Provoke him?"

Malsano heads to the toilets with his stomach wrenching. Corvo and von Baumgarten are left alone.

"We have to get the vampire into the light of day, we have to set out some bait. Do you know *Hamlet*?"

"The prince of Denmark."

"The twisted prince of Denmark."

"What's he got to do with the kidnapper?"

"There is a passage in *Hamlet* where he hires some comedians.

His father's been killed by his mother's new husband, and even though he is sure, he wants to show it. He pays some actors, as I said, to stage the death of his father so he can see the killer's reaction."

"Doctor, we don't know who kidnapped the king of Denmark."

"Talk to Teresina's parents. Organize an event for the girl. The monster will attend. He will be revealed."

"It's too elaborate."

"Do you have any alternative? If the girl is dead, we have to sit and wait for another one to disappear, and another, and another. If she's alive we have this chance."

Malsano returns, buttoning his pants.

"Did I miss something?"

"We have to talk to the Guitarts," Moisès Corvo informs him. "And also with that master of the vanishing act and artist of the mind."

Enriqueta lives locked away. She doesn't want to leave Teresina's side so she hasn't been out on the street in the last week. Meanwhile the girl isn't gaining weight, despite all the food she's been giving her. She changed the girl's name to Felicitat, and she repeats over and over that her parents are dead, and that she's her new mother now. She punishes her with pinches and smacks on the bum when she refuses to eat the vegetables and meats that Salvador Vaquer lifts from the Boqueria. Salvador always watches out to make sure that lad who beat him up isn't following him. Now that the woman is back at home, the risk has returned as well. And he is convinced that another thrashing like the one he got will leave him right ready for the pine box. Blackmouth, on the other hand, lives for Enriqueta. He's become obsessed with keeping her happy, even though she treats him somewhat shabbily, always so distant. He sees in her some sort of mother figure and he believes he can glimpse love in any small gesture towards him; the lad is so hopelessly doomed that he can't even interpret emotions. He will do whatever he has to for her, blindly, now that he has mistaken fear for love. He will kill again, without hesitation, if someone wants to hurt her.

Teresina and Angelina have become friends. They share a straw mattress, and at night they curl up together to stave off the cold. Angelina treats her like a doll, like a new toy she isn't sure how long will last. She strokes her and calms her, she dries her tears and sings her lullabies. One evening when they don't hear any noise in the flat, they go out into the hallway and tiptoe to the velvety bedroom, where the wardrobes are of fine wood and the mirrors have the most elegant golden frames.

"Mama has princess dresses," declares Angelina, but the wardrobe door is locked with a key and she can't open it.

"Your mama isn't good."

Angelina looks cross, getting angry for real.

"She's your mama too now."

Teresina breaks out in tears, I want my mama, I want my mama, and Angelina smacks her across the face, abruptly stopping the tears.

"I want to go home." Her cheek is all red.

"This is your house and you're not leaving, or Mama will punish you."

Teresina holds back her tears with all her strength. Angelina takes her by the hand and leads her to the kitchen. There she searches through some sacks piled up on the floor and pulls out a knife, with dried blood, sharpened, as long as the girl's forearm. With her free hand she caresses Teresina's hair and kisses her on the forehead. She grabs some dirty little dresses from inside the sacks and chooses one.

"Now I'll dress you and take care of you," she says, her eyes twitchy, moving like panicky flies.

13

"LADIES AND GENTLEMEN, welcome to the Cinema Napoléon. I am Balshoi Makarov, artist of the mind and master of escape, and for the next hour I ask for your full attention."

Applause, the audience packed, people standing in the sides, pickpockets having a field day in the aisles. Moisès Corvo and Juan Malsano behind the stage, watching as two spotlights dazzle the illusionist, dressed in a tuxedo, with his head shaved and his goatee pointy with Vaseline. Vladimir Makarov opens his arms, taking in the energy from the audience and continues:

"The spectacle you will now see is filled with mysteries and disappearances, but they are only illusions, lies that your brains are willing to believe, a return to the childhood you left behind so many long years ago… well, from here I can see some young ladies who only just left it behind recently" —laughter. "But yours truly is only able to make magic on stage, because real life is altogether different. And this is why we are here. This is a benefit performance for the return of Teresina Guitart, who disappeared the night of 10th February. Since I can't pull her out of a top hat, at least I can humbly contribute with this new show, which I present tonight for you, and Teresina's parents, Joan and Anna.

The lights focus on the couple in the first row, the man holding back his emotion and the woman with her face in several handkerchiefs. A long ovation resounds through the theatre and the audience stand up to underscore their applause. Makarov has his arm extended towards them, allowing them to be the centre of attention.

Enriqueta and Salvador are sitting six rows back, uncomfortable but curious. During the long week all talk has been about Teresina and the magician's performance at the Cinema Napoleón to raise funds for finding her. The whole street's been discussing it and they couldn't resist the temptation to show up, to know what's said, to find out what the prevailing suspicions are as to the identity of the kidnappers. In a way, they are as much protagonists as the girl's parents, but in anonymity. And Enriqueta hears the applause as if it were directed at her. Joan Pujaló is at the back, leaning on one of the doorways. Today he is jealous of Salvador, he'd never taken Enriqueta out on the town. He's dying to be by her side.

"There are rumours that Mayor Sostres would come," continues Makarov after a while. He furrows his brow and brings his hand up to it, creating a visor. "But I don't see him out in the audience"—a burst of gaiety from the seats. "It's for the best, I'll have a distinguished crowd"—the laughter grows. "I would like to thank the chief of police, José Millán Astray, for coming, and some of his best inspectors, for the many hours they are devoting to the resolution of this case"—widespread rebuke, grimace from Millán, sardonic smiles from Corvo and Malsano in the shadows. "And I would like to thank all of you for your co-operation in these moments of such difficulty for the family."

Balshoi Makarov makes an exaggerated movement with his arms, as if he wanted to shoot lightning out of his fingertips, and from the ceiling falls a rain of multicoloured confetti. Sebastián has everything prepared after a couple of days of intense rehearsals. The idea for the show was Moisès Corvo's, and Sebastián took it to the owner of the cinema, who gave it the go-ahead. There's no such thing as bad publicity. Vladimir Makarov, for his part, accepted immediately. His contract had ended at the beginning of the year and he hadn't found a promoter for his new show, so this presented him with an excellent opportunity to give his new number a baptism by fire and, at the same time, help the police in their investigation.

"First of all, I need a volunteer"—people look around as if saying, you, you, the boys pinch their girlfriends so they'll jump up and go on stage. The illusionist pulls a coin purse out of his pocket, opens it and looks at the identification inside. "I see we have here… Marina… Marina? Is there a Marina in the room who's missing this? Gentlemen of the police force, please, don't hold this against me."

A shriek and a girl gets up and runs towards Makarov. It is his assistant. I've seen you somewhere before, haven't I? No, no, no. And the show begins.

Balshoi Makarov is quite talented, and for a good long while he plays with the audience at guessing their dates of birth, the names of their parents or if the card they have in their trouser pockets, unbeknownst to them, is a three of spades. Half an hour later he pulls out a tank with glass walls filled to the top with water and asks a young man to tie up his hands and feet with some chains. Sebastián plays Beethoven's 'Clair de Lune' on a gramophone and prepares the projector. Makarov hangs himself from a hook that lifts him, using pulleys, up and over the tank. He laughs and falls inside, while the upper trapdoor closes and the curtain comes down. Sebastián plays the film *History of a Crime* by Ferdinand Zecca. It's more than ten years old, but he hopes to achieve the desired effect.

A thief enters a room where a man is sleeping, and he breaks into his safe. The noise wakes the victim up and he fights against the intruder, who pulls out a knife and sinks it into his chest, fatally wounding him.

Makarov has already got out of the fish tank through the back. When he fell, he landed in a half-empty compartment in the centre, covered up to his waist. Now he undoes the chains and goes down through a hidden trapdoor without anyone noticing.

"Did you see anybody?" asks Corvo.

"No, there's too much light. I'll look now, before the film ends." He wets his face and shirt to make it look as if he was in the water.

The thief in the film is at an outside café, surrounded by beautiful women, living the high life, when the gendarmes show up and arrest him. They take him to prison and there he falls into a deep sleep, watched over closely by a jailer. He dreams that he has a full, honourable life, with a wife and children and guests over for dinner, and that he is happy. But the long arm of the law wakes him up, and a priest prays the last words for his soul. They are taking him to the scaffold.

Makarov goes out to the side corridor to finish off the number. He has to get to the first floor, right beside the projection booth, and surprise everyone. He will have escaped the wings of death just as the film ends. He only has five minutes.

The criminal begs for forgiveness and faints as he sees the end approaching. The guillotine awaits him and he draws nearer, tied up like Makarov was before jumping into the box, and moaning. The public goes oh, and there are those who can't bear to look. The thief is stretched out and they are about to decapitate him.

Enriqueta thinks she's already seen enough, that it's all a pantomime and that she has better things to do than watch films and sleight of hand. She elbows Salvador Vaquer in the ribs. They stand up and leave the row of chairs, amid protests from the other spectators who want to see the end of the film. Makarov makes them out among the penumbras of the theatre and recognizes the gimp without a shadow of a doubt. He points to him and looks at the policemen, who are keeping a close watch on the audience from the other side.

Enriqueta Martí and Moisès Corvo exchange glances, and it seems they say it all. The police see Salvador, limping as fast as he can towards the exit.

"Pujaló," says Malsano in a hushed voice, just as *History of a Crime* ends and the curtain rises. "There, at the back."

Juan Malsano breaks into a run because Pujaló saw that something was going wrong and he vanished through the door. Moisès Corvo heads towards where Enriqueta and Salvador are fleeing. The spotlights illuminate Makarov, on the first floor, who is waving every which way. The applause is deafening.

"What's that one's name?" shouts Corvo to Staff Sergeant Asens, who is in charge of security for the performance.

"What?" He doesn't hear him, the ovation kills all other sound.

"What's that one's name?" And he points to the couple.

"Salvador?"

"The gimp. The fat gimp."

"Salvador Vaquer, a wastrel. And she is Enriqueta Martí."

Moisès Corvo feels a stab in his left arm, at the height of the bullet wound. His monster, just metres away.

He pulls out his revolver and quickens his step.

Joan Pujaló, sweating like a pig, crosses the Rambla and enters

Anselm Clavé Street. He isn't used to the exercise and he's gasping for breath. Inspector Malsano loses sight of him. He has to get him, no matter how, he is convinced he has something to do with it, running away as fast as your legs will carry you when the police have spotted you can only mean bad things. When he reaches Ample Street, there is no trace of the painter. The echo of Pujaló's shoes against the cobblestones fades out, and Malsano has to look in every doorway. He doesn't know if he's still running away or if he's now hiding. He opens some doors, but the blackness is his enemy. After a little while he lowers his arms, takes a deep breath, with burning lungs, and he admits defeat.

Moisès Corvo is getting increasingly closer to Enriqueta and Salvador. He, limping, and she, all dressed up, walk slowly. He grips the weapon in his hand, ready to use it, and shouts at them when he's got them in his reach on Sant Pau Street.

"Police!"

The couple stop, turn, and remain still, staring at the inspector.

"Don't frighten us, Officer," she says, the bodkin she always carries hidden in her sleeve slipping down to her hand.

"Hands in the air," demands Corvo.

"I think not," she says.

Blackmouth smacks a stick into the inspector's head with all his might. Corvo turns, unsure as to what's happened, and the lad wallops him again, this time laying him out on the ground.

Killing someone doesn't require intent. There are murders where the killer went too far, or didn't consider the consequences of certain actions. To kill someone, the only truly essential element is opportunity. Moisès Corvo lies with his head open, at Blackmouth's feet, as the lad winds up with the stick to finish him off.

"Enough!" shouts Enriqueta.

When Malsano returns to the Cinema Napoleón, with the performance still going on, he doesn't find Corvo. He asks Asens, who tells him he hasn't been seen since. And he repeats the names of the couple he was pursuing. Juan Malsano goes out to look for them, but he doesn't know where to start. He has a bad feeling, which grows with the passing hours. He doesn't find him at the police station on Conde del Asalto or the prefecture on Sepúlveda Street. He decides to head over to Corvo's flat, on Balmes Street, but doesn't find him there either. He hesitates about asking his brother if he's seen him, so as not to worry him any further. The next day Juan Malsano checks the hospitals, with no luck. Millán Astray has found out about the disappearance and calls Malsano in for an urgent meeting.

"Leave it in our hands. Rest. This matter is affecting you personally and your perspective on the big picture is getting muddled. We'll put every man on finding Inspector Corvo."

But Malsano can hear the echo of his words, that's how hollow they are. They're now not only taking him off the investigation, but also the search for his missing partner. The policeman doesn't mention the names Enriqueta or Salvador. He's afraid that if he does someone could catch them first and make them disappear. He has to arrest them himself.

Golem and Babyface are waiting for him right outside the police station.

"What did he say?" asks the big bloke.

"That I should go home and sleep."

"And what are you going to do?"

"Are you guys very busy?"

An hour later, Golem knocks down the door to the flat on

Picalquers Street and shouts police police police, while Babyface and Malsano enter crouched down and with their revolvers in hand, hammers cocked, ready to fire. In the darkness, every room is a mystery, every corner is a hidey-hole, every shadow an enemy. When they are sure it is empty, they begin the search. They know that it's completely illegal, that without the authorization of the judge this entry cannot be used as evidence in any trial, but they don't care. The priority is finding Moisès Corvo. Malsano takes the bedrooms, Golem the kitchen and Babyface the tiny parlour.

"Nobody's lived here for months."

The search yields jars filled with tallows, animal bones (they look like rabbit, or hare, or maybe cat, but not human), half-rotten hides and children's toys. There are no photos or portraits, nor a single mirror. The walls have yellowed paper and no decoration of any kind. In a chest of drawers appears a pile of papers, amid fines and receipts, which the policemen study carefully. In some of them there are repeated addresses, one on Riera Baixa Street, another on Tallers and a third on Ponent, which they mistake for Pujaló's and disregard.

Moisès Corvo is bound hand and foot, and hasn't seen anything for a few hours because they've locked him up in a pitch-black room. He can't speak: he has a handkerchief or a rag in his mouth. If he listens carefully he hears some muffled voices, but he can't really make out the words. He is stupefied and woozy, and his arm and head are seething with pain. They might have drugged him, because he has to fight to stay awake and he's awfully disoriented. He tries to figure out how many people there are, sounds like a man and woman, the ones he was following when he was attacked from behind. It's possible that the one speaking with a more nasal tone is Blackmouth, but he doesn't know if he can trust his senses right now. He would even say that sometimes there is a girl chattering, or two, or more.

"Let's just kill him." Declaration of intentions from Salvador Vaquer, who is scared to death. "It's too risky having a copper in the house."

"No. Not that." Enriqueta combs Teresina ineptly, ripping out tufts of her hair, which is now quite short. The little girl doesn't even dare to cry.

"How long before the scuffers tie up loose ends and show up here? Nobody's protecting us now, Enriqueta!"

"We still have many friends, Salvador. Many."

"Why don't we kill him and get it over with?"

"Because it's much more fun this way."

Salvador Vaquer doesn't comprehend Enriqueta's reasoning, but nor does he dare to run away. Maybe he should do as Pujaló did and vanish into thin air. But he knows full well that if she falls, she'll spill all the beans. And that before she even opens her mouth he'll be a dead man, because that boy from the other day—or some other one—will show up after dinner or while he's having a coffee with a splash of milk in a tavern and kill him without a word. They've lost all the protection they used to have, if it ever was a dependable safety net, and now he is in the hands of a woman who thinks that keeping a gagged policeman around the house is fun. It's a sinking ship, with the hull punctured and a captain convinced she's invincible.

Light inundates the room where Moisès Corvo lies on the floor, and the cockroaches flee in terror. The inspector holds back his vomit, because it would mean choking to death, and he inhales and exhales deeply through his nose. Two silhouettes approach, grab him by the legs and move him to a corner. One of the voices is that of the gimp, Salvador, but he doesn't recognize Pablo Martí, the evil woman's father, in the other.

"Are you sure he's unconscious?"

"Enough not to make trouble."

Moisès touches something spongy with his shoulder, but he doesn't know what it is. It seems like a bag filled with flesh, and gives off a stench of putrid potatoes.

"Help me prepare the mortar." It's the gravelly voice of Pablo Martí. "Not just anybody knows how to do this. It's an art. You have to get the perfect consistency, not too soft and not too damp."

"What do I have to do?" Salvador Vaquer looks at him, awaiting instructions.

"This is why you young people today are such useless loafers. Haven't got skill or drive. Don't know how to do anything."

When Moisès Corvo wakes up again, the false wall is half built and the two men have stopped for the day because the sun has gone down. We'll finish it first thing tomorrow morning. The policeman twists to get out of his ties, now that he's slightly recovered his mobility, but there isn't enough space: on one side the new barrier, on the other the wall, and right up against him, that noxious thing that seemed like a sack and is now rigid.

Enriqueta Martí comes in with a cup of hot broth in her hands. She pulls out the fabric that fills Moisès Corvo's mouth and whispers, "Don't try to scream, you can't. It's no use. Now drink, you need nourishment."

And she pours the clear soup down his throat. The policeman spits out the first swig, but she grabs him by the nape of the neck and forces him to ingest more.

After a little while Moisès Corvo is asleep again, sedated, right beside the corpse of Blackmouth, the lad who stopped being useful to the woman.

Despite busting down the doors of the flats on Riera Baixa and Tallers, the police find no one there. They both seem abandoned, and there is no trace of the couple, and much less Corvo. They turn them upside down, but there are no longer any strings to pull on. They try to locate the owners they rent from, but can't find them either.

"It's them, for sure," Babyface asserts.

"All we have is circumstantial evidence, nothing conclusive," says Malsano. "But it's them."

Salvador has priors for corruption of minors and he is the gimp who was seen trying to snatch a girl to take her to the Xalet del Moro, which seems to provide a network of child prostitution to the upscale neighbourhoods and is protected by powerful people, able to nip any police investigation in the bud. And erase priors like the ones Enriqueta had, because she doesn't show up anywhere and she fits von Baumgarten's limited profile perfectly. She moves in the shadows and has knowledge of folk medicine. The nameless monster has finally come out of its den to look upon its work. However, she has become invisible again.

"Pujaló has to be easier to find." Golem puts a hand on the inspector's shoulder. "He's a talker, and they're never able to hide for very long. They go on and on and their mouths do them in. Go home, Juan, we'll take care of it."

But Malsano knows that he won't be able to sleep, anxious because each minute that passes is a missed opportunity. He meets up with Quim Morgades in the offices of *La Vanguardia* daily.

"Publish it," he requests. "If somebody knows where Teresina is, it will lead us to Moisès. Write it. We don't have time. We have to find them."

Morgades makes a call to the trial court assigned to the missing girl's case and talks to the clerk, Miguel Aracil. After a few minutes he returns to the call and confirms that the judge, Ramon Mazaira, will allow the publication of the news. He is sick and tired of the police's incompetence and lack of results in a case that has provoked such social alarm. He is fed up with the prefect, who only two days earlier sent a statement to the press denying the facts of the kidnapping. Go ahead, says the clerk. The next day, Quim Morgades writes a short column asking for citizen collaboration to find Teresina.

"Good luck," says Malsano in parting.

When Inspector Corvo opens his eyes again, the darkness is absolute and the new wall already reaches the ceiling. He wants to move to hit it with his legs and take advantage of the fact that it must still be weak to knock it down, but he is stuck. He can't yell, he can't move. He can only wait. It is increasingly harder to hear the voices beyond the false wall, and he is losing hope of getting out of there alive.

On the 27th, first thing in the morning, Sergeant Major Ribot runs to tell Juan Malsano. Golem and Babyface have arrested Pujaló as he was entering his painting studio at daybreak.

"Are they at the station?"

"No."

The port, on a Monday, is quite a silent place, a forest where topmasts and funnels bob. The fishermen aren't there, the small Valencian boats with awnings are closed and the stevedores sit beneath canopies playing cards and chatting. The sound of splashing water and drowned shouts is all Juan Malsano hears when he gets there, leaving behind the city of tramcars and factories. But he only sees Golem and Babyface alone, on the dock, watching the water. When he approaches, he discovers Joan Pujaló staying afloat best he can, I can't swim, I can't swim!

"Where is your wife?" shouts Golem, squatting.

"Get me out of here! I'm drowning!"

He does the doggie paddle and gets close to the shore, but Golem extends a leg and uses his foot to push Pujaló's head a bit further into the water.

"Please, I—" He swallows water "—I'm drowning."

Pujaló is exhausted.

"This bastard was playing dumb when we caught him."

"Where's my partner?" bellows Malsano.

"Who?"

"Why were you running the other day?"

"I… I got scared!" He can barely speak.

"Why?"

"I don't know. I saw you and… since you had already talked to me…"

"What?"

"Help me. Get me out of here, I can't swim, please."

"Where is Enriqueta?"

"I swear I don't know." Ay, Joan would have his fingers crossed if he could, but he's got enough on his plate with just staying afloat.

"She is with Salvador."

For a moment, Joan Pujaló's face is transfigured.

"I don't know. Get me out of here."

"I'd let him drown," says Babyface. "If he doesn't know anything, he's no use to us. Let him sink."

He speaks loud and clear so Pujaló can hear him.

"Where is Salvador?" insists Malsano.

"I don't know, I don't know."

The inspector grabs his revolver and opens the cylinder. He pulls out three bullets and puts them in his jacket pocket.

"You like to gamble, huh? You like to bet."

"Believe me," he begs.

"You have a fifty per cent chance of winning, Pujaló." He aims at him. "Where are they?"

"I told you that—"

The shot hits the water and wounds the man's abdomen. He shrieks with pain and stops his paddling.

"Where are they?" Malsano repeats, slowly and deliberately, and the vapour that comes out of his mouth looks like sulphur emerging from hell.

"Ponent, Ponent. Help me, I'm dying." It didn't hit any vital organ, but it's dreadfully painful. "They're in Enriqueta's flat!"

"Where?"

"Twenty-nine Ponent, fourth flat on the first floor, with the girl. I don't know anything about your partner, I swear."

Staff Sergeant Asens helps Golem pull the man out of the water. Call an ambulance.

Malsano runs.

*

Few people plan on being buried alive. But many are afraid of it, a fear clinically named taphephobia and rooted in the Romantic poets such as Lord Byron and Percy Shelley. Famous composer Frédéric Chopin wrote in his will that, once he was dead, he wanted his heart ripped out to make sure he wasn't buried alive by mistake. It was Edgar Allan Poe who, in the story 'The Premature Burial', really captured the terror of being thought to be dead when one is actually still alive.

The false wall was up and Pablo Martí went back to Sant Feliu after finishing his work. She is my daughter, he justified, as if that excused anything. Salvador leant a mattress against it, and moved around a couple of little cabinets so it would look as if it had always been set up that way. I put one hand on the wall and speak.

"Moisès."

The girl's voice rouses him.

"Who are you?"

"Moisès, I'm here."

"Teresina?"

"Yes."

"Are you all right?"

"You don't have to worry any more."

"You have to let the police know, Teresina. You have to go out on the balcony and shout."

All of a sudden Moisès Corvo realizes that he can talk, in spite of the rag in his mouth having slipped down his throat until it is stopping up his trachea.

"The police are already on their way over. Soon I will be free, and you too, Moisès."

"Where is Salvador?"

"Doesn't matter. Salvador is a loser. It's always been her, Enriqueta. She was the one who snatched me, she was the one who took all the children."

"You have to hide, Teresina. If the police come she will try to kill you."

"She won't do anything to me. It's already been decided, all of it. And you've been important, Moisès. Without you they never would have found her. She knows that, and that's why she wanted to punish you."

"Who are you?"

"Teresina."

"Who are you really?"

"I'm a voice inside your head, nothing more."

"Help me out of here. We have to catch her, we have to make sure she doesn't get away. We have to finish off the monster."

"I can't help you, Moisès. I can only stay here, beside you, until the moment comes. You don't have to worry about her. She will go to prison. They will interrogate her. All the evil she has brought to this world will come to light. Many things will be revealed, but there will be many that are hidden. You already know that."

"She will get away with it: she is protected by very powerful people."

"Everyone forgets. Over time she won't be in the papers, the monster will be a hazy memory. A huge ship will sink, new diseases will come, a war unlike any ever seen will break out, and Enriqueta will be a legend told to scare children."

"She has to pay for what she's done."

"In a year from now, Moisès, Malsano will help Isaac von Baumgarten to get into the Reina Amàlia Prison. The doctor will sink a stake right into the middle of Enriqueta Martí Ripollès's chest and then he will decapitate her."

"And Conxita? And my brother? And Andreu?"

Moisès Corvo would cry if he could shed a tear.

"You found the girl," says Malsano to Staff Sergeant Asens. "Whatever happens in there. A lady neighbour told you that she had seen her and you went into the flat with some excuse."

"A hygiene inspection."

"Whatever. But you found the girl and you arrested Enriqueta."

"If I had known it was them," laments Asens, "...if I had suspected earlier..."

Juan Malsano knows that if they go into the flat on Ponent Street, if they arrest Enriqueta and take her into the station, they'll use any flaw in procedure to let her go free. If it's a municipal officer, an agent of the recently created force, they'll have a harder time of it. The Municipal Guard could use some prestige and publicity, like any police force, but this one has the added fact of a clean record because it is so new. What really matters now is finding Moisès Corvo, saving Teresina and, obviously, capturing Enriqueta.

"I'll wait here." Babyface chews on a toothpick and leans against the entrance. "No one comes in or out."

Malsano goes into the staircase and through the hall, taking the steps two at a time and gathering forces in front of the door. His hands are sweating. He doesn't want to think too much about what he'll find on the other side. The monster, Moisès, the girl. He chases the bad omens out of his head. And if?... No, no, no. Golem asks for permission with his gaze, and Malsano nods.

The wood around the doorknob breaks and the door opens wide as if surrendering. The two policemen enter with their revolvers aimed into the void. The beating, like a blacksmith's shop in their temples, is so intense it hides all other sounds. Is it empty? Is this flat empty too? In the back, as if kilometres away, a girl cries, and Golem doesn't think twice, running over there, while Malsano covers him from behind.

"The girl is here!" His voice comes from an indeterminate place in the dwelling. "On the floor, son of a bitch, on the floor!"

Malsano tenses up even more when he hears his colleague's orders. He doesn't know that he's found Salvador Vaquer in a corner of the bedroom, or that he found him with Moisès Corvo's weapon in his hand but then tossed it when he saw the giant entering the room. Juan goes into the parlour decorated with expensive furnishings and mirrors and sees Angelina seated in an armchair, her hands resting on her skirt, as if waiting her turn.

"Who are you?"

The girl is silent. She must be the daughter of Enriqueta and Pujaló. She has the lost gaze of madness. He continues to the kitchen, which is in shadow, and a silhouette moves slightly for a second.

"Halt!" bellows Malsano. "Hands on your head!"

He can't see her well, but he senses that she is obeying the order he has just spat out. The bulb is in the middle of the kitchen. He advances a couple of paces very slowly to pull the little chain and turn it on. When he does, it blinds him, and when he opens his eyes Enriqueta pounces on him, beside herself, gripping the knife like an enraged beast. She doesn't seem human, she isn't human. Malsano dodges her, but loses his balance and falls against the sink. Enriqueta recovers her position and confronts him face to face, but Malsano manages to aim his revolver at her, so that her impulse towards him places the barrel pressing on her ribs. That leaves her frozen in place, her face shaken, her arms in the air, the knife blade twinkling with the reflection of the bulb's light.

"Try it," warns Malsano. "Just try it and I'll blow you to bits."

Enriqueta hesitates, but doesn't back down. Juan Malsano holds her gaze a good long while, 500 or 600 years, and in it discovers the wickedest person he's ever met. She is pure evil, the devil, the monster, without a grain of humanity. And his skin bristles and his body trembles.

"He's not here." Golem appears with Teresina. He left Salvador handcuffed, crying. "I can't find Moisès."

Malsano straightens up but keeps his gun on her. Enriqueta challenges him, it even seems that she's smiling. She has a secret they can't get out of her.

"Where is my partner?"

She doesn't speak, she keeps her eyes glued on him, but she's already thrown the knife to the floor. A defenceless victim.

"Where is my partner?" he repeats, raising both his tone of voice and his revolver. If he were to shoot now, he would blow a hole right between her eyebrows.

"Juan…" Golem knows that if the inspector shoots everything would be worse.

He went too far with Pujaló, and he looks capable of venting his anger and frustration on Enriqueta. Golem takes a step towards Malsano. Juan…

"Where is Moisès Corvo?" He clenches his teeth, his finger tensing on the trigger.

Golem raises his hand and places it on the barrel. Juan. And he lowers it slowly. She smiles, the miscreant.

"We'll find him. And she will pay."

Juan Malsano winds up and smashes the butt of the revolver against Enriqueta's cheekbone. He breaks the skin and two teeth, leaving her on the ground, with the taste of her own blood in her mouth.

"Where is my friend?"

"Moisès, listen to me. In two weeks I will reveal where your corpse is hidden. It won't be made public. That wouldn't be good for anyone. Malsano will fake a robbery to get it, and he'll give you a burial. Your family will hold a wake, finally. They will say farewell, they will cry, and they will be proud."

"I didn't get a chance to say goodbye."

"You don't all leave this world the way you'd like, or the way you deserve."

"And what happens now."

"Nothing. It's over. You will sleep and never awaken. I'm here to keep you company. It's the least I can do. I owe you that, because you've always been with me and you haven't ignored me, you haven't pretended I don't exist."

"Why?"

"There is no answer, Moisès. There wasn't one that day with the Apaches, and there isn't one now, here. There is no why, just a how. And your how has been magnificent."

"I don't understand you."

"You don't have to understand it. You have to accept it. You were a great man, with many defects and many virtues. You've had a full life: you've seen it all, and there are people who love you and will miss you and remember you well. No one will say poor bloke, poor thing, poor little thing, which is what people repeat when someone is no longer by their side, in order to go on suffering, enjoying, working, playing and surviving. They will say: Moisès Corvo was my brother, my uncle, my husband, and they will be proud. He fought for what he believed in, against adversity. He gave it his all. And he pulled it off. Not everyone can say that, Moisès. Not everyone can reach the end, close their eyes and know that they are leaving a deep, lasting mark in the hearts of those who loved them. Living is fighting, not giving in and walking off with your head held high."

"It was good while it lasted, Teresina."

"No: it was very good."

"I won't argue with a girl who talks like a doddering old man."

Moisès Corvo's soul dies out the way it lived.

"Now I will say goodbye."

I kiss him, and the darkness swallows us up.

ACKNOWLEDGEMENTS

This novel couldn't have been written without the help of the Arús Public Library, the archival service of *La Vanguardia* newspaper, the endless source of stories that is Montse Aguilar, my co-workers who asked if all that was really true after listening to the story of Enriqueta over and over again; and all those people who, without realizing it, contributed a grain of sand.

PUSHKIN PRESS

Pushkin Press was founded in 1997, and publishes novels, essays, memoirs, children's books—everything from timeless classics to the urgent and contemporary.

Our books represent exciting, high-quality writing from around the world: we publish some of the twentieth century's most widely acclaimed, brilliant authors such as Stefan Zweig, Marcel Aymé, Antal Szerb, Paul Morand and Yasushi Inoue, as well as compelling and award-winning contemporary writers, including Andrés Neuman, Edith Pearlman and Ryu Murakami.

Pushkin Press publishes the world's best stories, to be read and read again. Here are just some of the titles from our long and varied list. For more amazing stories, visit www.pushkinpress.com.

THE SPECTRE OF ALEXANDER WOLF
GAITŌ GAZDANOV
'A mesmerising work of literature' Antony Beevor

BINOCULAR VISION
EDITH PEARLMAN
'A genius of the short story' Mark Lawson, *Guardian*

TRAVELLER OF THE CENTURY
ANDRÉS NEUMAN
'A beautiful, accomplished novel: as ambitious as it is generous, as moving as it is smart' Juan Gabriel Vásquez, *Guardian*

BEWARE OF PITY
STEFAN ZWEIG
'Zweig's fictional masterpiece' *Guardian*

THE WORLD OF YESTERDAY
STEFAN ZWEIG

'*The World of Yesterday* is one of the greatest memoirs of the twentieth century, as perfect in its evocation of the world Zweig loved, as it is in its portrayal of how that world was destroyed' David Hare

JOURNEY BY MOONLIGHT
ANTAL SZERB

'Just divine… makes you imagine the author has had private access to your own soul' Nicholas Lezard, *Guardian*

BONITA AVENUE
PETER BUWALDA

'One wild ride: a swirling helix of a family saga… a new writer as toe-curling as early Roth, as roomy as Franzen and as caustic as Houellebecq' *Sunday Telegraph*

THE PARROTS
FILIPPO BOLOGNA

'A five-star satire on literary vanity… a wonderful, surprising novel' *Metro*

I WAS JACK MORTIMER
ALEXANDER LERNET-HOLENIA

'Terrific… a truly clever, rather wonderful book that both plays with and defies genre' Eileen Battersby, *Irish Times*

SONG FOR AN APPROACHING STORM
PETER FRÖBERG IDLING

'Beautifully evocative… a must-read novel' *Daily Mail*

THE RABBIT BACK LITERATURE SOCIETY
PASI ILMARI JÄÄSKELÄINEN

'Wonderfully knotty… a very grown-up fantasy masquerading as quirky fable. Unexpected, thrilling and absurd' *Sunday Telegraph*

RED LOVE: THE STORY OF AN EAST GERMAN FAMILY
MAXIM LEO

'Beautiful and supremely touching… an unbearably poignant description of a world that no longer exists' *Sunday Telegraph*

THE BREAK
PIETRO GROSSI

'Small and perfectly formed... reaching its end leaves the reader desirous to start all over again' *Independent*

FROM THE FATHERLAND, WITH LOVE
RYU MURAKAMI

'If Haruki is The Beatles of Japanese literature, Ryu is its Rolling Stones' David Pilling

BUTTERFLIES IN NOVEMBER
AUÐUR AVA ÓLAFSDÓTTIR

'A funny, moving and occasionally bizarre exploration of life's upheavals and reversals' *Financial Times*

BARCELONA SHADOWS
MARC PASTOR

'As gruesome as it is gripping... the writing is extraordinarily vivid... Highly recommended' *Independent*

THE LAST DAYS
LAURENT SEKSIK

'Mesmerising... Seksik's portrait of Zweig's final months is dignified and tender' *Financial Times*

BY BLOOD
ELLEN ULLMAN

'Delicious and intriguing' *Daily Telegraph*

WHILE THE GODS WERE SLEEPING
ERWIN MORTIER

'A monumental, phenomenal book' *De Morgen*

THE BRETHREN
ROBERT MERLE

'A master of the historical novel' *Guardian*